GARCIA
THE CENTENARIAN
AND HIS TIMES

Da Capo Press Music Reprint Series

GARCIA
THE CENTENARIAN
AND HIS TIMES

By
M. Sterling Mackinlay

DA CAPO PRESS · NEW YORK · 1976

Library of Congress Cataloging in Publication Data

Mackinlay, Malcolm Sterling, 1876-
  Garcia the centenarian and his times.

  (Da Capo Press music reprint series)
  Reprint of the 1908 ed. published by W. Blackwood,
Edinburgh.
  Includes index.
  1. Garcia, Manuel, 1805-1906. I. Title.
ML420.G24M2 1976 782.1'092'4 [B]   75-40206
ISBN 0-306-70671-7

This Da Capo Press edition of *Garcia the Centenarian and His Times*
is an unabridged republication of the first edition published in
Edinburgh, London and New York in 1908.

Published by Da Capo Press, Inc.
A Subsidiary of Plenum Publishing Corporation
227 West 17th Street, New York, N.Y. 10011

Garcia the Centenarian

And His Times

Manuel Garcia

John S. Sargent

THE CENTENARY PORTRAIT OF MANUEL GARCIA BY JOHN S. SARGENT.
SIGNED BY THE MAESTRO SIX WEEKS BEFORE HIS HUNDRED-AND-FIRST BIRTHDAY.

Garcia the Centenarian

And His Times

Being a Memoir of Manuel Garcia's Life and Labours for the Advancement of Music and Science

BY

M. STERLING MACKINLAY

M.A. OXON.

AUTHOR OF 'ANTOINETTE STERLING AND OTHER CELEBRITIES'

WITH ILLUSTRATIONS

NEW YORK

D. APPLETON AND COMPANY

1908

THEIR MAJESTIES THE KING AND QUEEN OF SPAIN.

(FROM A PHOTOGRAPH SPECIALLY FORWARDED TO THE AUTHOR BY HIS MAJESTY.)

𝕯𝖊𝖉𝖎𝖈𝖆𝖙𝖊𝖉

TO

H.M. THE KING OF SPAIN

BY GRACIOUS PERMISSION

PREFACE.

_____

In presenting this Memoir of Don Manuel Garcia, I wish to thank those friends and pupils of the Maestro who have assisted me with reminiscences, photographs, and other material. But especially I would thank Mrs Alec Tweedie for the kind way in which she read through the MS., when it was still in a rough state, and made many invaluable suggestions with regard to its arrangement and improvement generally.

M. S. M.

Oxford and Cambridge Musical Club,
Leicester Square,
March 1908.

CONTENTS.

CONTENTS.

FOURTH PERIOD. RETIREMENT. (1895–1906.)

LIST OF ILLUSTRATIONS.

LIST OF WORKS CONSULTED.

'Albion.' (An American weekly newspaper published from 1823-1826.)
Appleton's 'Cyclopedia of American Biography.'
'Athenæum' (1848).
Brewer's 'History of France.'
Burney's 'History of Music' (1776-1789).
Colletta's 'History of Naples' (1734-1825). Horner's translation.
'Diversions of a Music Lover.' By C. L. Graves.
Eitner's 'Quellen Lexikon.'
Elson's 'History of American Music.'
Fétis' 'Biographie Universelle des Musiciens.'
'Fitz-Greene Halleck's Memoirs.' By General James Grant Wilson.
Fuller-Maitland's revised edition of Grove's 'Dictionary of Music.'
'Harmonicon' Musical Magazine (1823-1833).
Haydn's 'Dictionary of Dates.'
'Jenny Lind's Memoirs.' By Holland and Rockstro.
'Le Guide Musical.'
'Londina Illustrata.' By Wilkinson. (1819-1825.)
'Madrid.' By a Resident Officer. (1833.)
Mapleson's 'Memoirs.'
'Marchesi and Music.'
Mendel's 'Musikalisches Conversations Lexikon.'
'Mexico.' By Maria Wright.
Morse-Stephens's 'European Revolution.'
'Musical Reminiscences of Earl of Mount-Edgcumbe' (1824).
'Paris.' By G. L. Craik. (1834).
'Recollections.' By Bessie Palmer.
Sir Felix Semon's 'Zum hundertsten Geburstage Manuel Garcia's.'
    (Privately printed.)
'Sixty Years of Recollections.' By Ernest Legouvé.
'Student and Singer.' By Sir Charles Santley.
'Thirty Years of Musical Life.' By Hermann Klein.
Wyndham's 'History of Covent Garden.'

FIRST PERIOD

PREPARATION

(1805–1830)

CHAPTER I.

MANUEL GARCIA, the Centenarian.

How much do those words imply !—words which it is impossible to pen without a feeling of awe.

Garcia, a member of that family of Spanish musicians whose combined brilliancy has probably never been equalled in the annals of the musical world. The father and founder of the family, renowned as one of the finest tenors of his day ; as a prolific composer, and as a singing teacher of distinguished ability, as well as conductor and impressario ; in fact, a fine vocalist and an equally fine musician, which in those days was something of a *rara avis*.

The eldest daughter, Maria Malibran, a contralto whose brief career was one series of triumphs, while her gifts as a composer were shared by her sister, Pauline Viardot-Garcia, whose singing drew forth the praise and admiration of all, and whose retirement from the stage and concert platform brought with it fresh honours in the field of teaching, wherein she showed herself a worthy exponent of the high ideals of the Garcias.

And what of Manuel himself ? The subject of

our Memoir has a triple claim that his name should be inscribed on the roll of fame. As professor of singing, he is acknowledged to have been the greatest of his time. In the musical firmament he has been the centre of a solar system of his own, — a sun round which revolved a group of planets, whose names are familiar to all : Jenny Lind, Maria Malibran, Mathilde Marchesi, Henriette Nissen, Charles Santley, Antoinette Sterling, Julius Stockhausen, Pauline Viardot, and Johanna Wagner —these are but a few of them.

Many, too, out of the number have themselves thrown off fresh satellites, such as Calvè, Eames, Henschel, Melba, Scheidemantel, van Rooy. One and all have owed a debt of eternal gratitude to Manuel Garcia and his system.

Again, as a scientific investigator he has given us the Laryngoscope, which Huxley placed among the most important inventions of the medical world. Indeed, it is no figure of speech, but a statement of demonstrable fact, that millions have been benefited by his work.

Thirdly, as a centenarian, he is without question the most remarkable of modern times.

Of the men who have attained to that rare age, those who possess any claim upon our interests beyond their mere weight of years are but a comparative handful.

Of musicians one alone has approached him in longevity, Giacomo Bassevi Cervetto, who died on January 14, 1783, within a few days of his 101st birthday, but with little distinction beyond this fact. As to the rest who go to make up the

tale of the world's centenarians of recent years,
it has been generally a case of the survival of the
unfittest—

> "In second childishness and mere oblivion,
> Sans teeth, sans eyes, sans taste, sans everything."

How different Manuel Garcia when he celebrated
his 100th birthday : in the early morning, received
by the King at Buckingham Palace ; at noon,
entering the rooms of the Royal Medical Society
with short, quick steps, walking unaided to the
dais, mounting it with agility and then sitting
for an hour, smiling and upright, while receiving
honours and congratulations from all parts of the
globe. Which of those who were present will ever
forget how he attended the banquet that same
evening, in such full possession of his faculties and
bodily strength as to make his own reply to the
hundreds assembled to celebrate the occasion?
Could anything have been finer than this sight
of Grand Old Age?

Now the fame of each individual member of the
Garcia family would seem to demand that, in
addition to the story of the Maestro's own career,
considerable details should be given regarding that
of his father and sisters. Surely the three last
have claims to our attention beyond the mere fact
of being in the one case a parent who exercised
a very important influence upon Manuel Garcia's
character and choice of career in early days, and
who was, moreover, the fountainhead from which
flowed the stream of musical talent that in the
children broadened out into so grand a river,—in

the other case, the sisters, who were bound not only by ties of kinship but by a debt of gratitude for the part which their brother played in their vocal training.

This brings us to the first point, Señor Garcia's position as a teacher. There is a trite proverb to the effect that the proof of the pudding is in the eating. It is so in the present case. One can state the fact that he has been a great master, one can lay down a general outline of his teaching and applaud the soundness of his methods, but after all the outer world will in such matters be apt to judge by results alone. Or let us put it in another way. His knowledge is like the foundations of a house : experts may examine it closely and admire good points, but to a great extent the successes of his pupils are the bricks by which alone a wide reputation is built up.

For this reason I propose to sketch briefly the career of the more famous among those who studied under the old Spaniard, and in doing so I trust that the above circumstances will be considered sufficient excuse for the digressions which will be made at various points.

We now come to a second consideration.

The discovery of the laryngoscope, owing to its far-reaching results, is of such importance that the chapter dealing with it is bound to contain matter which will naturally appeal to the special rather than to the general reader. The desire that the many may not suffer for the sake of the few to a greater extent than is absolutely necessary has prompted me to quote but briefly from the text of the important technical papers which he presented to the Royal Society in 1854 and to the International Medical Congress in 1881.

In the former of these he sets forth a detailed account of the results which he himself obtained in connection with the human voice from the use of the instrument; in the latter he has told the story of the invention and given a full description of the laryngoscope.

Last of all, there is the question of his remarkable age. As a centenarian, he passed through many great historical events, and witnessed a number of changes not only in the musical world, but in the general advance of civilisation. To mention but a few cases of the former : his childhood in Spain was passed amid the scenes of the Napoleonic invasion, followed by those of the Peninsular War, while his boyhood in Naples caused him to witness the execution of the ex-king Murat, a few months after the despotic brother-in-law's final overthrow at Waterloo. His first visit to England was made when George III. was on the throne; his nineteenth year saw the death of Louis XVIII.; while his arrival in America to take part in the first season of Italian opera ever given there was at a time when New York was a town of 150,000 inhabitants, and the United States were preparing to celebrate the jubilee of the Declaration of Independence. In early manhood he joined the French Expedition against Algiers, and on his return found himself in the midst of the July Revolution, which resulted in the expulsion of Charles X. from the capital and the placing of

Louis Philippe on the throne; while he spent his last months in Paris as a member of the National Guard during another revolution, that of 1848, which ended in the flight of Louis and the proclamation of the French Republic.

The first fifteen years of residence in London saw the English nation throw down the glove to Russia, enter on the Crimean War, and bring it to a successful close with the fall of Sebastopol, which was followed by such events as the Indian Mutiny; the accession of William I. to the throne of Prussia, with Prince Bismarck as his chief adviser; the capture of Pekin; the American Civil War; the death of the Prince Consort, and two years later the marriage of the heir to the throne of England to the beautiful Princess of the Royal House of Denmark.

He was in his sixty-first year when Lord Palmerston died; as for the Franco-Prussian War and the Siege of Paris, they were looked on by him in his old age as things of but yesterday; while at various periods of his life he resided in Madrid, Naples, Paris, New York, Mexico, and London.

Again, in his work as a teacher, there came for lessons not merely the children of old pupils, but many even whose parents and grandparents had studied under him; while before his life was brought to a close England had been ruled by five successive sovereigns.

His father, whom we shall refer to in this Memoir as the elder Garcia, was born at Seville on January 22, 1775 — over a hundred and thirty years ago. At the time of his birth Seville could not boast a single piano. Such a thing seems hardly credible to us who live in the twentieth century, when it is the exception rather than the rule to come across a house that does not boast an instrument, which is at any rate sufficiently recognisable from its general contour for one to feel justified in saying, " Let it pass for a piano."

Whence the elder Garcia obtained his musical talent it is impossible to learn. Whatever the previous generations may have been, there is no record of their having made any mark among the musicians of their time. Garcia is a fairly common Spanish name, and we find mention of several musicians of the eighteenth century, and even earlier, who bore that cognomen ; none of these, however, can possibly have had any direct relationship to the family in which we are interested, and for an obvious reason. " Garcia " was only a *nom de guerre* which had been taken by the founder of the family when he entered upon a musical career, his baptismal name having been Manuel Vicente del Popolo Rodriguez. The fame of the new name, however, soon eclipsed the old, and hence in due course it came to be adopted by him and his descendants as their regular surname.

In the spring of 1781 the " elder ". Garcia, being now six years old, became a chorister in the cathedral of his native town. Here he quickly began to display an extraordinary talent and precocity, his first musical training being received at the hands of Antonio Ripa, and continued under Juan Almarcha, who succeeded Ripa as Maestro di Cappella at the cathedral. These two men were considered the first teachers in Seville, and under their able tuition his powers developed so rapidly, that even in his early teens he was already acquiring a reputation in his town not only as singer, but as composer and *chef d'orchestre.*

During the years which Garcia was thus spending in patient study, the neighbouring kingdom of France was approaching nearer and nearer to that vast upheaval which was to bring such fatal consequences. The populace had long been smouldering with discontent against the hated aristocrats, and at last in 1789 the country flamed up in that terrible revolution which culminated in that wonderful episode, the storming of the Bastille on July 14.

When this historical event took place the elder Garcia was in his fifteenth year. Two years later he made his *début* at the theatre of Cadiz in a "tonadilla" into which a number of his own compositions had been introduced. Not long after this he made his first appearance at Madrid in an oratorio, while his earliest opera was performed there under the title of "Il Preso." Such was his success in the Spanish capital that he was quickly recognised as one of the greatest tenors his country had ever produced.

The following year, 1792, found France overtaken by a succession of catastrophes : the invasion by Austria and Prussia, the storming of the Tuileries, the September massacre, and that tragic end of the French Monarchy, for the time being, with the execution of Louis XVI.

The last years of the eighteenth century were spent by the elder Garcia in building up an ever-

increasing reputation throughout Spain; while
during this period European history continued to
raise fresh landmarks for future generations to bear
in wondering memory, for when he was nineteen
there came the execution of Robespierre, and the
splendid victory of Lord Howe over the French fleet,
followed in 1789 by another glorious naval achievement in the Battle of the Nile.

The first years of the new century brought with
them the close of the elder Garcia's bachelor life
with his romantic marriage to Joaquina Sitchès.
The story of the meeting and courtship is one of
singular charm.

Joaquina, who was Spanish by birth, was gifted
with a somewhat mystical temperament, and early
declared her wish to pass her life in a convent. Her
parents raised no objection to her taking the veil,
and she forthwith commenced her novitiate.

In due course the time arrived when, according
to custom, she must go out into the world again for
a while, in order to prove whether her desire for the
religious life was genuine. Accordingly the beautiful
young novice went much into society, making her
appearance at balls, parties, theatres, and the other
gaieties of the capital.

One evening she was taken for the first time to
hear Garcia sing. He made a deep impression upon
her, and an introduction followed, which led to her
falling violently in love with the singer. He on his
side became no less completely a victim to her
charms, and lost no time in declaring his passion,
and that was the end, or should one not perhaps
say, the beginning? Joaquina paid a last visit to

the convent to bid good-bye to the mother-superior, and soon afterwards the lovers were united.

Señorita Sitchès was possessed of great natural gifts as a singer, and after her marriage became desirous of associating herself with his career. She therefore determined to put her musical talents to use and went on the stage, where she soon became a worthy second to her husband.

And so we come to the year 1805, which brings with it the birth of a son, the subject of this Memoir.

MANUEL GARCIA'S MOTHER.

CHAPTER II.

CHILDHOOD IN SPAIN.

(1805–1814.)

MANUEL PATRICIO RODRIGUEZ GARCIA — to give his full name—was born on March 17, 1805, four days before the death of Greuze. The place of his birth was not Madrid, as has been so often stated, but Zafra, in Catalonia.

What of the musical world in 1805 ? Beethoven had not yet completed his thirty - seventh year, Schubert was a boy of eight, Auber, Bishop, Charles Burney (who had been born in 1726), Callcott, Cherubini, Dibdin, Halévy, " Papa " Haydn, Meyerbeer, Paganini, Rossini, Spohr, Weber, these were all living, and many of them had yet to become famous. As for Chopin, Mendelssohn, Schumann, and Brahms, they were not even born ; while Gounod, Wagner, and Verdi were still mere schoolboys when Garcia was a full - blown operatic baritone.

The year of Manuel's birth was the one in which the elder Garcia composed one of his greatest successes, a mono-drama entitled " El Poeta Calculista." It was this work which contained the song that achieved such popularity throughout Spain, " Yo

che son contrabandista." When the tenor used
to sing this air he would accompany himself upon
the guitar, and by the fire and *verve* with which
the whole performance was given, he made the
audiences shout themselves hoarse with excitement.

Among the most enthusiastic of his listeners were
the weak old dotard Charles IV., King of Spain,
and his son, the bigoted and incompetent Ferdinand,
who had already made himself a popular favourite
and commenced his intrigues against the Throne.
Above all, one must not forget Don Manuel de
Godoy, Prince of the Peace, who was carrying on
a shameful intercourse with the Queen, and was
undoubtedly at the time the most powerful man
in the kingdom.

The two most faithful allies of England at the
beginning of the nineteenth century were the
small kingdoms of Portugal and Sweden.

In view of the sea - power which the Island
Empire had gained since the Battle of Trafalgar,
Napoleon decided that the strength of this alliance
must be broken. Accordingly, on October 29, 1807,
the Treaty of Fontainebleau was signed, by which
it was agreed that the combined armies of France
and Spain should conquer Portugal. The little
kingdom was then to be divided into three parts :
the northern provinces were to be given to the
King of Etruria in exchange for his dominions
in Italy, which Napoleon desired to annex ; the
southern districts were to be formed into an in-
dependent kingdom for Godoy, the Prince of the
Peace ; and the central portion was to be temporarily held by France.

In pursuance of this secret treaty a French army under General Junot marched rapidly across the Peninsula.

On receiving the news that the invaders were close to Lisbon, the Prince Regent, with his mother, the mad queen, Maria I., sailed for Brazil with an English squadron. Hardly had the Regent left the Tagus when Junot entered Lisbon on November 20, meeting with a favourable reception at the hands of the Portuguese, who resented the departure of the Prince Regent, and had no idea that there was a secret design to dismember the kingdom.

When the Franco-Spanish plans had thus reached a successful point in their development, the elder Garcia decided that the time was ripe for him to seek that wider success which he was ambitious of achieving. He had already made his name in Spain both as a singer and composer; but this did not satisfy him. Paris had long been the goal on which he had set his mind. And what more favourable opportunity was likely to arise than the present, when the successes of the alliance would naturally predispose the French people to give a warm welcome to any Spaniards who visited the country at such a moment? Accordingly he made his last appearance in Madrid in a performance of oratorio, and at the close of 1807 set out for Paris.

Soon after his arrival in the French capital he had an opportunity of making his *début*, for on February 11 he appeared in Paër's " Griselda." How bold a stroke this was may be realised from the fact that, apart from his never having properly

studied singing up to this time, he had not yet
sung in Italian.

The applause of Napoleon in the French capital
proved to be no less enthusiastic than had been
that of Charles IV. in Madrid—indeed, so great
was the tenor's success that he was appointed to
the post of *directeur du chant* in less than three
weeks, as well as becoming the leading tenor at
the Théâtre Italien.

The following month brought with it the birth
of his first daughter, Maria Felicita, who was
destined to become famous under the name of
Malibran.   Some ten months later the mono-
drama, "El Poeta Calculista," was given in Paris
for the first time, on the occasion of the elder
Garcia's benefit.   Its reception may be judged
from the fact that the performance of the operetta
had to be interrupted for several minutes, so
greatly was the singer fatigued by the constant
ovations and insistent demands for encores.   The
success which he achieved during this first season
in Paris laid the foundation of a world - wide
fame.

Now, when Señor and Señora Garcia left Spain
at Christmas 1807, they decided that it would be
best not to take with them so young a child as
Manuel then was, and accordingly he was left
behind in Madrid with his grandparents, in whose
charge he remained until his tenth year.   This
resulted in his passing through some historic
scenes, by the memories of which, in his old age,
he formed a link with the past which seemed
wellnigh incredible.

Those were years of war and bloodshed, for, during his childhood, Spain was convulsed first by the throes of the Napoleonic invasion, and then by the successive campaigns of the Peninsular War.

Let us take a glimpse of the swift march of events, of which he must have not only heard reports, but in many cases been the actual witness during his sojourn in Madrid.

First, however, we will try to get some idea of the Spanish capital as it was in the early years of the nineteenth century.

We obtain the best impression from a book published in the year 1835, "embodying sketches of the metropolis and its inhabitants," by a resident officer.

The most striking feature of Madrid at this time, according to this writer, was the irregularity in the height of the buildings. It was not uncommon to see a wretched tumble-down-looking house supporting itself against the palace of a grandee, displaying its checkered, moss-grown, weather-stained tiling in mockery of the marble and sculpture of its next-door neighbour.

"The quarters of Madrid known under the name of the 'Rastro' and 'Barrios Bajos' presented a most unwholesome and ungainly appearance, being chiefly composed of hovels, with mud walls and tiled roofing, which contained but a ground-floor, and were inhabited by the dregs of the population. They were the purlieus of vice and crime, and were not only a disgrace to the capital, but would have been so to any sixth-rate town in the kingdom.

B

This, and the great disparity in the buildings of Madrid at that time, may be accounted for by calling to mind the capricious way it commenced its importance as a capital.

"It had struggled on, a second-rate town, until the Emperor Charles V. of Germany (Charles I. of Spain), suffering under a severe fit of the ague, which he had caught in Valladolid, the royal residence at that time, came to Madrid for change of air, and recovered ; in consequence of which he continued to reside there till his death. Philip II. decided its prosperity by ultimately making it the seat of the Court, and after this it was augmented by bits and scraps as a building mania came on, or as the times permitted."

The same discrepancy prevailed in the style and mode of living : everything was in extremes, both in houses, equipages, clothing, eating, and drinking. Luxury and misery, comfort and squalidness, were constantly elbowing each other.

As to the inhabitants, had an Englishman been transported blindfolded into Spain and his bandage taken off when set down in Madrid, he might readily have believed himself in a seaport town from the great variety of costumes.

"The *Valencian*, with his gay-coloured handkerchief rolled about his head in the Moorish fashion, a brilliantly striped *mantā* thrown gracefully over his shoulder ; the *Maragato*, looking for all the world like a well-fed Dutch skipper in flesh and costume ; the man of *Estremadura*, his broad buff belt buckled about his loins, and a string of sausages in his hand ; the *Catalonian's* wild Albanian look and cut, a red woollen cap falling on his shoulder in the way of the Neapolitan mariners; the *Andalusian's* elegant dress, swarthy face, and immeasurable whiskers; *Galicia's* heavy, dirty son, dragging after him at every step a shoe weighing from two to three pounds, including nails, doublings, and other defences against a treacherous and ruinous pavement. All these might well have been taken for the inhabitants of regions hundreds of leagues asunder, differing as essentially in language as in costume."

But one of the most remarkable features of Madrid was the predominance of large convents in the finest situations and best streets, often monopolising more space than should have fallen to their share. The fronts of the holy houses extended themselves widely up and down the street, causing a dead blank, and destroying the symmetry of the *calle*. The monotonous appearance was, however, frequently relieved by the close - shaven heads of some of the "fathers" appearing at the little windows of their cells, condescending to look upon what was passing outside—faces, some fat, ruddy, and shining, others pale and sallow, with strange black beards and flashing eyes.

The nunneries, in point of usurping place and selecting the most frequented quarters of the town, yielded nothing to the male convents. There were no less than three of them in the Calle Alcala, perched in the very midst of the thoroughfare to and from the Prado.

The sisters used to have a number of latticed windows towards the street, whence they might see without being seen. These celestial spouses, as they called themselves, were very troublesome neighbours, for they were so chary of being seen, even when walking in their garden, that, not contented with running up a wall twenty feet high at least and spoiling a whole street, they insisted on doing the same service to all the houses which had the misfortune to be within eyeshot of them. Hence there would be seen whole balconies completely boxed up with sheet-iron opposite a long dead wall, with a few ascetic-looking cypresses peeping over it.

Here, then, we have some of the principal features of Madrid at that time, and it was not till several years after Manuel Garcia had left the capital that the first stir towards improving the place was made; for we read how in 1835 " commodious flagways are being laid down for the convenience and security of passengers. Moreover, the convents are to be pulled down," the same writer continues. " Few of these buildings merit respect from the shovels. Their architecture is vulgar and extravagant where the long dead walls do not constitute their only claim to admiration. Still I must confess I like to see a host of cupolas and minarets sparkling and towering in the glorious sunset. Nor does the flowing costume of the friars—black, blue, white, and grey — show amiss in the motley crowd of picturesque costumes paraded in the streets. Murillo has immortalised the cowl and cassock, and custom has rendered both favourites with the mass of the people, who will long regret the monks and their soup doled out at the convent gate."

And now to return to the point at which we left our narrative to set down these few details of Madrid at the time Manuel Garcia was residing there with his grandparents.

Spain had been the consistent ally of France since the Treaty of Basle in 1795. Nevertheless, Napoleon deliberately determined to dethrone his faithful friend, Charles IV.

Court intrigues gave him a splendid opportunity for interfering in the affairs of Spain. The heir to the throne, Ferdinand, Prince of the Austrians, hated his mother's lover, Godoy, and for sharing in a plot against the favourite was thrown into prison. He appealed for help to Napoleon, and Charles IV., on his side, did the same. Upon this, Napoleon began to move his troops across the Pyrenees, and a French army, under the command of Murat, approached Madrid. The population of the Spanish capital at once rose in insurrection and maltreated Godoy, who fell into its hands. Manuel Garcia was at this time just entering his fourth year, and the rising which he thus witnessed was one of his earliest memories.

Charles IV. at once abdicated, and was quickly forced to cede the crown to " his friend and ally," Napoleon, who conferred it on his brother Joseph, King of Naples, on June 6th.

But it was one thing to proclaim Joseph King of Spain, another to place him in power. The patriotism of the Spanish people was stirred to its depths, and they declined to accept a new monarch supported by French troops. In every quarter insurrections broke out and *juntos* were formed.

One was able to get a graphic picture of the horrors of that outbreak from the reminiscences which Señor Garcia used to give, for it made an impression on his childhood which remained undimmed throughout the successive years of his life. Indeed, it was more than ninety years later that I recall his speaking of these scenes one afternoon when the ill-starred war, which his beloved country was at the time carrying on against the United States, brought to his mind the memory of that other war nearly a century before.

"During the weeks which succeeded Joseph Bonaparte's assumption of the Spanish throne," he said, "there arose great bitterness between the peasants and the invaders. Daily, when the roll-call was read, a number of French soldiers failed to answer to their names: during the preceding night the unhappy men would have been murdered in their beds by the inmates of the houses in which they had been quartered in the surrounding villages."

The French exacted terrible reprisals for this, and he vividly recalled the long line of men, youths, and even boys who were forced to run the gauntlet between the rows of soldiers on their way to wholesale execution. "Shoot every one old enough to hold a gun." So ran the cruel order, given out day after day to the soldiers in many districts.

On the 2nd of May a wholesale massacre of the French took place in Madrid, and the survivors were driven out of the town by the mob. In consequence of this, Murat was forced to retire with his soldiers beyond the Ebro, while the province of Asturias rose *en masse.*

But mobs and undisciplined militia can never stand against regular troops. The Spanish army was defeated, and on the 20th of July young Garcia witnessed the entrance of Joseph Bonaparte into the capital as King of Spain.

That same day, however, brought serious disaster to one of the flying columns which had been sent out in various directions. The Spanish insurgents at once rose in every quarter, and a guerilla warfare was begun which proved more fatal to the French army than regular defeats would have been. Napoleon for the first time had to fight a nation in arms, and Joseph Bonaparte was forced to evacuate Madrid within three weeks of making his royal entry, and to retreat beyond the Ebro, as Murat had done two months before.

Here he was joined by his brother-in-law with 135,000 men, and a rapid advance was made on Madrid, with the inevitable result that the Spanish capital was forced to capitulate, and on December 13 the young Manuel had the excitement of seeing the entry of the great Napoleon into the town at the head of the French troops.

The events of the next three years of the Peninsular War were not witnessed by him, for the place remained in the hands of the French until 1812, when he saw Madrid evacuated by Bonaparte, and occupied on August 12 by Wellington and his troops after the battle of Salamanca.

With his main army the English general now

advanced on Burgos, which, however, resisted all his assaults; and the Anglo-Portuguese army had to retire once more into Portugal, while for the last time Joseph returned to the Spanish capital.

In the summer of 1813 Wellington broke up from his quarters, and, marching in a north-easterly direction, attempted to cut off all communication between France and Madrid. The movement completely overthrew the French domination in Spain, and Joseph Bonaparte fled with all the troops he could collect. Wellington followed, and came up with the French army at Vittoria, where he defeated them.

This victory, by which the invaders were driven back into France, was followed by a burst of national enthusiasm. The Spanish guerillas destroyed every isolated French post, and on October 8, 1813, Wellington crossed the French borders with his army.

A few months later Ferdinand VII. was restored to the throne of Spain.

Such were the events through which his native land was passing during the childhood of Manuel Garcia, and which he was able to recall in after life.

What memories and experiences must he have had to pour into the ears of his parents when, in the summer of 1814, he was summoned to join them at Naples, where they had settled two years previously, having been forced to leave Paris owing to the strong feeling against Spain!

MANUEL GARCIA'S FATHER.

CHAPTER III.

NAPLES.

(1814–1816.)

WHEN Manuel Garcia joined his parents in Italy
in the summer of 1814, being at the time in his
tenth year, he found Naples under the rule of
King Murat.

Here he saw for the first time his sister Maria,
who was now six years old, while his father he
found installed in the position of principal tenor
in the chapel choir of King Murat. The elder
Garcia had held this post for about two years, having been appointed immediately on his arrival from
Paris. Since then he had been devoting himself
to a complete study of the art of singing under
his friend and teacher, Ansani.

This celebrated tenor was able to hand on to him
the Italian vocal traditions of that "Bel Canto"
school which had come down from the old Neapolitan maestro, Porpora.

Soon after Manuel came to Italy he was taken
by his father to see Ansani, who not only heard
him sing, but gave him a few informal lessons. It
was a case of winter and spring, for while the
pupil was in his tenth year, the teacher was ap-

proaching his seventieth. With this fact we are brought face to face with an almost incredible link with the past. Ansani was nearly twenty when Porpora died, in his eighty - second year. A remark which Manuel Garcia once made rather points to the possibility that Ansani may have had a few lessons from Porpora himself. Whether this was absolutely true I know not,—at any rate it may well have been so. Accept the supposition, and those who had the honour of studying under the "centenarian" would at once be placed in a position to say that they were pupils of one whose master had himself received lessons from a man born in 1687. The possibility is a fascinating one.

Giovanni Ansani himself was an interesting personality. Born in Rome about the middle of the eighteenth century, it has been reported that he once met Bach. As, however, the German composer died in the year 1750, about the time that Ansani was still busying himself with the feeding-bottle—or its eighteenth-century equivalent—the story must be regarded with some suspicion, to say the least of it.

After a musical training received in Italy, he sang in various parts of the Continent. Twenty years before the close of the century he made his appearance in London, and at once took the first place. He soon left, however, on account of disputes with Roncaglia.

In 1781 he returned to England, and Dr Burney, who heard him sing in that year, has described him as the sweetest, albeit one of the most powerful, tenors of his generation. He was a spirited actor, and had a full, fine-toned, and commanding voice, while, according to Gervasoni, he had a very rare truth of intonation, great power of expression, and most perfect method both of voice emission and vocalisation. His wife, Maccherini, was also a singer, and accompanied him to London on his second visit. He himself was always noted for a quarrelsome disposition, and as a prima donna his wife had an almost equally bad temper. Such jealousy in fact existed between them that, when either was applauded for singing, the other was accustomed to go into the pit and hiss.

In 1784 Ansani appeared at Florence, and toured Italy. At the age of fifty he retired and settled in Naples, where he devoted himself to teaching. It was some twelve years later that he began to give lessons to the elder Garcia.

When Manuel joined his parents, he at once commenced to study singing under his father's guidance. The training of those days was a much slower process than that which is deemed necessary at the present time. Months, indeed years, would be spent in the practice of simple solfeggi, to be followed by exercises in rhythm and studies for intonation.

The monotony of the first portion of this training evidently became very wearisome in time, for Señor Garcia would afterwards recall how one day, after being made to sing an endless variety of ascending scales, his desire for a change became so great that he could not resist bursting out, " Oh dear! mayn't I sing down the scale even once?" The training of those days was indeed a hard one, but it turned out artists who had a very wonderful command over their voices.

After a time Manuel began to find these severe studies irksome. He seems, moreover, to have had no particular vocation for the lyrical stage, and the bent of his mind, even at that early period, had a leaning towards science.

As a boy, he had a soprano voice of beautiful quality, and it has been asserted that during the stay in Italy he was appointed to a place in the cathedral choir. Absolute verification of this statement is practically impossible to obtain, though there seems no reason for doubting its truth. On the other hand, there is a strong likelihood that it may have been confused with the fact that the *elder* Garcia (whose name was also Manuel) was in the chapel choir.

From this time the training of his voice continued practically without intermission, under his father's tuition, till his twentieth year. It was largely due to the fact that work was not stopped during that dangerous period at the commencement of puberty, that he assigned the break-down of his voice in after years.

The elder Garcia took the greatest delight and pride in the early education and musical training of his son, and among many other valuable lessons, he impressed upon him that a singer must not only know how to use his voice, but must, above all, be a thorough musician.

As we have already seen, Manuel was taken to see Ansani, who gave him a few lessons. In addition to this, much help was received from

Zingarelli, when the elder Garcia was too busy to take him. His intelligent brain could therefore make a blend of Spanish and Italian methods. To this he added in after life his own observations on the human voice, and applied the scientific theories which he formed and eventually corroborated by means of his laryngoscope. It was by the wise combination of this knowledge that he was able to evolve the magnificent Method which produced Jenny Lind.

Zingarelli was a man whose name is worth pausing over for a moment, for some episodes of his life are of considerable interest. In 1804 he had succeeded Guglielmi as Maestro di Cappella of the Sistine Chapel in Rome.

When Napoleon in the zenith of his imperial power gave his son the pompous title of " King of Rome," he ordered rejoicings throughout his kingdom, and a " Te Deum " was arranged to be sung at St Peter's in Rome. When, however, the authorities, both French and Italian, were assembled for the performance of this servile work, Zingarelli refused to have anything to do with it, and added that nothing would induce him to acknowledge the rule of the Corsican usurper. Upon this he was arrested, and, by Napoleon's orders, taken to Paris. Here he was immediately set free and granted a pension, owing to the fact that Napoleon preferred his music to that of any other composer.

In 1810 he left Paris for Naples, where three years later he was appointed director of the Royal College of Music, and he was holding this import-

ant post when Manuel came from Spain. Some
eighteen months later, just before the Garcia
family left for Paris, he succeeded Paisiello as
Maestro di Cappella at the Neapolitan Cathedral;
and these two positions he continued to hold until
his death at the age of eighty-five.

During the sojourn in Italy the elder Garcia
was not only in Murat's private choir, but was
also *primo tenore* of the King's Opera Company
at the San Carlo. I remember Señor Garcia one
day giving an amusing account of his father's first
appearance there.

Before he set out for his opening rehearsal he
had come to the conclusion that it would be a
splendid thing if he could hit upon some way of
proving to the members of the orchestra that he
was not one of the ordinary small fry possessed
of a voice and little else. He wanted to gain
their respect both as a musician and as a singer.
This is how he managed to accomplish his desire.

His opening aria in the opera to be rehearsed
was in the key of E flat. The orchestra played
the introductory bars, and waited with a casual
interest for the new singer's opening phrase. The
tenor commenced, but, instead of doing so in the
key in which they were playing, he began to sing
a semitone higher, in E natural. At first they
were horrified at the discords which resulted.
Gradually, however, as the aria went on, and the
vocalist still sang exactly a semitone above the
key in which they were playing, it began to dawn
upon them that, instead of being sharp through
nervousness or lack of ear, he was keeping

a half tone too high intentionally throughout the piece. Consequently, when they heard him continue in E natural, without a moment's hesitation, or a single false note (for so great a musician was he that he could abstract himself entirely from his surroundings and from the sound of the instruments), their disgust turned to surprise, then admiration, and finally enthusiasm. When the aria was concluded there was an enormous burst of applause and the wildest excitement among them all, for they saw what a really great singer they had found in this newcomer. Of course he sang the remainder of his part in the proper key, but by this novel entry he won the lasting respect of his comrades.

The anecdote afforded a good illustration of his exceptional powers. The elder Garcia was certainly a wonderful man, and in some ways a unique figure in the history of music, for it is doubtful if any other singer has duplicated his extraordinary talent and versatility. Attention has already been called to the fact that he was conductor and impresario. As a composer he was responsible for over forty operas, of which number seventeen were Spanish, nineteen Italian, and seven French; and in many cases he was even responsible for the libretto. The greater number of these works were performed in Spain, France, and America.

When he was in Paris "El Poeta Calculista" was given, as we have already said, with the greatest success in 1809, and three years later "The Caliph of Bagdad" received no less appreciation. His power as an actor was equal to that as a singer, while his Spanish temperament gave a fire to his impersonations which could not but awaken enthusiasm. " J'aime la fureur andalouse de cet homme," wrote a contemporary critic; " il aime tout."

But of all his qualities that which perhaps stood out most was a remarkable gift of extemporisation. It was this which first attracted the notice of Rossini, and led him to write the tenor *rôle* in " Elisabeth " for the elder Garcia. The result was so satisfactory that when he set to work on his next opera, " Il Barbiere di Seviglia," he wrote the part of Almaviva specially for him.

The story of this production, as Manuel Garcia related it, was an interesting one.

In the December of 1815 Rossini had bound himself to produce a new opera by the 20th of the following month. He hesitated at first about accepting a libretto which Paisiello had treated so successfully, but having obtained that composer's permission he wrote the entire score in a fortnight. To avoid all appearance of rivalry with Paisiello he named his work first of all, " Almaviva, or The Useless Precaution "; and it was accordingly pro- duced under this title in Rome at the Argentina Theatre on February 5, 1816, with the follow- ing cast :—

Rossini	.	.	Signora Giorgi Righetti.
Berta	.	.	Signorina Rossi.
Figaro	.	.	Signor Luigi Zamboni.
Bartolo	.	.	Signor Botticelli.
Basilio	.	.	Signor Vitarelli.
Count Almaviva		.	Signor Garcia.

The theatre was packed with the adherents of the older composer, who resented the new effort as an intrusion on his rights. In consequence of this the work was unmercifully damned, but it was kept on the stage and continually grew in favour until it became one of the most popular comic operas ever written.

These two operas, "Elisabeth" and "Il Barbiere," were not by any means the only ones in which the elder Garcia undertook the tenor *rôle* at the initial performance, for in the course of the long career which followed he had the honour of creating a number of other parts.

As a singer, according to his son, his forte lay in the rendition of the lighter and more florid music, the voice being remarkable for its extraordinary flexibility. It was this faculty which gave his inventive powers their full scope in the extemporisations which he was wont to introduce into the various arie. This custom, it may be well to point out, was quite in accordance with the tastes and actual wishes of the composers of that time.

Among the old musicians it used to be customary to write a mere outline or suggestion of the voice part. Particularly was this the case when there was a return to the original theme, while it applied equally to the conventional ending found in nearly all arie of that time. The singers were expected to elaborate the simple melody given them, and to raise upon this foundation a graceful edifice, adorned with what ornaments their individual taste dictated, and suited to their own powers of execution.

C

The following illustration will prove the truth of the above assertion. It is a story from the lips of the maestro.

While his father, the elder Garcia, was at Naples, one of the old Italian composers came to produce a new opera.

At the opening rehearsal the tenor was given his part to read at sight. When his first aria had been reached he sang it off with perfect phrasing and feeling, but exactly note for note as written. After he had finished the composer said, " Thank you, signor, very nice, but that was not at all what I wanted." He asked for an explanation, and was informed that the melody which had been written down was intended merely as a skeleton which the singer should clothe with whatever his imagination and artistic instinct prompted. The writer of the music asked him to go through it again, and this time to treat it exactly as though it were his own composition.

The elder Garcia was skilful at improvising : consequently, in giving the aria for the second time, he made a number of alterations and additions, introducing runs, trills, roulades, and cadenzas, all of which were performed with the most brilliant execution. This time, when the end of the music was reached, the old composer shook him warmly by the hand. " Bravo ! Magnificent ! That was my music, as I wished it to be given."

It may be noted that Lord Mount-Edgcumbe, in his ' Musical Reminiscences ' (published in 1824), refers more than once to the same thing. In speaking of the famous male soprano, Pacchierotti,

who made his *début* in London in 1778, the following passage occurs :—

His voice was an extensive soprano, full and sweet. . . .
His powers of execution were great; but he had too good
taste and too good sense to make a display of them where it
would have been misapplied, confining it to one *bravura* song
(*aria d'agilità*) in each opera, conscious that the chief delight
of singing lay in touching expression and exquisite pathos.
. . . He could not sing a song twice in exactly the same
way, *yet never . . . introduced an ornament that was not
judicious and appropriate to the composition.*

Again Lord Mount-Edgcumbe writes :—

Many songs of the old masters would be very indifferently
sung by modern performers, not on account of their difficulty
but their apparent facility. Composers when writing for a
first-rate singer noted down merely a simple *tema* with the
slightest possible accompaniment, which, if sung as written,
would be cold, bald, and insipid. It was left to the singer
to fill up the outline, to give it the light and shade and all
its grace and expression, which requires not only a thorough
knowledge of music but the greatest taste and judgment.

But to return to the elder Garcia and his family.
It was during this stay at Naples that little
Maria made her first public appearance, when she
was barely five years old. The anecdote was one
which Manuel Garcia was very fond of relating.

The opera in which the diminutive vocalist made
her *début* was Paër's " Agnese," in which there was
a child's part.

In the second act there is a scene where the
husband and wife have quarrelled and are re-
united through the intervention of their daughter.
The tiny Malibran attended the rehearsals and

knew the whole opera by heart. On the night of the performance the prima donna either forgot her part or hesitated a moment. Lo! the little girl instantly took up the melody, and sang with such vigour and resonance that the entire house heard her. The prima donna was about to interrupt when the audience shouted, "Bravo! don't stop her. Let her go on."

It was a period in which the public loved infant prodigies, both musical and dramatic, and Marietta was actually permitted to sing the part of Agnese throughout the rest of the scene—a piece of audacity which delighted the hearers and called forth an exhibition of true Italian enthusiasm. Two years after this the tiny musician commenced to study solfeggi with Panseron, while Hérold gave her the first instruction on the piano.

In the autumn of the year 1815 an event occurred which brought the Garcia family into a vivid realisation of the changes which had been taking place in European affairs during the earlier part of the year, with the battle of Waterloo.

Scarcely had the news of Napoleon's downfall reached Naples when the townsfolk witnessed the closing scene in the life of his brother-in-law. The month in which Napoleon landed in France King Murat declared war against Austria, whose queen, it will be remembered, had but recently died. He was defeated at Tolentino, and retired first to France, then to Corsica. In the autumn the brilliant but headstrong ex-king of Naples was mad enough to make an attempt to regain his forfeited throne, on which Ferdinand had been reinstated by the Congress of Vienna. Having landed with about thirty followers on the coast of Lower Calabria, he was almost instantly arrested by a detachment of the Neapolitan troops, by whom he was handed over to a court-martial and sentenced to death.

The closing scene is well described in Colletta's 'History of Naples' :—

After the passing of the sentence the prisoner was led into the courtyard of the castle of Pizzo, where a double file of soldiers was drawn up, and, as he refused to have his eyes bound, he looked calmly on while their weapons were made ready. Then, placing himself in a posture to receive the balls, he said to the soldiers, 'Spare my face and aim at my heart.' After these words the muskets were discharged, and he who had been King of the two Sicilies fell dead, holding in his hand the portrait of his family, which was buried with his sad remains in the very church which had owed its erection to his piety. Those who believed in his death mourned it bitterly, but the generality of the Neapolitans beguiled their grief by some invention or other respecting the events of Pizzo.

Manuel Garcia was in his eleventh year when the tragedy took place, and in after years would recall the sensation which the gruesome incident made among the Neapolitans.

Almost immediately after Murat's death the Neapolitans found cause for great affliction and terror in the appearance of the plague, which seemed to them almost a judgment from Heaven.

The epidemic had only ceased a few months in Malta when it broke out again in Dalmatia, spreading thence from place to place, till it attacked the inhabitants of Cadiz at one extremity of the Mediterranean and Constantinople at the other.

At the same time it reached Noia, a small city of Puglia, situated on the Adriatic.

Eagerness for gain by men carrying on illicit trade caused its introduction with some goods from Dalmatia.

The first death occurred on November 23, 1815, but a cordon was not placed round the city till six weeks later; traffic went on as usual, people left the city and returned, and merchandise was carried into the provinces and as far as Naples. Fortune, however, or divine providence, saved the kingdom and Italy, for out of the number of men and quantity of goods leaving Noia, none happened to be infected.

At last, on January 1, precautionary measures were taken, and the unhappy city was surrounded by three circuits of ditches, one at a distance of sixty paces, the next at ninety, and the third, which was rather a boundary-line than a barrier, at ten miles. Sentries were placed along these, and numerous fires lighted up the country at night. Whoever dared to attempt passing the line was punished with death; and more than one case is recorded of a poor wretch, maddened with the horrors of the town, rushing across the boundary-line, only to fall instantly under the musket-fire of the soldiers.

Throughout the winter the Garcias, in common with the other inhabitants of Naples, lived in constant fear that the plague might break out in the town.

Since, with the coming of spring, the danger showed little sign of ceasing, the elder Garcia determined to leave the country and remove with his family to Paris, from which he had been more than four years absent. It must have been just about the time of their departure that the theatre in which the tenor had been appearing during four successive seasons was destroyed by fire.

The scene which took place is well described by Colletta. The opera company, it appears, were on the spot rehearsing when the fire broke out, and at once fled in consternation. Their cries, with the volumes of smoke issuing from the building, made the danger known, and people hastened from all parts of the city, but too late. The conflagration spread, the king and royal family left the palace which adjoined the theatre, and the fire, catching the whole of the immense structure that composed the roof, sent forth raging and brilliant flames, which were reflected on the Monte St Elmo and in the sea below. The sky, which had been calm, became stormy, and the wind blew the flames in the direction of Castel Nuovo, until they licked the bare walls of the castle.

Happily the danger did not last long, for in less than two hours the noble structure was burned to ashes; and the mistake of having from financial avarice abolished the company of firemen was now acknowledged too late.

The king ordered the theatre to be rebuilt in the shortest possible time, and in four months it rose more beautiful than ever, though Manuel Garcia was never to see it after its phœnix - like re-appearance.

CHAPTER IV.

PARIS AND LONDON.

(1816–1825.)

In the spring of 1816 the elder Garcia left Naples, and with his family set out for Paris, which he had decided to make his home once more.

When he had last been in that city, upwards of four years previously, Napoleon had still been all-powerful; when he returned Louis XVIII. was on the throne and Bonaparte in hopeless exile at St Helena.

After he had settled down he continued the singing lessons of his son, whose general education was looked after by private tutors,—Reicha, Basbereau, and others. As to himself, he was at once engaged as *primo tenore* at the Théâtre Italien, then under the management of Catalani, —a woman whose story we will dwell on for a moment.

At the age of twelve she had been sent to a convent near Rome, being introduced by Cardinal Onorati. Here her voice soon became a great attraction owing to its extraordinary purity, force, and compass, which extended to G in altissimo. On leaving the convent, where sometimes the congre-

gation had openly applauded her splendid notes
in the services, she found herself compelled to perform in public, owing to the sudden poverty of her
parents.

At the age of sixteen she obtained her first
engagement at the Fenice Theatre in Venice, and
thence she went to other opera houses in Italy,
meeting everywhere with wonderful success.

In the year of Manuel's birth, Catalani signed
her first agreement with the managers of the King's
Theatre in the Haymarket at £2000 per annum,
and remained in England for seven years. She
was, however, a prima donna of the deepest dye,
capricious as she was extravagant. Neither would
her disposition endure the possibility of rivalry,
nor would the size of her increasing demands allow
the managers to engage any other singers of position. At last with the close of 1813, having un-
successfully attempted to purchase the King's
Theatre outright, she fell out with the directors
and left London.

With the fall of Napoleon she went to Paris,
where Louis XVIII. gave her the management of
the Théâtre Italien, with a subvention of 160,000
francs. Subsequently, during the Hundred Days,
she fled before the advance of the despot, fearing
his wrath, and paid a tactful visit to Germany and
Scandinavia. It was only after the capture of the
Emperor that she dared return, and even then she
did so by way of Holland, instead of coming direct,
lest at the last minute he might somehow free
himself and come back into power. However, all
was well, Catalani returned to her position at the

Théâtre Italien, and at once engaged Garcia *père* on his arrival in Paris.

In the autumn of the year the tenor and his family paid their first visit to England, but only made a short stay. The little daughter Maria, who was now eight years old, accompanied them, and was left in England for some years, her education being carried on in a convent school at Hammersmith. It was to this fact that in after life she owed her success in this country as a singer of oratorio and English songs.

Upon the elder Garcia's return to Paris, the " Caliph of Bagdad " was revived, as well as another of his operas, " Le Prince d'Occasion." As *primo tenore* of Catalani's troupe, he appeared as Paolino in Pergolesi's " Matrimonio Segreto," and sang in all the operas which were in vogue at that time,—a very different repertoire to that which audiences are accustomed to hear nowadays.

At last an unfortunate quarrel arose between Catalani and himself, and at the end of 1817 he went once more to England. This was only a few months after " Don Giovanni " had been given in England for the first time at the Italian Opera House, with Mesdames Fodor, Camporese, and Pasta ; Signori Crivelli, Ambrogetti, and Agrisani.

His success in London was great during the ensuing season. He made his *début* with Mme. Fodor in " The Barber of Seville," his performance of Almaviva being, according to a critic of that time, " commensurate with his transcendent talent," while he appeared in other operas with equal *éclat*. During the same season he created a further sensation by singing at the chapel of the Bavarian

Embassy in Warwick Street, where several masses of his own composition were given.

In 1819 he returned to Paris and became once more a member of the company at the Théâtre Italien, Catalani having failed and resigned the reins of management during his absence in England. Here he repeated his old success in "Otello" and "Don Giovanni," and also took part, on October 26, in the first performance of "Il Barbiere" ever given in Paris, at the Salle Louvois. It was again received coldly, as had been the case on the original production in Rome three and a half years before. Once more the critics demanded the "Barbiere" of Paisiello, which was accordingly put on the stage at the Théâtre Italien, only to meet with dismal failure; and thus in the end Rossini triumphed with it in the French capital, as he had in that of Italy.

The cast of this Parisian *première* was as follows:

Rosina	. .	Mme. Ronzi de Begnis.
Figaro	. .	Signor Pellegrini.
Bartolo	. .	Signor Graziani.
Basilio	. .	Signor de Begnis.
Almaviva	. .	Signor Garcia.

In addition to appearing at the opera Garcia *père* continued to compose prolifically. "La Mort du Tasse" and "Florestan" were produced at the Grand Opera, "Fazzoletto" at the Théâtre Italien, and "La Meunière" at the Gymnase, while three others were finished but never performed.

Moreover, he devoted a good deal of attention to teaching singing, his fame attracting a number of pupils, while at the close of the year 1819 he published a book on his 'Method of Singing.'

In the spring of the following year, in which took place the accession of George IV. to the throne of England, Manual Garcia paid a flying visit to Spain. It was destined to be the last time he ever saw his native country. The fact is a curious one when we remember his intense love for Spain, which was so strong that, in spite of his spending the last fifty - eight years of his life in England, nothing would have induced him to become a naturalised British subject.

On his return from Madrid he commenced the study of harmony, for, as has been already stated, his father was a firm believer in the necessity of every singer being a musician in the broadest sense of the word. For this work he was placed under François Joseph Fétis, who had just succeeded Elen as professor of counterpoint and fugue at the Conservatoire. This was six years before Fétis became librarian of the institution—a position in which he was enabled to prepare his famous 'Biographie Universelle des Musiciens,' which is one of the greatest monuments to the achievements of musical genius ever reared. He was indeed a remarkable man, who displayed talent not only as teacher, but composer, historian, critic, and author of various theoretical works.

In 1821, the year of Napoleon's death, Mànuel's youngest sister was born — Michelle Ferdinande Pauline,— who was in after years to become no less famous than Maria. The second and third names were given her in honour of her sponsors, Ferdinand Paër and Princess Pauline Galitzin.

In the spring of 1823 the elder Garcia was

again appearing at the King's Theatre, and during the season he founded his famous school of singing in London. It was at this time, too, that he first began seriously to take Maria's musical training in hand, since she was now approaching her fifteenth birthday. His daughter soon showed the individuality of her genius, in spite of a certain fear inspired by her father's somewhat violent disposition.

He made his reappearance at the King's Theatre in May in Rossini's "Otello," given with the following cast :—

Otello	Signor Garcia.
Desdemona . . .	Mme. Camporese.
Elmiro	Signor Porto.
Roderigo . . .	Signor Curioni.
Iago	Signor Reina.
Emilia	Signora Caradori.
Doge	Signor Righi.

In speaking of his return to London, the 'Harmonicon' tells us: "Garcia's voice has an extensive compass and considerable power, and is round and clear. Its flexibility is remarkable."

On June 5 we find the tenor taking part in the first performance of Rossini's semi-serious opera, "Ricciardo e Zoraide," with this cast :—

Agorante . . .	Signor Garcia.
Ricciardo . . .	Signor Curioni.
Ernesto	Signor Reina.
Ircano	Signor Porto.
Zoraide	Mme. Camporese.
Zomira	Mme. Vestris.
Fatima	Mme. Graziani.

Four weeks later he is appearing at the *première* of another of Rossini's works with the strange title, "Matilde di Shabran e Corradino, ossia Il Trionfa della Belta," with the principal parts distributed thus :—

Matilde di Shabran	. .	Mme. Ronzi di Begnis.
Corradino . . .	.	Signor Garcia.
Isidoro . . .	.	Signor di Begnis.
Raimondo . . .	.	Signor Reina.
Edvardo . . .	.	Mme. Vestris.
Contessa d'Arca .	. .	Signora Caradori.

From all this, it will be seen that Manuel Garcia lived in a musical world day and night. Awake or asleep, music and musicians surrounded the boy.

At the close of the London season his father returned to Paris.

An exceptional insight into the musical and artistic circles of the French capital at this time, when Manuel was a young man of eighteen, is given by the following paragraph from a paper of that day :—

" On November 15 some of the principal musical composers and theatrical performers of Paris united to give a dinner to Signor Rossini, in the great room of M. Martin, Place du Châtelet.

" Signor Rossini was seated between Mdlle. Mars and Mme. Pasta. M. Lesueur, placed exactly opposite to him, had Mme. Colbran Rossini on his right and Mdlle. Georges on his left; Mmes. Grassari, Cinti, and Denuri sat next to these. MM. Talma, Boieldieu, Garcia, and Martin were in the midst of this group of elegance and beauty.

All the arts, all the talents, were represented by MM. Auber, Hérold, Cicéri Panseron, Casimir Bonjour, Mimaut, Horace Vernet, &c.

" When the dessert was served, M. Lesueur rose and gave the following toast—'To Rossini! whose ardent Génius has opened a new path and formed an epoch in the art of music.'

" Signor Rossini replied by this toast—'To the French School, and to the prosperity of the Conservatoire.'

" M. Lesueur then gave—'Gluck.'

" Signor Garcia proposed—'Gretry! the most sensible and one of the most melodious of French musicians.'

" Signor Rossini then gave—'Mozart.'

" M. Boieldieu offered his toast in the following words—'Mehul! I see Rossini and the shade of Mozart applaud this toast.'

" M. Hérold proposed—'Paisiello! Full of ingenuity and passion, he rendered popular in all parts of Europe the Italian School.'

" Finally M. Panseron (for M. Auber) gave— 'Cimarosa! the precursor of Rossini.'"

With this the proceedings were brought to an official close and an unofficial commencement of others, which were doubtless continued into "the sma' wee hours."

In the January of 1824 the Garcias returned to England once more, for we find the following announcement made in one of the London musical papers—

" The Italian Opera (King's Theatre) is to open towards the end of the present month. Signor

Rossini is engaged as composer and director of the music : he is to superintend the performance of his own operas, and to produce a new one. The engagements both for the opera and the ballet are upon a liberal scale. Among these are—

Mesdames — Ronzi di Begnis, Colbran — Rossini, Pasta, Vestris, &c.
Signors — Garcia, Curioni, Franceschi, Remorini, di Begnis, Porto, &c.
Conductor — Signor Coccia.
Leader — Signor Spagnoletti.
Poet — Signor Vestris.
In the Ballet will appear — Mme. Ronzi Vestris; Mdlle. Legras, Mdlle. Idalise Grener, Mdlle. Noblet; M. Albert, M. Charles Vestris, M. Ferdinand, &c.
Principal Ballet-master — Mons. Aumer."

The season opened on January 24 with " Zelmira," a new opera conducted by " the universally fashionable composer of the day, Signor Gioacchiso Rossini."

How strangely reads the repertoire of the representations given at the King's Theatre during the next months ! Two only are heard at Covent Garden nowadays, and those but rarely —" Don Giovanni " and " Il Barbiere," which latter was given with Mme. Vestris as Rosina, di Begnis as Bartolo, Benetti as Figaro, and Garcia in his old part of the Count. One may perhaps add to the number of those still heard occasionally the " Nozze di Figaro "; but this is only given at the most attenuated intervals.

As for the rest, what can we say of Zingarelli's

"Romeo e Giulietta" and Rossini's "Otello," in
which Mme. Pasta makes her *rentrée?* Add to these
"Ricciardo e Zoraide," "Semiramide," "Turco in
Italia," "La Donna del Lago," and "Il Fanatico
per la Musica" which Catalani chooses for her
reappearance.

But there are other musical events worthy of
attention during these months.

We read that "Master Liszt, the young German
pianist, had a concert at the Argyll Rooms, when
he exhibited talents that astonished all the leading
professors who were present."

Further, we find Signor Rossini giving two subscription concerts at Almack's Rooms, — how
strangely the names of the fashionable concert
rooms of the past sound to us now!—"Tickets
two guineas."

They are announced "To Begin at Nine o'clock";
while the composer has the assistance of the leading operatic artistes of the day—Catalani, Pasta,
Vestris, Garcia, di Begnis, *et hoc genus omne.*

But what is of especial interest is the fact that
Rossini not only conducted, but *sang.* He gave
"a cavatino (*sic*) from Figaro," and a duetto with
Mme. Catalani, "Se fiato in corpo avete" by
Cimarosa.

The second of these subscription concerts, given
on June 9, 1824, is worthy of our attention, for
we find "Mdlle. Maria Garcia" making apparently
her first appearance in London, taking part with her
father in a duet, "Di Caprici," and adding a solo,
"Nacqui al'affano," both by Rossini.

With the close of the London season the elder

D

Garcia returned to Paris. Here his " Deux Con-
trats" was performed at the Opéra Comique. But
the early autumn of this year is principally memorable for the fact that he allowed his daughter to
make her first appearance in Paris as a professional
singer,—the concert in which she took part being
given at a musical club which he had just established in that city.

Two months later the entire family went to London,
and here Maria's musical education was continued in
the singing-class which her father had established.
The elder Garcia was again engaged as first tenor
at the Royal Opera, his salary having now risen
from £260 (1823) to £1250. Here he continued to
gain still greater fame as a teacher, while his fertility as a composer was shown by two Italian operas,
" Astuzia e Prudenza" and " Un Avertimento."

On June 7, 1825, Maria had the opportunity of
making her *début* in London at the King's Theatre,
as Rosina in " Il Barbiere," under the directorship
of Mr Ebers.

It was owing to a fortuitous combination of circumstances—the sudden return of Mme. Pasta to
Paris, Ronzi losing her voice through illness, Vestris
seceding to the stage, and Caradori, an excellent
seconda donna, being *hors de combat*—that Maria
found herself engaged to fill the gap.

Manuel Garcia, by the way, in after years used
sometimes to recall the effect which Pasta's singing
made on him, when he heard her in his youth. He
spoke of her as possessing a voice of ravishing beauty,
together with perfection of fioriture and grandeur of
dramatic conception, but in spite of this there was

no doubt in his mind as to his preference for the singing of Maria. Indeed, he would always declare that his sister was the most natural and most precocious genius with whom he had ever come in contact.

With her *début* at the King's Theatre Maria achieved a triumphant success, which was witnessed by her brother; and she was engaged by the management for the remaining six weeks of the season for a sum of five hundred pounds.

Once more we find that curious repertoire of operas in favour at that time which contrasts so strangely with the taste of the present day, and serves to illustrate the important changes in the form and character of music which Manuel Garcia witnessed during his life.

We may, moreover, in this year trace the first introduction of Meyerbeer's music to English audiences, for we read in the July 'Harmonicon'—

" On the 23rd of last month there was brought out ' Il Crociato in Egitto,' the new grand opera of Meyerbeer, a composer whose name was completely unknown in this country only a few weeks ago. . . . Mdlle. Garcia, disguised in male attire, performed the part of Felicia with great ability, both as a singer and actress."

Turning from opera to the concert world of 1825, we learn that " The only regular subscription concerts now supported in London are the Ancient and the Philharmonic," though we find Mme. Catalani during May giving a series of four concerts at the Argyll Rooms, assisted by Mrs Salmon, Mr Sapio, and Signor Remorini.

In the way of private musical entertainments, the
Duke of Devonshire gave a fashionable concert in
May, with Pasta, Velluti, the last male soprano who
ever trod the boards in opera in this country, Puzzi,
and a pianist with the mellifluous cognomen "Szy-
manowska"; while on June 15, a state concert
was given by his Majesty King George IV. at
—Carlton Palace!

Among the artists taking part in the latter we
find Signor and Mdlle. Garcia, Caradori, Begrez,
di Begnis, Curioni, Remorini, Velluti, and Crivelli.

At the end of the season the elder Garcia, together
with his wife, son, and daughter, sang at several
provincial concerts, and their names appear in the
programmes of two of the Gentlemen's Concerts at
Manchester on August 15 and September 9.

Four members of the family appearing together
was surely a remarkable event!

In the same month Maria was one of the soloists
at the second York Festival.

The committee had tried to get Catalani, but,
after pecuniary terms had been arranged, the treaty
failed in consequence of a stipulation on her part
that several songs should be transposed into a
lower key to suit her voice.

"The committee had conceded," says the 'Harmonicon,' "to the condition with regard to detached
airs, but refused for those which are connected with
choruses. Then they tried to get Mme. Pasta, but
this was refused, as they could not give her permission to come without materially compromising
the interests of the Italian Theatre Royal. Thus
disappointed, they entered into negotiations with Mr

Braham and other eminent performers, and finally succeeded in obtaining the following assemblage of talent :—

Mr Greatorex, *Conductor.*
Dr Camidge, *Assistant-Conductor.*

Principal Vocalists.

Miss Stephens.	Mr Braham.
Miss Caradori.	Mr Vaughan.
Mdlle. Garcia.	Mr Sapio.
Miss Travis.	Mr Knyvett.
Miss Wilkinson.	Mr Terrail.
Miss Goodall	Mr Bellamy.
and	Mr Phillips.
Miss Farrar.	Signor di Begnis.

A Grand Chorus of 350 voices, and 248 Instrumentalists in the Orchestra."

A perusal of the programme brings home to us the change which has taken place in the last eighty years.

Handel naturally figured largely, while Mozart was represented by his Jupiter Symphony, Beethoven by his Symphonies in C and D and one of the Leonora overtures. Such names, however, as Pepusch, Spontini, and Salieri have long since disappeared. Again, the style of Festival programme was then of a very mixed, and, as regards some of the numbers, of a very " popular " kind. Festivals of the present day are of a much more serious character.

Mdlle. Garcia we find set down for such items as " Gratias " by Gugliemi, " Alma invitta " from " Sigismondo," " O patria " from " Il Tancredi," a terzetto from " Il Crociato in Egitto," and one of her "chevaux de bataille," "Una voce poco fa" from " Il Barbiere."

With the York Festival the visit to England was brought to a close, and at the end of the month the Garcia family embarked at Liverpool for New York, where Manuel was to take part in the first American season of Italian Opera.

Before following them there, let us seek a glimpse of some of the operatic and theatrical events between the year of Manuel Garcia's first visit to England and his trip to America.

In 1816 John Kemble was playing Coriolanus at his London season; Charles Kean was at Drury Lane; and at Covent Garden Mrs Siddons reappeared as Lady Macbeth, while Charles Mathews brought to an end his contract with that theatre.

Next year Henry Bishop's operatic drama "The Slave" was produced at Covent Garden, and a novel pantomime entitled "Robinson Crusoe," with Grimaldi as Friday. It was, moreover, on June 13 of this season that Kemble played Coriolanus for the last time, and retired. In 1818 Macready appeared in an acting version of "Rob Roy,"—a novel which Sir Walter Scott had published shortly before.

This year, moreover, saw the birth of Gounod, and the death of Mrs Billington, heroine of so many Covent Garden triumphs. In 1819 several oratorios were given under Henry Bishop, with Samuel Wesley the church musician as conductor; while on June 9, at the benefit of Mr and Mrs Charles Kemble, Sarah Siddons appeared on the stage for the last time in her life: a few months

before this the beautiful Miss O'Neill retired from
the boards.

Shelley passed away in 1822 (the year which
followed that of the coronation of George IV.);
while within a few weeks there took place an
interesting benefit performance, at which "The
Rivals" was acted, with the following cast:—

Sir Anthony . . .	Munden.
Captain Absolute . .	Charles Kemble.
Faulkland . . .	Young.
Acres	Liston.
Lydia	Mrs Edwin.
Mrs Malaprop . . .	Mrs Davenport.

The next year is specially noteworthy for the
production, in May, of Henry Bishop and Howard
Payne's opera, "The Maid of Milan," which contained the air "Home, Sweet Home"; while in
the following December, a tragedy by Mrs Hemans
saw the light under the title "The Vespers of
Palermo."

The year is, however, perhaps most important
to us from the, at that time, unparalleled constella-
tion of stars who were appearing at Drury Lane:
Macready, Kean, Young, Munden, Liston, Elliston,
Terry, Harley, Knight, Miss Stephens, and Mme.
Vestris.

In 1824, the year of Byron's death, Henry Bishop
left Covent Garden for Drury Lane, and Carl Von
Weber was engaged in his place, in honour of
which event "Der Freischütz" was brought out
at the English Opera House, being also produced
in the autumn at Covent Garden, where it was

given for no less than fifty-two performances during the season of 1824-25.

And what of the salaries which were being received by theatrical stars at the beginning of the nineteenth century?

The great Charles Mathews writes at this time of a proposed engagement, "Now to my offer, which I think stupendous and magnificent, £17 a-week." John Kemble, for acting and managing, was receiving £36; Miss O'Neill, at the most brilliant portion of her career, never had more than £25 a-week; while Mrs Jordan at her zenith had thirty guineas; and Charles Kemble, until he became his own manager, never received more than £20 a-week.

Strange reading, indeed, when we compare it with the salaries which theatrical stars were receiving during the last few years of Garcia's life.

CHAPTER V.

OPERA IN AMERICA.

(1825–1826.)

THE earliest operatic performances in America were
derived not from Italian but from English sources.
Elson tells us in his book on American music that
" The Beggar's Opera," which created such a furore
in Great Britain, probably was the first entertainment of the kind given in the colonies, being performed in New York as early as December 3, 1750,
and innumerable times thereafter. This was followed by a series of other ballad operas.

" From the conglomerate Ballad Opera, often the
work of half a dozen composers," Elson continues,
" New York passed on to a more unified art-work,
and the operas of Arnold, Storace, and Dibdin were
given with some frequency. During the British
occupation, in revolutionary days, the English regi-
mental bands often assisted in the orchestral parts
of the operatic performances. At a later period
many refugees, driven from France by the Revolution, were to be found eking out a precarious livelihood in the orchestra.

" At the beginning of the nineteenth century
Charleston and Baltimore entered the operatic

field, and travelling troupes came into existence, making short circuits from New York through the large cities, but avoiding Boston, which was wholly given over to Handel, Haydn, and psalms.

"In March 1825 New Yorkers heard a great opera for the first time, for 'Der Freischütz' came to America by way of England. It was adapted and arranged with the boldest of alterations and makeshifts. Extra dances were introduced to charm the audience, and the incantation scene was often given without singing, as melodrama that is, recitation with orchestral accompaniment, while the fireworks let off during the scene won public favour at once.

"But the real beginning of opera in New York, and in a certain sense in America, occurred in the autumn of this year, when the elder Garcia arrived with his well-equipped opera troupe. Well might a critic of that day speak of the Spanish tenor as 'our musical Columbus.' The whole season of opera during that memorable period was a revelation to the new world."

The company which the elder Garcia brought with him from Europe consisted of the following principal artists. His daughter Maria, who was seventeen years old, undertook all the contralto *rôles*, while his wife and Mme. Barbieri were the soprani. He himself was, naturally, *primo tenore*, being assisted by the younger Crivelli as the *secondo*. The latter artist, the son of Gaëtano, one of the best Italian tenors, had first met the Garcia family in Naples, where he had spent some years in vocal study under Millico and Zingarelli.

During the last year of Garcia's stay in Italy
Crivelli had written an opera, which was performed
by the San Carlo company, of which it will be
remembered the elder Garcia was a member.

The baritone for the New York season was
" Garcia, jr.," as the subject of this memoir was
advertised, and the cast was completed by d'Angri-
sani as the *basso cantante*, and Rosich as the *buffo
caricato*. The chorus, which was collected and
organised by Garcia only with the greatest difficulty, consisted chiefly of mechanics settled in
America, who were accustomed to serve in choirs
and could read music.

Of the circumstances which brought about this
scheme of giving Italian opera in America we may
read in the biography of the poet, Fitz-Greene
Halleck. In it the author, General James Grant
Wilson, tells us that Halleck was one of the two
thousand New York pupils of Signor Daponte, who
was for many years professor of Italian literature
in Columbia College there. " To this Signor
Daponte, the personal friend of Mozart, and writer
of the libretto of 'Don Giovanni,' the poet told me,"
says the biographer, " that we were indebted for
the introduction of Italian opera here, he having,
with the late Dominick Lynch and Stephen Price,
induced the elder Garcia to visit them with his
troupe, and appear at the Park Theatre, of which
Price was the manager."

When the elder Garcia arrived in New York
he was at once visited by this Daponte, and it is
reported that he rushed up to the Italian librettist
and embraced him with the greatest warmth, sing-

ing all the while the aria "Fin ch'han dal vino," the Drinking Song from "Don Giovanni," for the words of which Daponte had been responsible.

During October and November, in addition to appearing in oratorio, the Garcia family gave a number of concerts, during which the tenor delighted to show the perfection of his method. He had a custom of striking a single chord, and then with his wife, son, and daughter, rendering a difficult operatic quartette, unaccompanied. At the end he would strike the chord again, to show that they had not deviated from the pitch to the extent of even a hair's-breadth. They certainly formed a quartette of pre-eminent ability; indeed, Chorley, one of the greatest musical authorities of his day, wrote of them, "The family of Spanish musicians are representative artists, whose power, genius, and originality have impressed a permanent trace on the record of the methods of vocal execution and ornament."

The first mention of their arrival we find in the 'Harmonicon,' which had a notice on October 25, to the effect that "The Spanish family of the Garcias, consisting of husband, wife, son, and daughter, have been engaged by Mr Price."

Some three weeks later a preliminary notice of their forthcoming venture appeared in a New York paper called 'The Albion, or British, Colonial, and Foreign Weekly Gazette.' In its issue of November 19 there was printed the following prospectus, which may be quoted in full, as it contains several points of interest :—

" Signor Garcia respectfully announces to the

American public that he has lately arrived in this country with an Italian troupe (among whom are some of the first artists in Europe), and has made arrangements with the managers of the New York Theatre to have the house on Tuesdays and Saturdays, on which nights the choicest Italian operas will be performed in a style which he flatters himself will give general satisfaction.

" For the succeeding eight days the names of persons desirous to take boxes or benches for the season of three months, or for one month, will be received at the box office at the theatre, and the applicants for the longest term and greatest number of seats will be entitled to the choice of boxes. The seats in the pit will also be numbered, and may be taken for the same periods.

" The price of the box places will be two dollars ; of pit, one dollar ; and of gallery, twenty-five cents.

" The opera of ' Il Barbiera (*sic*) di Seviglia ' is now in rehearsal, and will be given as soon as possible.

" Tickets of the permanent boxes will be transferable. Performance to commence at 8 o'clock."

In the next issue of the paper we read that

" Signor Garcia has the honour to announce to the public that the opera of ' Il Barbiere di Seviglia ' will be performed on Tuesday next. The books are now open, and places may be taken at the Box Office."

The advertisement goes on to state that " the best operas of Cimarosa, Mozart, and Paisiello, with others by Rossini, will be immediately put in rehearsal."

The opening performance was given at the Park

Theatre on November 29, 1825, the opera being "Il Barbiere," cast as follows :—

Almaviva . . .	Garcia, Senior.
Figaro . . .	Garcia, Junior.
Rosina . . .	Maria Garcia.
Bertha . . .	Madame Garcia.
Bartolo . . .	Rosich.
Basilio . . .	d'Angrisani.
Fiorello . . .	Crivelli.

'The Albion' gave the opera company an encouraging send-off in the following naïve announcement :—

"We have been disappointed in not receiving a *scientific* critique, which we were promised from a professor, on the Italian Opera of Tuesday night; we shall, however, have something to say later, and meanwhile can state that the experiment has proved completely successful, and the troupe may be assured of making a fortunate campaign."

It is recorded further that "an assemblage of ladies so fashionable, so numerous, so elegantly dressed, has probably never been witnessed in an American theatre."

General Grant Wilson gives us some further details of this fashionable audience, for, according to him, it included Joseph Bonaparte, the ex-King of Spain, and the two friends, Fenimore Cooper and Fitz-Greene Halleck, who sat side by side, delighted listeners. Another account refers to the representation in these terms :—

"We were last night surprised, delighted, enchanted : and such were the feelings of all who witnessed the performance. The repeated plaudits

with which the theatre rung were unequivocal, un-
affected bursts of laughter. The best compliment
that can be paid to the merit of the company was
the unbroken attention that was yielded throughout
the entire performance, except that every now and
then it was interrupted by judiciously bestowed
marks of applause, which were simultaneously given
from all parts of the house. In one respect the
exhibition excelled all that we have ever witnessed
in any of our theatres — the whole troupe were
almost equally excellent : nor was there one whose
exertions to fill the part allotted to him did not
essentially contribute to the success of the piece.

"Signor Garcia indulges in a florid style of
singing : with his fine voice, fine taste, admirable
ear, and brilliancy of execution, we could not be
otherwise than delighted. . . . Signorina Garcia's
voice is what is denominated a fine contra-alto "—
the gentleman is nothing if not correct, while we
trace in the next words the unquestionable fact that
he has been comparing notes with our " scientific "
friend of ' The Albion.' " Her science and skill are
such as to enable her to run over every tone and
semitone with an ease and grace that cost apparently no effort." The sentence reads for all the
world like a twentieth-century eulogy of an ardent
motorist, if we substitute for tone and semitone
the words woman and child.

He concludes with a vivid little sketch of Maria
Garcia as she was at the age of seventeen :—

" Her person is about the middle height, slightly
embonpoint; her eyes dark, arch, and expressive ; and a playful smile is almost constantly the

companion of her lips. She was the magnet who attracted all eyes and won all hearts."

This was Manuel Garcia's operatic *début:* it was not his first appearance before the public, for, as we have seen, he had already been singing previously at several concerts. It has been asserted by some that his *début* in opera was made in Paris in the preceding year, but he himself declared this was untrue; while his sister, Pauline Viardot-Garcia, has stated most definitely that it took place in New York.

His voice was never powerful : he had sung with charm as a boy, and when his voice broke it developed into high baritone — not tenor, as has been asserted by many. The latter mistake probably originated in the fact that sometimes, as will be related later, he undertook the tenor parts when his father felt indisposed ; but on these occasions he always altered the melody of the higher passages to suit his baritone voice.

In the first and subsequent performances of "Il Barbiere" his artistic singing of the air "Largo al factotum" made a considerable stir in New York, and his popularity was thereby considerably increased, but from the criticisms it is obvious that Manuel Garcia would never have been an operatic artist of the first rank, and, as we shall see, he was to find his *métier* in another field of music.

On the last day of the year we read in 'The Albion' that "The celebrated opera of 'Tancredi' will be produced at the Park Theatre this evening."

The paragraph which followed immediately after the above announcement recalls the mixed receptions which the immortal Kean sometimes experienced when he made his earlier appearances on the American stage :—

"Mr Kean has returned from Boston. The managers of the Boston theatre declare in an address to the public that they had no reason whatever to suppose that any serious or organised opposition existed against Mr Kean until 4 o'clock of the evening of his appearance.

"That amiable lady and excellent actress, Mrs Hilson, takes a Benefit at the Park on Wednesday, on which occasion Mr Kean has offered to perform in a favourite part."

In the next issue, January 7, 1826, we find the criticism of the performance of "Tancredi." One of the company had apparently discharged the duties of scene-painter for the production, and with success.

"'Tancredi' has been performed twice to crowded houses by Senior (sic) Garcia and his admirable troupe. Nothing could exceed the enthusiasm with which it was received. The scenery, painted by one of the troupe, is of matchless vigour and beauty, displaying magnificent ruins, paintings, &c., so peculiar to modern Italy.

"The corps has received a most efficient auxiliary in the person of Madame Barbiere (sic). Signorina Garcia takes the part of Tancredi. The piece, from its own intrinsic merits and the excellent manner in which it is performed, cannot fail to have a good run."

Evidently the Italian language was not a strong point in the office of 'The Albion.' We have already seen how "Il Barbiere" figured as "Il

E

Barbiera," and Madame Barbieri as "Barbiere," while Signor Garcia appeared as "Senior." A still stranger mistake occurred in the notice of the *première* of "Otello" on February 11 :—

"Rossini's opera of 'Otella' (*sic*) has been produced by the Italian troupe. It was a most fortunate effort, and the piece, we trust, will have a good run. Signor Garcia astonished the audience with his masterly powers, many of whom had no conception that so much tragic effect could be given in recitative.

"After the performance Signor Garcia was addressed by Mr Kean behind the scenes, who complimented the highly-talented vocalist on the great talent he had that night displayed, and expressed in the warmest terms the gratification experienced in listening to him. Several of the troupe were present on Wednesday to see Mr Kean in the part of Othello."

In this American *première* of Rossini's "Otello," one of the greatest successes of the season, we find the parts distributed as follows :—

Otello . . .	Signor Garcia.
Iago . . .	Signor Garcia (junior).
Elmiro . .	Signor Angrisani.
Doge . . .	Signor Crivelli.
Roderigo . .	Madame Barbieri.
Emilia . .	Signora Garcia.
and	
Desdemona . .	Signorina Maria Garcia.

It must be many years since any operatic version of "Othello" has been performed other than that of Verdi, which was produced in Milan exactly sixty-one years after the performance of Rossini's setting just described. Indeed at the date of this American *première*, Giuseppe Verdi was but a lad entering his teens.

Another important production of the season was "Don Giovanni," given on May 23, with the elder Garcia in the title - *rôle*. His son appeared as Leporello, and, as the criticism in 'The Albion' stated four days later : " In the part of Saporello " —the office shines once more in spelling—" the younger Garcia exhibited more musical ability than he has been generally thought to possess. His duet with Don Giovanni in the banquet scene was spirited enough."

Some other portions of this critique read rather quaintly. It will be remembered how the editor of the paper was perturbed after the opening performance of the season at not receiving the " scientific critique, which we are promised from a professor." He is evidently "still harping on my daughter," for one reads with infinite regret that —" To enter into any minute examination of ' Don Giovanni's ' *scientific* merits is beyond our space and purpose " ; while later we learn that " Madame Barbiere's taste is pure, and her *science* considerable."

The critic comes to the regrettable conclusion that " Garcia Senior is not at home in the simple melodies of Mozart," the reason which he gives for this fact being set forth in a delightful bit of phraseology,—" He must have a wide field for display : he must have ample room to verge enough for unlimited curvetings and flourishes."

Maria was able to satisfy this most learned and scientific judge, and we may presume that she found sufficiency of verging - room in Mozart, for we are told, "Mdlle. Garcia's Zerlina, though not so simple and rustic as Fador's (*sic*), the great Zerlina of Europe, is much more pleasing and fascinating. It was admirably acted, which for a singer is high praise. The celebrated 'Batti, batti,' was never better sung."

"In proportion as she is excellent," the notice concludes, "must we regret that a few nights longer and she will disappear from the public gaze."

Why the good gentleman should have been so perturbed it is a little difficult to see, for the season did not terminate for four months. Perhaps the explanation is that, just as other scientific men declared that the seven days of the World's Creation really meant seven periods, each extending over hundreds of years, so this one in saying "a few nights," took each night to stand for a period of a month. After all, as has been observed in Lewis Carroll's immortal book, it is only a question of who is to be master, the man or the word.

On August 26 we are informed that "'Il Barbieri de Siviglia'"—mark the dazzling array of fresh mistakes in spelling—"was performed last night for the fortieth time without any abatement of attraction."

Finally we are told of the approaching end of the season :—

"*Sept.* 16*th.*—The Italian operas are about to

close in this city. We believe it is not finally
arranged how the troupe is to be disposed of, but
the Philadelphia papers express strong hopes of
having this delightful entertainment"—enchant-
ing phrase for such an occasion—"in that city.
The following is Signor Garcia's card :—

" 'Signor Garcia respectfully announces to the
public that his engagement is limited to five
representations of Italian operas, and will positively conclude on the 30th inst. On Saturday,
September 16th, the benefit of Garcia, jun.' "—this
was how Manuel appeared on the bills throughout
the New York season—" 'Tuesday the 19th, benefit of Mme. Garcia ; Saturday the 23rd, benefit
of Signor Garcia, Tuesday the 26th, benefit of
Signorina Garcia, concluding Saturday the 30th,
this being positively the last night of performance.' "

And so, on September 30, 1826, the first
American season of Italian opera was brought to
a close, after lasting ten months,—seventy - nine
performances in all.

As to the repertoire, we have already set down
the names of " Il Barbiere," " Don Giovanni,"
" Tancredi," and " Otello" ; besides these we find
Zingarelli's "' Romeo e Giulietta," which in later
years was to be ousted as completely from the field
by Gounod's version as Rossini's " Otello" was
fated to be by Verdi's. The list was completed
by " Cenerentola," " Semiramide," " Turco in
Italia," and two operas specially written by the
elder Garcia, with a view to showing off his
daughter's talents, " L'Amante Astuto," 'and " La
Figlia dell' Aria."

As to the composition of the orchestra, we learn that it consisted of seven violins, two violas, three violoncellos, two double - basses, two flutes, two clarinets, one bassoon, two horns, two trumpets, and drums,—twenty-four performers in all. The first violin and leader was De Luce, while a M. Etienne presided at the pianoforte. That the orchestral standard was by no means as high as that of the vocalists, may be readily surmised from the following criticism of one of the earliest performances :—

"The violins might be a little too loud; but one soul seemed to inspire and a single hand to guide, the whole band being throughout the magic mazes of Rossini's most intricate flights under the direction of M. de Luce ; while M. Etienne presided in an effective manner at a piano, of which every now and then he might be heard to touch the keynote by those whose attention was turned that way, and just loud enough to be heard throughout the orchestra, for whose guidance it was intended."

As has been already stated, the performance took place on Tuesday and Saturday evenings. The latter was a very great mistake, owing to the strong religious feelings of the city, which kept the inhabitants from going out on this evening for fear of interfering with preparation for the Sabbath. As we may read in a notice of the season, which was sent over by the New York correspondent to one of the English papers: "Saturdays were fixed on in imitation of London, but on the night which is your best nobody goes to the theatre, for we are very *serious* in this city, and do not go to the late amusements on Saturday."

However, in spite of this *contretemps,* the season turned out a complete success, for the 79 performances brought in gross receipts of 56,685 dollars (ranging from 1962 dollars on the best night to 250 dollars on the worst), which made an average of some 700 dollars at each representation.

It is rather ludicrous to read some of the articles which appeared in the New York papers during the earlier months of the Italian Opera. In them advice was given to those who had written asking questions as to how to dress in a fashionable way for the opera nights, according to the European manner, and how to behave during an opera performance.

In fact, it was thought " the thing " to go to the Park Theatre season, and the whole affair created the greatest excitement among the fashionables of Manhattanville.

Finally, we read towards the end of September of the future plans of the company :—

" They have been invited to New Orleans and also to Mexico, and it is believed that they will go to the latter place when their engagement here is over."

With the 1st of October 1826 the New York opera season had become a thing of the past, and on October 2 the dramatic season of Macready, a thing of the present, for on that date the tragedian trod the boards of an American stage for the first time. One cannot perhaps bring the chapter to a more seemly close than with the announcement which the ever-fascinating 'Albion' made in speaking of the opening performance :—

"Mr Macready appeared in the character of Virginius, in the presence of an audience of the most respectable description, and comprising all the talent and critical acumen of this great city." One can only pray that the scientific acumen was not absent on that memorable and respectable occasion.

CHAPTER VI.

NEW YORK AND MEXICO.

(1826–1827.)

PICTURE to yourself Señor Garcia sallying forth into the streets of New York on February 4, 1826, and purchasing a paper, to be confronted with this piece of up-to-date intelligence :—

" The following despatch was transmitted from Strasburg to Paris on Saturday afternoon, ' The Emperor Alexander I. of Russia died at Taganrog on December 1st, after a few days' indisposition.' The express which brought this intelligence left Warsaw on the 8th inst."

Here, then, we find that it has taken exactly nine weeks for important Russian news to reach New York. A fortnight later a short article appeared in one of the American papers which gives a rather good insight into the state of civilisation at that period. It has been sent over by a London correspondent. Above the contribution is the heading, in large type, " STEAM GUN EXPERIMENTS." I quote some of the more interesting portions :—

" At length this formidable weapon, destined, if ultimately adopted, to change the whole system of modern warfare, has been so perfected by Mr

Perkins that the effects of its projectile power from a musket bore and with a lead ball may be fully judged. A trial was made last month at Mr Perkins' manufactory in the Regent's Park before the Duke of Wellington and staff." A strange piece of reading indeed.

"The adoption of the most destructive implements possible in war will be most friendly to humanity, by shortening its duration. Offensive war will profit much less than defensive. A fort may be made impregnable against an attacking force, and a breach (could such a thing be made under the fire of steam artillery) could not be stormed. It is impossible to foresee what changes this discovery may not make in the history of nations.

.   .   .   .

"It is not exceeding the bounds of probability to suppose that we shall ere long as commonly see vessels propelled by Perkins' steam-engines undertaking the most distant voyages, as we now see them employed on our coasts. In this case, calms, contrary winds, and tides will be comparatively of little consequence, since a steam vessel, under such favourable circumstances, can always make some way on her voyage or retreat into harbour."

Here I may be permitted to quote a series of paragraphs culled from 'The Albion' of March 25 of this same year, as being good specimens of the news which the maestro was accustomed to read. They give a series of vivid glimpses into the days when he was a young man. First, let us see some of the tit-bits of up-to-date gossip and fashionable news which the London correspondents have to retail to their subscribers in New York :—

" Mr Charles Mathews, the celebrated comedian, is on a visit to Sir Walter Scott at Abbotsford."

" Madame Pasta was expected to be in London by the first of April." Inauspicious date !

" His Majesty [this would be George IV.] on his return to town will occupy apartments at St James's. Carlton House will not again be the Royal residence."

" The expense of postage of letters through the medium of the Twopenny Post Office by Alderman Thompson's Committee, when he first announced himself as one of the candidates for the presentation of the City, amounted to no less a sum than £128."

" *Industry and Talent.*—It is a notorious fact that Sir Walter Scott unites drudgery with lofty genius, and has put his hand to almost every department of literay (*sic*) labour, without being scared by occasional want of success."

Farther on we find this heading, in large type, under " Intelligence received, by the *Bayard*, from Havre "—

" SPEECH OF THE KING OF FRANCE,
" Delivered at the opening of the Chambers,
January 31st."

Then follows a full report of the address which Charles X. had given eight weeks before.

Next we come to a piece of geographical dis-covery :—

" The operations of the British armies against the Burmese enable us to correct many errors and to

add to our limited knowledge of the geography of
the East.   A short time since, we announced the
important fact that a branch of the Irrawaddy
had been discovered to discharge into the Bay of
Bengal.   This discovery has been fully confirmed,
various stragglers from Sir Archibald Campbell's
army at Prome having found their way to the coast
in that direction, and there got on board English
vessels."

The last quotation which I will make from the
issue of that date refers to the " Seizure of a
slave vessel in England."   In it we read how
" The French vessel was boarded and subsequently
seized by Lieutenant Rye of the coastguard service.
She was found well fitted out with all the ordinary furniture of a slave-trader, her hold adapted
in the usual way to the reception of slaves.
Among her other stores there were, of course, found
manacles and shackles in great abundance : a
long chain to confine the unfortunate creatures
in gangs, with all the usual implements of negro
torture that would not be understood by their
names, we are happy to say, by most of our
readers."

These, then, were the special plums of " Latest
Intelligence " from Europe, which the twenty-year-
old Manuel no doubt devoured with keenest relish
on that morning eighty odd years ago.

I should like to make one more quotation from
the same paper, two months later, for it gives us a
glimpse of both the artistic and military doings of
Europe at this time.   The article in question is an
appreciation of the President of the Royal Academy.

" Sir Thomas Lawrence is confessedly at the head of the English school of portrait-painters. He is about forty-seven years of age. The Kembles and Mrs Siddons have been his favourite associates. At one time he was a particular friend of the late Queen Caroline. His portraits of George IV. are excellent. In 1818 he was commissioned to visit the Congress of Aix-la-Chapelle for the purpose of painting the monarchs, warriors, and statesmen of Europe. During that visit the doors of his *atelier* were open to his friends, and it is impossible to fancy a more interesting sight than his morning levée. The Emperors of Russia and Austria, the King of Prussia, Wellington, Richelieu, Blücher, Bernstoff, and a long train of distinguished personages, were almost always to be met there."

During the opera season of 1826 two strange events took place which Señor Garcia would recall in after-years. At the time the one filled the inhabitants of New York with the wildest excitement, the second with the deepest gloom.

On April 8—three weeks, that is to say, after the future centenarian had celebrated his twenty-first birthday—the extraordinary duel took place between John Randolph, United States Senator from Virginia, and Henry Clay, Secretary of State. The meeting was on the right bank of the Potomac within the state of Virginia, above the Little Falls Bridge—pistols, at ten paces. Each of the principals was attended by two seconds and a surgeon, while Senator Benton was present as a mutual friend. Needless to say, it ended in the way which was to become so fashionable among French duel-

lists in later years. The daring combatants escaped
scatheless and shook hands, — the gentlemanly
Anglo-Saxon alternative for each rushing into the
other's arms with a wild cry of "Mon ami! mon
ami!" and saluting his late adversary with an affec-
tionate kiss on either cheek.

As to the second event, one cannot do better
than let the story be told by the notice which
appeared in one of the New York newspapers:—

"JUBILEE OF DECLARATION OF INDEPENDENCE.

"FOURTH OF JULY CELEBRATIONS.

"SUDDEN DEATH OF TWO EX-PRESIDENTS.

"The death of John Adams, late President of the United
States, took place on July 4. He was the second President
of the United States and the first Minister sent by this
country to Great Britain after the acknowledgment of the
Independence.

"He departed this life, full of years and honours, on the
evening of the 4th inst., as the bells were ringing for the
conclusion of the celebration of the auspicious day. The
venerable patriot rose in his usual health, rejoicing that he
had been spared to witness the jubilee of his country's
freedom. Towards noon he became ill, grew gradually
worse, and at six fell asleep. He was one of the earliest
and ablest and most fearless champions of his country's
freedom, and his name fills a wide space in its history. Only
two of the signers of the Declaration of Independence now
survive.

"DEATH OF MR JEFFERSON.

"Mr Jefferson, late President of the United States, died
at his residence in Virginia, on July 4, at 10 to 1 o'clock.

It is a strange coincidence that these two venerable personages should have paid the debt of nature on the same day,
and that day the Fiftieth anniversary of that Independence
which they so essentially contributed to achieve."

On September 30, as we have seen, the New
York venture of Italian Opera was brought to a
conclusion.

A few days later the elder Garcia set off for
Mexico, where he had arranged to initiate a season
at the Opera House. He was accompanied on the
journey by the whole troupe, with the exception of
his daughter Maria.

The reason of her remaining behind was that on
March 23 of that year she had given her hand to
Monsieur Malibran, a French merchant three times
her own age, and by repute a very wealthy man.
It can scarcely have been a love-match, for the
union appears to have been a most unhappy one
from the start. As to the reason for the marriage,
some light has been thrown by Fitz - Greene
Halleck's biographer, in a conversation which I
had with him recently.

It will be remembered that Halleck was present
at the opening night of Italian opera in America,
in the company of his friend Fenimore Cooper.
The latter must have been busy correcting the
proofs of his latest book, 'The Last of the
Mohicans,' since this was published in New York
soon after the New Year, — a literary event
which of course Manuel Garcia could quite well
remember.

Halleck at once fell under the spell of Maria's
voice and personality. Of his admiration for her

singing he wrote these lines, alluding to his own death :—

> " And when that grass is green above me,
> And those, who bless me now and love me,
>   Are sleeping by my side,
> Will it avail me aught that men
> Tell to the world with lip and pen
> That once I lived and died ?
>
> No ! if a Garland for my brow
> Is growing, let me have it now,
>   While I'm alive to wear it ;
> And if, in whispering my name,
> There's music in the voice of fame
>   Like Garcia's, let me hear it."

Was ever a more beautiful compliment paid to a singer ?

It was not long before the poet obtained an introduction to his ideal. The acquaintance thus began quickly ripened, and Fitz - Greene Halleck became deeply attached to her. This warmth of feeling was undoubtedly returned, and there seems every probability that Maria, girl of seventeen as she was, might have been well content to wed the American poet. Her father, however, intervened, and sternly refused to allow things to go farther.

Here we have a possible explanation of the tragedy which ensued. Monsieur Malibran came upon the scene and offered himself, and Maria perhaps decided to accept him in order to escape from the discipline of an exacting parent. There certainly must have been some very powerful reason at work to bring about her union with a man older than her own father, at an age when youth and romance would naturally appeal to her most

strongly, and such a wedding of May and December
could not but appear repulsive in the extreme.
Certainly it can hardly have been the man's re-
puted wealth which tempted her to take such a
step, seeing that she was already well advanced
on the road to becoming one of the greatest operatic
stars of her day.

After the wedding and her family's departure
for Mexico, the unhappy Maria discovered that her
husband's affairs had for some time past been in
a very bad state, and that he had really been
counting on the income which would accrue from
her talents.   Matters grew rapidly worse, and
within a year of the marriage he was declared
bankrupt and thrown into prison.   Under these
circumstances Maria at once, of her own accord,
determined to resign, for the benefit of her
husband's creditors, the whole of the provision
which had been made for her by the marriage
settlements.   It was a noble act, which gave rise
to strong manifestations of favour and approbation on the part of the American public.

For some months after this she remained in New
York, singing on Sundays at Grace Church, and
occasionally appearing at the Bowery Theatre in
English operettas, such as "The Devil's Bridge"
and "Love in a Village."

By this time, however, the youthful contralto
had had her eyes thoroughly opened as to the
character of the man to whom she had given
herself, and at last she bravely decided to cut
the Gordian knot by leaving her husband and
returning to Europe.

F

Accordingly her final appearance on the American stage was announced for September 28, 1827, and on this night she took her farewell benefit at the Bowery Theatre, in Boieldieu's "Jean de Paris." Of the closing scene of that evening we read—

" When the programme had been completed, the Signorina came forward and seated herself at her harp, but seemingly overcome with emotion again rose. Mr Etienne, the pianist, thereupon took up the prelude to a farewell song, specially written for the occasion, and this, on regaining her composure, she sang in a most touching and effective manner."

Within a few days of this performance Maria set out for Paris, where, as we shall see, she was to be joined almost immediately by her brother.

And now we will turn to the fortunes of the rest of the Garcia family, who had left New York to inaugurate a season of opera in Mexico.

Upon arriving at the end of the journey, the elder Garcia soon found that the duties of impresario, composer, conductor, chorus master, and even machinist and scene-painter, must all centre in himself.

But this was not the worst, for at the very outset a calamity fell upon the company which with any one else would have been sufficient to bring the season to a close before it had opened, as an Irishman might have put it.

On reaching the Opera House in Mexico city, they at once began to prepare for their forthcoming season. Everything was unpacked, and they commenced going through scenery, dresses, properties, and the rest. All these they found in order. When, however, they began to look for the music score and orchestral parts, they found, to their horror, that nearly the whole of the music had been left behind or lost *en route.*

What was to be done? Their season was advertised to commence in a few days, and without music it was utterly impossible. The artists were in despair, and completely lost their heads. The elder Garcia alone remained calm in the midst of turmoil. They could not perform without music; very well, he must write out fresh copies of the scores as best he could. What was advertised for the first night? "Don Giovanni"? *Bien;* then he would make a start on that. Without losing a moment he set to work, and actually reproduced the whole of the full orchestral score from memory! As each number was finished it was given out to copyists, who prepared the separate parts for the various instruments.

This task being ended, the marvellous man set to work on "Otello" and "Il Barbiere," which with the first named had always been the most important in his repertoire. How successfully he carried out his self-imposed task may be judged from the fact that when "Don Giovanni" was given, no one present could tell that it was not the original score. As if this had not been enough work, he promptly proceeded to compose eight operas for his company to perform; nor was this all, for finding that the words of the Italian operas were not understood, and that the people had not the northern affectation of liking them better on that account, he translated into his native Spanish every work which was performed. And here a few words may be said upon the memorising of new operas.

It was customary in those days for managers to allow their artists nine days to learn a two-act opera. For three acts the time would be increased to twelve days, and for four acts sixteen. That the elder Garcia did not always allow so much is borne out by the statement which Maria Malibran used to make that, on one occasion, her parent bade her learn a *rôle* in two days and sing it at the opera.

"I cannot do it, father."

"You *will* do it, my daughter; and if you fail in any way, I shall *really* strike you with my dagger when I am supposed to kill you on the stage."

"And he would have done it, too," she would add, "so I played the part."

Manuel himself was ever a phenomenally quick "study" in the memorising of any fresh *rôle*. Short though the periods would be which were allowed in the ordinary way for learning a work, they were for him a great deal too long. He was able to commit to memory the whole of his part in two or three days, while at the end of ten he had picked up the parts of all the other singers as well, so that if necessary he was perfectly able to prompt them during the final rehearsals.

His father used to take advantage of this extraordinary memory, and, when feeling indisposed, would say, "You must go on, and take my part to-night." The son would proceed to do so, and get through the performance successfully, singing the tenor *rôle*, in which he would alter the high passages to suit his own voice.

All this hard work, however, was not accomplished without leaving its mark, and in a few months he began to feel the effects of the strain involved in this perpetual rehearsing and singing not only of his own baritone parts but on occasions of the tenor music. His father was a hard taskmaster, and the son, though he had a fine voice, found the work involved by an operatic career too hard for his physical resources. At last things reached a point at which, as he once told me, he went through every successive performance in a state of fear lest his voice should leave him suddenly when he was on the stage.

His father and mother laughed at this feeling as absurd, and told him that he must study for a time in Italy, and then make his *début* there, as they had set their hearts on it. Partly, therefore, to please them, partly, it may be, to comfort and assist Maria, of whose intention to set out for Paris in the September he must have been well aware, Manuel Garcia left his parents to continue their season in Mexico, and in the early autumn of 1827 set out for Europe alone.

CHAPTER VII.

OPERATIC CAREER ABANDONED.

(1828–1830.)

MANUEL GARCIA, in the January of 1828, was present at the operatic *début* of his sister, Maria Malibran, in Paris, the details of which he once gave to me. On another occasion he stated most distinctly that he left his parents in Mexico about the middle of their stay, set out for Paris, and, arriving there not long after his sister, remained with her till after her *début*. He added that during this period she continued her vocal studies under his tuition.

Under these circumstances one may safely assume that he arrived in the French capital either in October or in the early part of November, 1827.

With regard to Mme. Malibran's *début*, the following is the story as he gave it. I related the episode in 'Antoinette Sterling and Other Celebrities,' from which I am enabled to quote here and elsewhere in the present memoir by courtesy of the publishers, Messrs Hutchinson.

Rossini was director both of the Théâtre Italien and of the Grand Opera House, where French alone was performed. He was a great friend of both

Maria Malibran and her brother, and frequently came to visit them at their house. Moreover, he heard the young contralto sing many times at social functions, often indeed himself accompanying her at the piano. Yet, though perfectly aware what a splendid singer she was, the composer never made her any offer to appear under either of the two managements.

At last her opportunity of making an operatic *debut* in Paris arrived, but from quite another source. Galli, a famous basso of that time, who was having a benefit at the Italian Opera House, called one day and told her that he would put on "Semiramide" if she would like to sing the title part. After consulting with Manuel, she decided to accept the offer.

Of the performance itself one of the Paris journals gives a graphic account :—

"The singer, at her entrance, was greeted with warm applause. Her commanding figure and the regularity of her features bespoke the favour of the public. The noble and dignified manner in which she gave the first phrase, 'Fra tanti regi e popoli,' justified the reception she had obtained, but the difficult phrase, 'Frema il empio,' proved a stumbling-block which she could not surmount. Alarmed by this check, she did not attempt the difficult passage in the 'da capo,' but, dropping her voice, terminated the passage without effect, and made her exit, leaving the audience in doubt and dissatisfaction. The prodigious talent displayed by Pisaroni in the subsequent scenes gave occasion to comparisons by no means favourable to Mme. Malibran. On her re-

entrance she was coldly received; but she soon succeeded in winning the public to her favour. In the
andante to the air, ' Bel raggio lusinghier,' the young
singer threw out such powers, and displayed a voice
so full and beautiful, that the former coldness gave
way to applause. Encouraged by this, she hazarded
the greatest difficulties of execution, and appeared
so inspired by her success that her courage now
became temerity."

From that night she was the idol of the French
public.

Another French critic writes, " If Maria Malibran
must yield the palm to Pasta in point of acting, yet
she possesses a decided superiority in respect to
song."

" Since that time," remarks Mr Hogarth, " the
superiority of Malibran to Pasta in song became
more and more evident; while in respect to acting,
though no performer has ever approached Pasta in
her own peculiar walk of terrible grandeur, yet none
has ever surpassed Maria Malibran in intelligence,
originality, vivacity, feeling, and those ' tender
strokes of art ' which at once reach the heart of
every spectator. Her versatility was wonderful.
Pasta, it has been truly said, is a Siddons : Malibran
is a Garrick."

On the morning following the Parisian *debut* a
note came asking Señor Garcia to go round to
Rossini's rooms. Upon doing so he found him in a
tremendous state of excitement, and prepared to
give Maria Malibran a four years' exclusive engagement, at the rate of more than a hundred thousand
francs per annum, if she would bind herself to sing

exclusively at the Grand Opera House during that period.

The terms were immense for those days. In spite of this, after careful consideration, the contralto decided to refuse them, feeling that it would be unwise to abandon Italian and confine herself to French for so long a time. She *did*, however, appear for him in a few operas, at enormous fees, with, if possible, greater success than before, at the Théâtre Italien during April and May.

Now it seemed very extraordinary to Señor Garcia and to his sister that Rossini should have heard her sing again and again in society without even mentioning such a thing as engaging her, and yet, after hearing her at the Opera House in music which she had sung before him on so many occasions, he should at once make her a magnificent offer for a term of years. Why was it? They could not understand it at all, and accordingly asked one day for the explanation.

"It is true," answered Rossini, "that I knew Maria Malibran was a brilliant singer from listening to her at private houses. But I had never heard her in a big place before a large audience. Consequently I felt that I could not make her a definite offer which would at all gauge her true value. Either I should be offering her less than she was worth, and by this be doing *her* an injustice, or I should be offering her more than she was worth, and so be doing *myself* an injustice. But now that I have heard her sing in front of an audience, and have observed what effect they mutually had each on the other, I can offer the very largest sum which her singing is intrinsically worth. That is the explanation of what I have done."

After remaining for a time to see his sister successfully started on her Parisian career, Manuel Garcia set out for Italy, and took up his residence there for some months. During this period he made the acquaintance of Lablache, whose voice was of the most marvellous power. There is a story which the maestro used to tell of the basso and Carl Weber which illustrates this fact.

Lablache was originally a double-bass player, and his first appearance in opera as a singer came about through a happy chance. A celebrated vocalist was suddenly indisposed just before the performance one night, and Lablache was induced to take his place and attempt the *rôle*. His rendering of the character was entirely successful, and he abandoned his old career for this new one.

A few months afterwards Weber, who had known his massive figure in the orchestra, heard him sing in opera. After listening to the enormous voice and magnificent basso notes, the composer exclaimed, "Mein Gott! he is still a double-bass."

The size of Lablache's voice aroused the emulation of Garcia, who, as his sister Mme. Viardot puts it, proceeded to play the part of the frog that wanted to make itself as big as a bull. In trying to imitate this Gulliver of *bassi* he undoubtedly did further injury to his voice, which had already been much overstrained by the hard usage it had received in Mexico.

When, therefore, about the beginning of 1829, he made a public appearance at Naples, as his parents had persuaded him to do, he did not come through the ordeal with much success. "Il débuta à Naples, je crois," says Mme. Viardot, "et il eût ce qu'il désirait, un four noir."

The next day Manuel collected copies of the newspaper critiques, which were unanimous in recommending him to tempt Fate no more on the stage, but to abandon the lyric career for which he was unfitted. These articles he dispatched to his father with a letter in which he wrote : "You see from these notices that I can never hope to become an operatic artiste." (" Je ne puis être artiste.") "From now onward I am going to devote myself to the occupation which I love, and for which I believe I was born." With this letter he definitely abandoned the operatic calling.

He then made his way back to France, and there joined his parents, who had arrived from Mexico in the late autumn of 1828.

During the period of the elder Garcia's stay in Mexico, political events occurred which were the very reverse of propitious to any musical venture.

In 1828 the candidates for the Presidency were Generals Pedraza and Guerrero. On the election of the former the opposite party took up arms, and a bloody contest ensued, which terminated in the downfall of Pedraza's Government and in his flight from the country on January 4, 1829. The months which followed were full of turmoil, and at last in March it became necessary for all Spaniards to leave.

Owing to this state of affairs the elder Garcia, after some eighteen months of hard work and considerable financial success, was obliged to bring his Mexican season to a hasty conclusion. He accordingly prepared at once to journey to the coast with the £6000 which he had made during his stay in America.

Owing to the disturbances he had the greatest difficulty in obtaining the necessary passports. At last, however, he succeeded, and set off for Vera Cruz with his wife and younger daughter Pauline, who was now seven years old.

He was provided with a guard of soldiers, which, however, proved to be too weak, or, what is far more likely, too faithless, to protect his goods. At a place called Tepeyagualo, in the valley of Rio Frio, the convoy was attacked by brigands, and he himself obliged to lie flat on his face while his baggage was plundered of a thousand ounces of gold — the savings of two and a half years' work. Not only this, but the men seized everything else which was of value : in fact, he was left with practically nothing save a small sum of money which he was carrying in a belt around his body.

After this disastrous experience Garcia and his family made their way to the coast, embarked at Vera Cruz, and finally arrived in Paris, without any financial result to show for all the time they had spent in America. The blow of losing £6000 in cash and all his properties affected him less than most men : his disregard for money and his love of work for its own sake were a byword among his friends.

Upon his return the elder Garcia made a few appearances at the Théâtre Italien in " Don Giovanni" and " Il Barbiere." His voice, however, was no longer what it had been. He was warmly welcomed by his old admirers ; but these quickly perceived that his travels and misfortune, if not the advance of age, had much impaired his powers. He himself realised the change, and almost at once retired from the operatic stage, being in his fifty-fifth year, and devoted himself exclusively to the teaching which he had already started in Paris before leaving for America.

Among those who studied under him one may recall Mmes. Ruiz-Garcia, Rimbault, Favelli, and the Countess Merlin, who in later years was to publish a life of Maria Malibran, which can be looked on as little more than a fairy romance woven round a fascinating personality. Then there was Mme. Meric-Lalande, a brilliant stage soprano, who came to him as a natural singer of light opera, and after receiving some stricter training from the old teacher, was highly successful in Vienna, Paris, and the principal opera houses of Italy.

Of the men, Jean Geraldy is deserving of mention, since he afterwards became well known both as vocalist in the operas of Rossini and as a composer of many popular songs and operettas.

But of all the elder Garcia's pupils the tenor Nourrit was by far the greatest. It was for him that

Rossini wrote the part of Arnold in " William Tell," and Meyerbeer the parts of Roberto in " Robert le Diable" and of Raoul in " The Huguenots "; while he also created the parts of Masaniello, and of Eleazar in Halévy's " La Juive."

Nourrit commenced his studies before the elder Garcia set out on the American trip. When the teacher returned in 1829, his old pupil, who had now been leading tenor at the opera for four years, came to resume lessons. Of these Mme. Pauline Viardot still has a strong recollection. She was then a child not yet ten years old, but, in spite of this fact, used to assist her father by playing for him when he gave his lessons. When, therefore, among the others, Adolph Nourrit came to the house, she often used to accompany him at the piano at the lessons, — an experience which she still recalls with the greatest delight.

Of her many memories of that time none is more interesting than the fact that she read off with Nourrit the first melodies of Schubert which arrived in Paris, and of which theirs was the only copy in the city.

Nourrit's end was a sad one. After having been leading tenor for many years, he resigned eventually because Duprez was associated with him for the interpretation of the principal *rôles;* and this fancied slight so preyed on his spirits that at last, after singing at a benefit concert at Naples, he threw himself out of the window and perished miserably.

While Garcia *père* was giving lessons to his pupils, he would compose at the side of the piano delightful airs which, in the moments when the pupils were resting their voices, he would give his daughter to play at the piano. Moreover, he used to write for the use of his little Pauline many excellent studies; for she had been gently using her voice under his guidance since she had been but four years old. One of these studies commenced with a shake on the words "Aspri rimorsi atroci; figli del fallo mio." And while uttering the phrase he would make her throw herself completely into the feeling of the words, as well as into the vocal rendering of the music.

As a teacher the elder Garcia was strict and vigorous, a man of rugged discipline, so that the musical training which he gave his children was of the most rigid and thoroughgoing type.

Something of this has been already alluded to in setting down the experience of Manuel's early studies. There is, further, a well - known story, doubtless authentic, of a stranger passing near their house in Paris, and hearing sobs and objurgations proceeding from within. He at once inquired what was the meaning of these noises, and was answered, "Ce n'est rien. C'est Monsieur Garcia, qui fait chanter ses demoiselles." However that may be, there can be no question of the excellent results of his teaching.

As regards the accusations of violence, strictness, and tyranny which were brought against him, Madame Viardot asserts that he was much calumniated both as a father and as a man. "How often," she says, "have I heard my sister Maria remark, 'Si mon père n'avait pas été si sévère avec moi, je

n'aurais rien fait de bon; j'étais paresseuse et in-
docile.'   As for myself," she adds, " I never saw my
father lose his patience with me while he taught
me the solfège, music and singing."

When Manuel Garcia returned to France after
his *début* at Naples, he did not immediately begin
teaching at the vocal conservatoire which his father
had started.   His predilections had always been
scientific, and he was passionately fond of all such
studies, but specially of anatomy and all that had
to do with the human body.   On his arrival he
was suddenly seized with an idea that he would
prefer a seafaring life, and without thinking the
matter over twice he resolved to become an officer
in the French mercantile marine.   With this object
in view he began the study of astronomy and
navigation, and pursued the work with so much
diligence that he obtained a post on a ship.   He
was, in fact, on the point of going on board to take
up this new career when his mother and sisters
besought him with tears and supplications to
relinquish his intentions.   So ardently did they
implore him, that when actually starting he was
overcome with emotion and gave way to their
entreaties.

Upon this he settled down with his parents in
the Rue des Trois Frères in Montmartre, and was
of great assistance in helping the elder Garcia to
give lessons at the vocal conservatoire.   The hall
porter of their house was no less a person than the
father of Henry Mürger !   Manuel often used to
catch up the boy Henry in his arms and kiss him as
he ran about the passages.   " Little Mürger was a

most charming child," recalls Mme. Viardot, "full of fun and the pet of the house. At that time he was winning prizes at school, and used to arrive home with his arms full of them. Perhaps he was rather ashamed of his origin, for in the day of his success he never came to see us. We should have been so happy if he had."

And what a day of success it was! After having commenced as a notary's clerk, he gave himself to literature, and led the life of privation and adventure described in his first and best novel, ' Scènes de la Vie de Bohème,' published in the year when Manuel Garcia was celebrating his fortieth birth- day. During Mürger's later years his popularity was secure and every journal open to him, but he wrote slowly and fitfully in the intervals of dissipation, and died in a Paris hospital over forty-five years ago.

Unhappily Manuel with his nature found, on settling down in Paris with his parents, that the somewhat overbearing manner of his father was difficult to get on with, considering that he himself was now twenty-five years of age.

At last, after a few months, he made up his mind that it would be best to absent himself from Paris for a time, in the hopes that this might result in a pleasanter state of things on his return.

It happened that the turn which events took in Algiers brought an opportunity for carrying out this desire. A dispute arose about the payment of seven million francs,—a debt incurred by France in the Egyptian expedition. Of this sum $4\frac{1}{2}$ millions had been paid, but the balance remained unsettled till certain counter-claims could be adjusted.

"After a tedious delay, Hassein, the Dey of Algiers, the principal creditor, became impatient," —I quote from Dr Brewer—"and demanded immediate payment. To this request no answer was vouchsafed; and the next time the French consul presented himself at court Hassein asked him why his master had not replied to his letter. The consul haughtily replied, 'The King of France holds no correspondence with the Dey of Algiers'; upon which the governor struck him across the face and fiercely abused the king.

"An insult like this could not, of course, be overlooked; and it was at once decided by the French Government that a squadron should be sent to receive the consul on board, and revenge the insult."

As soon as this news became known Manuel talked the matter over with his sister, Maria Malibran, and through her influence with the Commander-in-chief he was enabled to obtain an appointment in the commissariat of the army which was to accompany the expedition.

Accordingly he embarked at Toulon on May 11, 1830, and took part in the severe conflicts which ended in less than two months with the bombardment of Algiers and its surrender to the French armament under Bourmont and Duperré, the deposition of the Dey, and the total overthrow of the barbarian government. After the fall of Algiers the young Spaniard returned to Paris to find the capital in a state of uproar.

On July 26 the obnoxious ordinances were made known regarding the press and the reconstruction of the Chamber of Deputies, which had been dissolved in May. This at once let loose the furies of revolution, and hostilities were commenced with the raising of barricades on the very next day. Repeated conflicts took place between the army and the police, the latter ultimately aided by the National Guard. On the last day of the month Charles X. retired to Rambouillet, and the flight of the Ministry took place. On August 2 Charles abdicated, and five days later the Duke of Orleans accepted the crown as Louis Philippe I.

These events were quickly followed by the publication of the Constitutional Charter of July and the retirement of the ex-King to England. The closing scene of the drama took place in the December of the year, when Polignac and the other Ministers, who had been members of the administration of 1829, were tried and sentenced to life-long imprisonment.

During the last months of 1830 Manuel Garcia attached himself to the military hospitals. His reason for taking this step was that he had determined to go through a course of preliminary study in the scientific side of singing before devoting his life to the career of teaching. At the hospitals he took up medicine and some specialised studies which embraced the physiology of everything appertaining to the voice and the larynx, for he had already perceived the importance of physiology as an aid to the rational development of the voice. His labours were crowned with success, and contributed much to the determination of the exact anatomy of the vocal cords.

During this time he used to carry home in his pockets the most extraordinary things from his anatomy class. Madame Viardot speaks of it thus :—

"What do you think he brought? You would never guess. The throttles of all kinds of animals, —chickens, sheep, and cows. You would imagine that these would have disgusted me. But it was not so. He would give me a pair of bellows, which I would insert in these windpipes, one after another, and blow hard. Heavens! what extraordinary sounds they used to emit. The chickens' throttles would cluck, the sheep's would bleat, and the bulls' would roar, almost like life."

At the remembrance of these rather gruesome incidents Madame Viardot laughs, much in the spirit, one may suppose, of the delicate Spanish beauty who applauds the thrusts of the matador at a bull-fight.

With the end of the year 1830 we find the first portion of Manuel Garcia's life brought to a close, the period of preparation. During the first twenty-five years we have found him brought up in music, learning the old Italian method of singing from his father and Zingarelli, with a few lessons from Ansani; while harmony he has studied under Fétis. He has acquired practical knowledge as an actor and singer upon stage and concert platform : he has heard nearly all the greatest operatic artists in Italy, France, and England : he has already had some experience of teaching, and is well acquainted with the lines followed by the famous *maestri* who have gone before him. Moreover, when he makes his regular start as *professeur de chant* in 1831, he is able to apply his medical knowledge to the greatest advantage.

With all these advantages, added to a fine intellect, intuitive perception, and extraordinary patience, what wonder that when once he embarks on his career as a singing-master he never again looks back, but speedily establishes himself as a scientific teacher, with a reputation unequalled by any of his contemporaries?

SECOND PERIOD

PARIS

(1830–1848)

CHAPTER VIII.

AND now let us take up the career of Maria Malibran, since the next six years of Manuel Garcia's life are chiefly concerned with the triumphs of this his first pupil. We have already seen how, shortly after her return from America in the early autumn of 1827, she had been joined in Paris by Manuel; how the two lived there together for some months, while he helped his sister with her singing and coached her in her operatic work, and how, after a brilliant *début* at Galli's benefit in the January of 1828, the youthful contralto was engaged for the Italian Opera season in Paris, commencing in the following April.

In 1829 Maria Malibran returned to London, where she had made her *début* at the King's Theatre four years previously. On this second visit she received from Laporte sixty-six pounds a performance for a three months' season, two appearances a - week (40,000 francs in all); while the principal parts which she undertook were Desdemona, Semiramide, Romeo, Tancredi, Ninetta, and Zerlina.

This was the scene of that rivalry with Mme. Sontag which wrung from her the words, "Pourquoi chante-t-elle si bien, mon Dieu?" During the London season they shared the success, which brought about such coldness between them that it took all the tact and diplomacy of the Countess Merlin to persuade them to sing the duet from "Tancredi" together in her drawing-room.

On January 3 of the following year the two stars again appeared together in Paris in "Il Matrimonio segreto," given at the benefit of Mme. Damoreau - Cinti. A few days later they took part in "Tancredi." Rarely had Sontag given so beautiful a performance as she did in this her last appearance in the part before retiring into private life. At the close of the evening, as if to beg her rival's forgiveness for her triumph, she offered to Malibran, with a charming gesture, the flowers which had been thrown at her feet on the stage.

On the 18th of the month Henriette Sontag made her last bow before the public, and retired from the operatic world upon her marriage to Count Rossi. Thus Maria Malibran found the field clear, and remained without a rival among the contralti of her time. After this she appeared regularly each season in Paris and London during that brief career in which she took the world by storm. Like a meteor she dazzled all by a brilliancy beside which other stars seemed dim, and like a meteor she was to pass away as suddenly as she had arrived, within nine years of her *début* in Paris.

The salary which the famous contralto used to receive was for those days almost unprecedented.

Maria F. Malibran

(FROM AN OLD ENGRAVING WHICH BELONGED TO MANUEL GARCIA.)

Having received in the operatic season of 1829 sixty-six pounds a performance, as already stated, the following year found her salary increased to £125 a-night, nearly double what she had had, while in the next one she was paid £2775 for twenty-four performances.

Her tours through Italy were a series of triumphs. In Rome she was overwhelmed with praise; at Bologna the enthusiasm was such that the public subscribed for a bust to be executed in marble and placed in the theatre; while at Naples, her grandest triumph of all was achieved on the night when she took leave of the audience in the character of Ninetta. Six times after the fall of the curtain was she called forward to receive the reiterated plaudits and adieus of a public which seemed unable to bear the idea of separation from its new idol. The singer, for her part, had only strength and spirits left to kiss her hand to the assembled multitude, and indicate by expressive gestures the degree to which she was overpowered by fatigue and emotion. Nor did the scene end within the theatre, for a crowd rushed to the stage-door from all parts of the house, and as soon as their favourite's sedan-chair came out they escorted it, with loud acclamations, to the Palazzo Barbaja, and renewed their salutations as the artist ascended the steps.

Of her first appearance in Milan Señor Garcia gave me a delightful account. At that time Pasta was a great favourite in the city, her most effective part being Norma. Such enormous success had she made in this *rôle*, in fact, that the Milanese always used to allude to her as "Norma" instead of making use of her own name.

Upon her arrival Maria Malibran was asked by the director of the Opera House in what part she would like to make her first appearance. She at once replied, "Norma, signor."

"But, madame, do you forget Pasta?"

"Eh, bien? I am not afraid of Pasta. I will live or die as Norma." Bellini's opera was therefore announced.

At the opening night Pasta came to hear the newcomer, and took up her position in the middle box of the grand tier amidst loud applause from the populace. Maria Malibran made her first entrance without any sound of encouragement, and the aria was received in deliberate, stony silence. Her next number was the terzetto. After one of the passages which she had to render the audience suddenly forgot themselves and shouted out, "Bravo!" This was instantly followed by cries of "Hush!" "Silence!" The trio came to an end. Not a hand! Instead were heard sounds of dispute from all parts of the house: "She is great;" "She is nothing of the kind;" "She is better than Pasta;" "She is not;" and these remarks went on for the rest of the evening.

Upon the second night Pasta did not come to hear her new rival. This time, when Malibran entered and sang her aria, her rendering was greeted with immense applause, which continued throughout the evening in ever-increasing enthusiasm. At the close she was called before the curtain again and again, and when she left the

Opera House to drive home, the populace took out the horses and themselves dragged her to the hotel. From that moment she was the pet of the Milanese public : Pasta's reign was over. Señor Garcia added that the latter was a most finished vocalist, but cold, whereas the singing of his sister was full of warmth and fire.

Strange to say, Maria Malibran soon found herself mixed up with the Italian Liberal politics. At Naples already her sympathy for the Carbonari had excited some talk. At Milan she was *fêted* by all the aristocracy, who hated the Austrian rule. On the first night of Donizetti's " Marie Stuart," while taking the title-*rôle*, she had to reproach Elizabeth with her irregular birth, calling her " vile bastard." The whole audience at once saw in this expression an allusion to the usurpation of Lombardy, and broke out into loud shouts. Next day the Austrian governor ordered the scene to be suppressed, and at the same time threatened Maria Malibran with prison if she did not submit. The singer, however, resisted, declaring that the composer alone could make alterations in his work ; and in consequence of this action the opera was withdrawn from the bill. This only increased her popularity, and in all political manifestations the cry would be raised, " Vive Malibran," as in after years " Vive Verdi " became synonymous with " Vive Victor-Emmanuel."

Similar difficulties arose in Venice. The governor was afraid of Liberal manifestations, and was for that reason opposed to the engagement of the contralto at the Fenice Theatre ; indeed it was the intervention of the Emperor alone which made him

waive his objection.   A sumptuary law of the six-
teenth century, which had never been repealed,
enacted that all gondolas must be painted uni-
formly black.   Maria Malibran wished to change
this.   "I have introduced a novelty here," she
writes, "which will mark an epoch in my career : I
have had the outside of my gondola painted grey
with decorations in gold.   The gondoliers wear
scarlet jackets, hats of pale yellow, the edges bound
round with black velvet, blue cloth breeches with
red ribbon down the side, in the French style,
sleeves and collar of black velvet.   The awning
over the boat is scarlet with blue curtains."

When she went out in this for the first time the
police at once reminded her of the regulations, but
she refused to yield, saying that, rather than do so,
she would leave Venice.   The governor was afraid
of a public riot, such was her popularity, and he
feared still more the observations of the Austrian
Court, so determined to shut his eyes to the matter.
But the singer had her revenge, for one day when
he had gallantly conducted her to her gondola, she
obliged him to take a seat in it, and then took him
through all the canals, while they were met by the
ironical cheers of all whom they passed.

In 1831 Maria Malibran built herself a handsome
villa near Brussels, and from that time on made it
a custom to retire to this home whenever she had
a few weeks' rest.

Here in the summer of the following year she
received a visit from Lablache, who was passing
through the town on his way south.   During con-

versation he suggested that they should make a tour in Italy: the idea pleased her, and without more ado they set off with an opera company, with the result that they made a perfect triumphal progress through the principal cities.

On June 2, 1832, Manuel Garcia's father passed away at the age of fifty-seven.

We have already seen what a prominent figure the elder Garcia was in the musical world of the early nineteenth century. No less gifted as an actor than as a singer, his greatest performances were given in such contrasting characters as Almaviva, Don Giovanni, and Otello. Again, as a composer he was responsible for over forty operas in Italian, French, and Spanish, many of which are still treasured among the municipal archives of Madrid. Lastly, as a teacher of singing he made his mark both in Paris and London, and a great many of the best qualities of the modern school of vocalists depend on the joint teaching of the elder Garcia and his son Manuel; for while the latter was the first to conduct vocal training on correct scientific principles, the former undoubtedly laid the foundation of the school from which sprung Grisi, Sontag, and Alboni. Truly a remarkable man, to whose abilities Rossini bore striking testimony when he said to Manuel, after the elder Garcia's death, "Si ton père avait autant de savoir - faire que de savoir musical, il serait le premier musicien de l'époque."

The spring of 1833 saw Maria Malibran at Drury Lane, receiving £3200 for forty appearances, in addition to two benefits, which brought an additional £2000; and on May 1, we read that she appeared in the first performance of an English version of "Somnambula," in which part "she drew the town in admiring crowds, tickling the ears of the groundlings with the felicity of her roulades."

In this opera she had already appeared in the Italian version with greater success even than Pasta, for whom Bellini had written the *rôle*. Further, the old Italian musician found in her his ideal interpreter for one of his most beautiful works, "Norma," with which he had only made a moderate success at La Scala.

On the night of its production in London, as the composer advanced to thank her, Maria Malibran rushed towards him with open arms, and sang the words, " Ah, m'abbracia."

" Mon émotion fut indescriptible," Bellini said afterwards in speaking of the incident. " Je me croyais en paradis. Je ne pus ajouter un mot, et je restai comme étourdi."

After the London season of 1833 Mme. Malibran returned to Naples, remaining there till the May of 1834, when she went to Bologna and Milan till the end of June, while July was spent in London. The following August saw her reception at the Court of Lucca, and of this visit a charming description is given in a letter written by the violinist de Bériot, to whom she had promised her hand as soon as her ill-fated marriage with Mons. Malibran should have been dissolved,—a lengthy process in those days.

"Lucca, *August* 31, 1834.

" Dear Sister,—We arrived at the baths of Lucca yesterday, and have been spending two delightful days. It would be impossible to find a reigning prince with more geniality and amiability than the Duke of Lucca. The same might be said of the queen-mother of Naples.

" The evening which I told you about in my last letter took place at her house on Friday last. Mariette sang ten songs, among the number being the one by Coutiau, which sent everybody into fits of laughter,—not that fashionable affected sort of laugh such as is considered etiquette at the Court functions in France and Belgium, but the hearty gaiety of the people, for here you do not have to put a restraint on yourself at the Court. When you enter the room you make your bow to the Queen and the Duke: after that you put your hat in a corner of the 'salon' and do whatever you like. I should become a furious royalist if we were allowed as much freedom as this at other courts.

" The day after the 'soirée' the Queen sent by her secretary some splendid presents. Maria received a magnificent diamond cluster for her forehead, while I was given a single stone of great value, set in a ring for the little finger of my left hand; so in future I am always sure to have a brilliant cadenza. Then there was a very nice ornament in the shape of an eagle for Mariette's sister, Pauline. But that was not all, for there was a purse of gold, more than sufficient to cover all the expenses of the journey. That is what I call behaving really handsomely.

" The rest of the evening was spent at Prince Poniatowski's. The Duke was present. He had been very full of fun during the dinner, over which he presided, sitting at the middle of the table. In his hand he held a big ruler to kill the wasps, of which there are great numbers in this country. He never missed one of them.

" After dinner he gave himself up to dancing, singing, and romping, taking every one by the hand, as Labarre used to do when he was in good spirits. At last the Duke sat down at the piano and sang a *buffo* duet from the 'Mariage Secret' in piquant fashion.

H

" At this moment a little incident interrupted the music, but added considerable picturesqueness to the evening. A couple of bats flew in at the window, attracted by the light, and amused themselves by fluttering and sporting around our heads.

" The ladies all took to their heels and fled into the next room, but the rest of the party, including S.A.R., armed ourselves with sticks and whips, and after two hours' conflict succeeded in killing the bats.

" My letter, my dear Constance, has been interrupted by an excursion into the country, organised on the spur of the moment. We purpose spending two more days at Lucca, at Prince Poniatowski's, with S.A.R., who has made himself as charming as usual.

" When I was in Paris I bought a cane with a knob made of lead. It took the fancy of the Duke, and I have given it to him. He has given me his own in exchange, and as it has a knob of gold it has a double value.

" Сн. DE Bériot."

With 1835 we come to an important advance of Manuel Garcia's position as a teacher, the first official recognition of his growing fame. When at the close of 1830, fresh from his anatomical studies at the hospital, he had joined his father in his work, he at once resolved to apply the knowledge thus gained. It was, therefore, his custom to insist that every pupil who presented himself should undergo a vocal and medical examination, while at the same time he made him submit to a special treatment, if the larynx appeared to him to demand it.

This scientific method of approaching singing made a great stir, and he soon found himself surrounded by an ever-increasing *clientèle*. With his pupils, both amateur and professional, he gained such continuous success that at last, in 1835, he

was appointed to a professorial chair at the Paris
Conservatoire, and this naturally marked a very
distinct step in his career.

It has always been stated that he was given the
post by Auber, but investigation proves this to be
incorrect.   Auber was not appointed to the directorship of the Conservatoire until the year 1842.   At
the time Señor Garcia joined the staff Cherubini
was at the head of affairs, having been made
director in the year 1821 (after being professor of
composition there for five years), and he remained
in that position until the close of 1841, when he
retired at the age of eighty-one, to be succeeded by
the younger composer.

In the year of Manuel Garcia's appointment to
the Conservatoire, his sister, Maria Malibran, was
in London during May and June, having been
engaged by the management of the Royal Italian
Opera at Covent Garden for twenty-one performances at a fee of £2775.

How little did those who listened to her in
London that summer foresee that with the close
of the season they were to hear her in the capital
no more, and that in little over a year her life was
to be brought to a tragic end !   Yet such was to be
the case.

After the close of the London season the contralto
retired to Brussels for a rest, and then in the early
autumn set out for Naples.

Immediately on her arrival she received an
urgent visit from Giovanni Gallo, the director of
the little theatre of "St Jean Chrysostôme."   The
interview led to a delightful episode.

The unhappy impresario was on the verge of bankruptcy, and came to beg her aid. Maria Malibran refused, but offered to sing for him at his theatre for a fee of three thousand francs.

The company and orchestra, who had already half dispersed, were hastily reassembled, and de Bériot himself directed the rehearsals for " Somnambula." The announcement of the forthcoming performance created tremendous excitement,—seats fetched incredible prices ; and on the night itself the hall was crammed to overflowing. The tenor was so affected that he suddenly stopped short, and for some minutes could not sing a note. The public began to murmur, and the whole success of the evening was in jeopardy, until Malibran came to the rescue. She at once commenced to sing the tenor music, and rendered it with such virility of accent and gesture that the public shouted with enthusiasm. What was more to the purpose, the tenor was able to recover himself after a few moments and take up his rôle again. At the fall of the curtain the ovation was tremendous,—indeed it seemed as if the applause would never come to an end.

Her generous action had been noised abroad throughout Venice, and when she went out people fought over bits of her shawl, her gloves, even her handkerchief, while all the gondolas formed a guard of honour as far as the Barbarigo Palace where she was staying. Scarcely had she entered when the Syndic of the gondoliers was announced. On being shown in, he presented a golden cup filled with wine, and begged her to touch it with her lips. From her balcony she saw the cup passed from hand to hand down that long flotilla, stretching away down to the "Riva del Carbone." Each boatman took a sip, but so small a one, fearing lest the wine should be exhausted before it had circulated among all his comrades, that when it came back into the hands of the Syndic it was still half full : seeing which, he poured the rest of the wine into the Grand Canal as a libation.

The total receipts of the performance were 10,500 francs, but nothing less than 15,000 could save the unhappy Gallo from bankruptcy. When he presented himself next day with the 3000 francs, as arranged, the tender-hearted artist discovered his predicament, and not only let him off her fee, but provided him with the further sum necessary for the settlement of his debt. Perhaps Alfred de Musset was thinking of this act of generosity when he wrote the lines—

> " Cet or deux fois sacré qui payait ton génie
> Et qu'à tes pieds souvent laissa ta charité."

In remembrance of this memorable performance, the municipality of Venice decided that the Theatre of Saint Jean Chrysostôme should be called henceforth the Théâtre Malibran.

The ensuing winter the prima donna spent at Milan, where the Duke of Visconti, director of La Scala, had offered her a contract for 185 performances, spread over two and a half years, for which she was to receive 450,000 francs. This visit to Milan marked the zenith of her fame, and is still referred to as " the glorious year." Here she pursued still further the studies, which she had

already commenced, with regard to the reform of
costume and scenery.   Towards the realisation of
her dreams she was supported by the Duke of
Visconti, who, besides his connection with the
opera house, was superintendent of the Academy
of Art and Science.   Reviving the ideas of Talma,
she wished to introduce in the theatre artistic and
archæological truth, and, with this aim in view, she
had copies made of a quantity of costumes from
the archives of Venice, and from the miniatures
in some old manuscripts.   From these designs
dresses were made for many of the operas, notably "Otello."   So great an interest did she take
in the carrying out of this reform, that she always
used to refer to it as "la grande affaire."

There are still extant not only a great number
of the designs, which were copied by her orders,
but several albums of sketches for which she was
herself responsible, and these exhibit considerable
dexterity, besides giving proof of the deep interest
which she took in the scheme.

In the midst of all this work, and of numberless
receptions at which she was ever the principal
attraction, she made frequent appearances at the
Scala in "Otello," "I Capuletti," "Norma," "Somnambula," and "Giovanna Grey."   The enthusiasm
of the public had never reached such a pitch before,
and it is from this year that those stamps dated
which bore her head, and were used to close
letters: specimens of these are still to be seen,
but they are extremely rare.

On the day of her departure her comrades at
the theatre presented her with a finely executed

medal of gold, in which she was depicted in the
costume of " Norma "; while the governor expressed the hope of seeing her quickly back again.
But it was never to be consummated.

On March 26, 1836, the contralto's marriage
with Monsieur Malibran was finally annulled by
the courts of Paris. This unworthy husband, soon
after her return to Europe, had heard of her success in the French capital and followed her thither,
demanding a share of her professional emoluments.
With this claim she very properly refused to
comply. He had obtained her hand by means of
deception, and she had acquitted herself of any
claim he might have had as her husband, by re-
signing in favour of his creditors the property
which had been settled on her.

Three days after the marriage had been annulled,
she was wedded to Charles de Bériot, the violinist,
and we read that " the Queen of France presented
the bride with a costly agraffe, embellished with
pearls."

Next day de Bériot and his wife arrived at
Brussels, and shortly afterwards were heard there
for the first time together at a concert given for
the benefit of the Polonais, and in another performance at the Theatre Royal.

Then came that fatal day in April when the
singer had a terrible fall from her horse, being
dragged some distance along the road and receiving injuries to her head from which she never
recovered, though her wonderful energy enabled
her to disregard the results for a time. She retired to Brussels, and went thence to Aix - la -

Chapelle, where she gave two concerts with de Bériot.

In September they made a rapid journey from France, arriving at Manchester on Sunday the 11th, where she had been engaged as the principal attraction for the Festival. The same evening she sang no less than fourteen pieces in her room at the hotel to please some Italian friends. On the Monday she took part in the opening performance. Next day she was weak and ill, but nevertheless sang afternoon and evening. On the Wednesday her condition became still more critical, but she managed to render "Sing ye to the Lord" with thrilling effect; and this was the last sacred piece she ever sang, for that same evening brought her grand career to its tragic close.

The scene was one which none forgot who were present on that fatal night.

Before Maria Malibran had even reached the hall she had already fainted several times. Yet with an indomitable courage she nerved herself to go through the coming ordeal. With tears in their eyes, her friends begged her to return without attempting the strain for which she was so ill-prepared. But no; Maria Malibran refused to break faith with the public whom she had served so long, so gloriously. Even though her heart was chilled with presage of impending doom, she forced herself to enter on her self-appointed task, and carried it through with such success that when her final duet had been sung, "Vanno se alberghi in petto," none who had listened to that rich contralto voice guessed that they had been present at the closing scenes of their favourite's career.

Her task was over, she had fought in an unequal combat and prevailed. But still an enraptured audience clamoured to hear her yet again, and the noisy demand grew ever more insistent, until Maria Malibran came forward to repeat the closing movement.

As she sang, an agonised expression came over her face, her limbs trembled, her efforts became more and more painful. It was the struggle of a brave woman against sinking nature, the vivid glare of an expiring lamp. Higher and higher rose the voice, paler and paler grew the singer. Then came a last wild note of despair: the swan song was ended, and Maria Malibran staggered from the platform, to sink exhausted into the arms of loving comrades.

A grateful public vied each with the other in doing honour to their heroine, but, alas! those thunders of applause fell on ears that heard them not. Maria Malibran lay hovering 'twixt life and death.

But the end was not yet. She rallied, and was borne across to her room at the hotel, and here she lingered for nine days in a fever before the end came. On her deathbed her poor brain was in song-land, and almost with her last breath she sang snatches of her favourite airs.

On October 1, 1836, her burial took place at the south aisle of the Collegiate Church, Manchester, but the remains were afterwards removed to Brussels, where they were reinterred in a maus-

oleum erected by her husband. Here for many
years, on each succeeding anniversary of her death,
the musicians of Brussels were wont to ·deposit
their visiting - cards at the grille of the now
deserted mausoleum, the cupola of which still
towers above the surrounding tombs. It was not
long after the singer's death that "Tom Ingoldsby"
—a stripling of seventeen in the year of Manuel
Garcia's birth—put into the mouth of his Lord
Tom Noddy the oft-quoted lines—

> "Malibran's dead, Duvernay's fled,
> Taglioni has not yet arrived in her stead."

Of Maria Malibran's powers as an artist her
brother could never speak too highly. She was
richly endowed with the artistic genius of the
family, and was possessed of a contralto of marvellous purity and richness, being at the same time
gifted with great histrionic powers. Her singing,
as has been already stated, was always full of fire
and warmth, while, besides her passion, there was
gentle pathos, which had great effect on the
listener. As a girl she was *petite* and slight,
with burning cheeks and flaming eyes. Though
not a beautiful woman, she was extremely attract-
ive. Her head was well shaped, her mouth rather
large, but her smile very sweet, and she had the
most perfect set of teeth, while her pretty figure
was full of graceful curves.

Her versatility was shown not only in her
extraordinary vocal and histrionic achievements
and skill in vocal improvisation, but in her powers
as a linguist, while as an artist her sketches were

good, and sometimes amusing. Moreover, her vivacious temperament and ready wit found an outlet in a love of fun and mimicry. An instance of this is related by John Parry, the composer and singer of refined comic songs. The incident took place at an evening party in Naples.

"Such a merry-making, frolicsome sort of party I never witnessed," he says. "We had much *good* singing, as you may suppose; but Mazzinghi's comic duet of "When a little farm we keep"— which I had the honour of singing with Malibran —carried all before it, in consequence of the exquisite manner in which she sang the *do re mi* part of it; and when she repeated it she executed the florid divisions so delightfully, and so brilliantly, yet quite differently from the first time, that the company was enraptured. . . . The prima donna requested Lablache to sustain the low F, me to sing B flat, and others the harmonic intervals above, then to place the finger on the side of the nose, so as to form a drone, while she imitated the squeaking tones of the bagpipes in such a manner as to cause the loudest laughter, especially when we sank our voices very slowly together, as if the wind in the bellows was nearly exhausted."

Maria Malibran was, moreover, a veritable tomboy when she was in the company of children, being up to all sorts of tricks, and rested by painting beautiful pictures; would dress as a man, and drive the coach from place to place, and when she arrived, brown with the sun and dust of Italy, would sometimes jump into the sea. Then she would go straight to the opera and, having sung "Amina," "Norma," or "The Maid of Artois," as we shall perhaps never hear them sung again, return home to write or sing comic songs. At cock-crow she was out galloping her horse off its legs before a rehearsal in the morning, a concert in the afternoon, and the opera at night.

Such was Maria Malibran, untiring in energy, scarcely resting a moment. Little wonder that she did not live to the same age as the rest of her family, for she died at twenty-eight, whereas her mother lived to be eighty-three, and her sister Pauline is still living, approaching her ninetieth birthday, while Manuel entered on his 102nd year before the Reaper summoned him.

Well did Lablache say of Maria Malibran, "Son esprit est trop fort pour son petit corps."

Pauline Viardot

CHAPTER IX.

AFTER the death of Malibran in 1836, the ensuing years of Manuel Garcia's life were spent in steady progress of fame as a teacher. The next event of importance in his career took place four years later. These intervening years were, however, brightened by much reflected glory, for as the period between 1830 and 1836 saw the triumphs of his eldest sister and pupil, Maria Malibran, so this next one brought the success of his youngest sister, Pauline Viardot, also his pupil.

Her first lessons had been received as a child at the hands of her father, but seeing that she was only eleven years old when he died, it may be certainly claimed that her brother was responsible for the greater part of her training.

It was in 1837, the year which saw the accession of Queen Victoria, that she made her *début* as a singer at Brussels. This was not, however, her first appearance on the platform, for she had already shown herself to be an admirable pianist. Her earliest lessons in pianoforte had been received in New York from Marcos Vega, being afterwards continued under Meyssenberg; but the most important part of her study was done under Liszt.

The German pianist had already made considerable success by the time his father died in 1827, when he himself was but sixteen years old. The event brought a great change in his circumstances, and made it necessary for him to keep himself by teaching. His services were at once in demand among the best families, and in due course Pauline was placed under him. Though she refers to her talent on the instrument as "passable," Liszt counted her one of his best pupils.

After studying for some time she made her appearance as a pianist at several concerts organised by her sister and de Bériot in Belgium and Germany. Composition, too, she learned under Reicha, and it was to him that she owed that grasp of the technique of her art by which she was able to give full scope to the richness of her own inspiration.

In 1837, as we have already said, her *début* as a vocalist was made at Brussels. After this she went on a concert tour with de Bériot, and sang at a concert in Paris in 1838 at the Théâtre de la Renaissance, when her powers of execution were brilliantly displayed in a *cadence du Diable*.

After these preliminary appearances, which were designed to make her "feel her feet," Pauline Garcia, on May 9, 1839, made her London *début* at Her Majesty's Theatre, as Desdemona in "Otello." Her success was instantaneous: without hesitation the public favour which had been bestowed on her sister was given to her also, with almost greater enthusiasm. From the commencement it was conceded that she was a remarkable artist.

She was a mezzo-soprano, with fine clear upper notes, and a wonderful execution in bravura passages. Moreover, as an actress she was equally successful in tragedy or comedy, besides being a perfect musician. And yet, as Señor Garcia would remark, there was not in her case a "phenomenal voice," as there had been in that of the lamented Malibran. It was, according to her brother, by no means a great one, and the voice alone would in ordinary circumstances have been placed in the second class.

There is a well-known story of a certain painter being asked by one of his sitters: "Tell me, with what do you mix your paints to get these wonderful effects?" "Madame," was the reply, "I mix them with my brains." So, too, Pauline Garcia may be said to have sung with her brains.

It was indeed the triumph of mind over matter. With her it was another case which went to uphold the truth of the well-known dictum that "Genius is the capacity for taking infinite pains." She possessed the will-power and determination to rise above all obstacles, as Demosthenes had possessed it centuries before, when he made up his mind to become a leading advocate, and, in order to attain greater clearness of enunciation, spent hour after hour by the seashore, where he would recite, his mouth filled with pebbles. With

what a result! The Athenian ended by becoming
one of the world's greatest orators : Señor Garcia's
youngest sister became one of the world's greatest
dramatic singers.

In the autumn of 1839 she went tó Paris
for a season at the Théâtre Italien, for which
she had been engaged by the impresario, Mons.
Louis Viardot, a distinguished writer and critic,
and founder of the 'Revue Indépendante.' Here
she shared in the triumphs of Grisi, Persiani,
Rubini, Tamburini, and Lablache ; while her principal parts were three *rôles* as different as they
were characteristic — in the operas of "Otello,"
"Cenerentola," and "The Barber of Seville."

Many tributes were paid by those who heard
her. Liszt, under whom she had studied the
piano, wrote of her in these terms—

"In all that concerns method and execution,
feeling and expression, it would be hard to find
a name worthy to be mentioned with that of
Maria Malibran's sister. In her, virtuosity serves
only as a means of expressing the idea, the
thought, the character of a work or a *rôle*."

George Sand called her " the personification of
poetry and music," and set down her impressions
on listening to the singer thus : " The pale, still,
—one might at the first glance say lustreless,—
countenance, the suave and unconstrained movements, the astonishing freedom from every sort
of affectation,—how transfigured all this appears,
when she is carried away by her genius on the
current of song ! "

Her first appearance in Paris was greeted by

Alfred de Musset, the poet of Romanticism and warm friend of Victor Hugo, in those well-known lines—

"Ainsi donc, quoi qu'on dise, elle ne tarit pas
La source immortelle et féconde
Que le coursier divin fit jaillir sous ses pas."

When de Musset wished to crystallise in prose his feelings on hearing her sing, he expressed himself in these words—

"Si Pauline Garcia a la voix de sa sœur, elle en a l'âme en même temps, et, sans la moindre imitation, c'est le même génie. . . . Elle chante comme elle respire. . . . Sa physionomie, pleine d'expression, change avec une rapidité prodigieuse, avec une liberté extrême, non seulement selon le morceau, mais encore selon la phrase qu'elle exécute. Avant d'exprimer, elle sent."

Again, Richard Wagner pays a remarkable tribute to her powers in a letter to L. Uhl relating to his stay in Paris in 1859, and to the attempts to arrange for the production of "Tristan" there. In it the composer recounts how the same difficulty of reading the *rôles* of this work was encountered in Germany, which militated much against its production. "Madame Viardot," he writes, "expressed to me one day her astonishment that in Germany people always spoke of this difficulty of reading the music of 'Tristan.' She asked me if in Germany the artists were not then musicians? I for my part hardly know how to enlighten her on this point; for this grand artiste sang through at sight, with the most perfect expression, a whole act of the *rôle* of Isolda."

I

Such was the artiste whose *début* in London in 1839 was followed by so brilliant a career.

We now come to 1840—a year made noteworthy in the life of Garcia by another important advance in his career.

Since his appointment to a professorship at the Paris Conservatoire, his reputation had continued to be steadily consolidated, and his *clientèle* included, besides those who were being trained for the musical profession, a great number of amateur pupils, among whom were to be found not only some of the most distinguished names in Paris, but many members of the royal family itself. Throughout this period he had been steadily working to increase his knowledge relative to the mechanism of the voice, and at last, in 1840, he found that his investigations had reached a point at which they might be found of interest to others.

Accordingly, in this year he set down the result of his studies in the classical paper which he submitted to the Académie des Sciences de France under the title, "Mémoire sur la voix humaine," to which was added the rather odd-sounding subtitle, " Description des produits du phonateur humain." In it he embodied the various discoveries which he had made relating to the larynx.

Among the principal points to which he drew attention were the following :—

(1) The head voice does not necessarily begin where the chest voice ends, and a certain

number of notes can be produced in either register.

(2) The chest voice and the head voice are produced by a special and spontaneous modification of the vocal organs, and the exhaustion of the air contained in the chest is more rapid in the proportion of four to three in the production of a head than a chest note.

(3) The voice can produce the same sounds in two different timbres—the clear or open, and the sombre or closed.

The memoir on the human voice was duly reported on by Majendie, Savart, and Dutrochet at a public meeting which was held on April 12, 1841, the result being that this resolution was passed : " The thanks of the Academy are due to Professor Garcia for the skilful use which he has made of his opportunities as a teacher of singing to arrive at a satisfactory physical theory of the human voice." The circumstance gave occasion for a somewhat acrimonious discussion concerning certain points of priority as between Garcia and MM. Diday and Pétrequin, two French scientists.

This was followed up by the publication of the ' Method of Teaching Singing,' in which Garcia cleared up the confusion which had hitherto existed between " timbre " and " register."

He defined the expression " register " as being a series of consecutive homogeneous sounds produced by one mechanism, differing essentially from another series of sounds equally homogeneous produced by another mechanism, whatever modifications of "timbre" and of strength they may offer. "Each of the registers," he added, "has its own extent and sonority, which varies according to the sex of the individual and the nature of the organ."

At this time he stated that there were two registers; but in later years, with the invention of the laryngoscope and the examination of the vocal cords which resulted from it, he altered the original division from two to three — chest, medium, and head-voice,—and this is accepted by all as scientifically correct according to the definition of "register" laid down by him.

The year which found Manuel Garcia presenting his paper to the Académie des Sciences saw his sister Pauline married to Monsieur Viardot, by whom she had been engaged for her first season at the Paris Opera House. Almost immediately after the wedding her husband resigned his position, so as to accompany her on her tours through Italy, Spain, Germany, Russia, and England.

At Berlin, such was her success, that after her performance as Rahel in Halévy's "La Juive," she was serenaded by the whole orchestra. Here, too, she astonished all by volunteering at a moment's notice to sing the part of Isabelle in "Robert le Diable" in addition to her own of Alice, when the artiste who had been engaged for the former *rôle* was suddenly taken ill.

Her actual *début* in Germany was made at a State concert in Berlin,—an official ceremony, but still a private one. The first public appearance in the country was made at an evening concert at the Gewandhaus of Leipsic in 1843.

Pauline Viardot was twenty-two at the time. With a charming appearance, and already ablaze with the reflected glory of her sister, Maria Malibran, the *débutante* quickly roused the sympathetic curiosity of her audience to enthusiasm. The entire press praised her virtuosity, artistic feeling, and nobility of countenance, but above all they expressed admiration for her gift of revealing the innermost beauty of the grand musical works in which she lived and felt so profoundly.

They admired, too, that unique talent which wrapped every phrase in the exquisite charm and grace which she brought to bear. For that reason the bravura air of Persiani's " Inès de Castro," the final rondo from Rossini's " Cenerentola," and an unpublished air of Ch. de Bériot, earned for her at this first concert as much applause as the great air from Handel's " Rinaldo " and the lighter French, Spanish, and German songs which she sang in the same programme. These last three varieties of song she gave with a national colour so characteristic that, as one of the critics said, " Elles parurent chantées par trois voix et par trois âmes totalement différentes."

As was her usual custom, she accompanied herself on the piano to perfection. Clara Schumann, who took part in the concert, was dumfounded, and never forgot the occasion. Another musician who appeared that evening was a young violinist, an infant prodigy, twelve years old, who was to become in later years the great master, Joseph Joachim.

Between 1840 and 1843 Mme. Viardot added to her successes many fresh operas, principal among them being "Tancredi," the "Gazza Ladra," and "Semiramide," in which she took the part of Arsace. By the year 1845 her repertoire comprised, in addition to those already mentioned, "Somnambula" and "Norma," "I Capuletti" (in which she played Romeo), "L'Elisire d'Amore," "Lucia di Lammermoor," and "Don Pasquale"; as well as in German, "La Juive," "Iphigénie en Tauride," "Les Huguenots," "Robert le Diable," and "Don Juan," in which she played sometimes the part of Zerlina, at others Donna Anna.

In 1848 she was in Paris again, and enraptured Meyerbeer with her rendering of Fides in "Le Prophète," a *rôle* which she subsequently sustained on over two hundred occasions in all the chief opera houses in Europe, being — *teste* Moscheles — "the life and soul of the opera, which owed to her at least half of its great success."

Three years later came another triumph, when, at Gounod's request, she created the part of Sapho. In 1855 she added to her laurels "Le Mariage Secret." Then came the evenings at the Théâtre Lyrique in 1859, with "Orpheo" and "Fidelio," and finally her season of opera in 1861, with "Alceste," "Favorita," and "Il Trovatore."

At the end of a career lasting over a period of twenty-five years, the artist retired, and in 1865 settled in Baden-Baden as a teacher, her principal pupils being Désiré Artot, Marianne Brandt, and Antoinette Sterling. Here in her own grounds she had a private theatre built, a small square building, capable of holding about a hundred people, in addition to a diminutive orchestra, stage, and anteroom. In this hall she was wont to give concerts, to which were invited celebrities from every land, representatives of the various branches of art and science, poets, painters, diplomats, and the like; while on more than one occasion the old Emperor of Germany himself honoured her with his presence.

At one of these, Mme. Viardot's pupils performed an operetta of her own composition, while Mme. Artot sang a scene from an opera, and several others from among the greatest German artists took part in the programme. These included Joseph Joachim and Ferdinand David, the latter of whom was at this time Concertmeister in Leipzig.

Antoinette Sterling, who was then studying with Mme. Viardot, sang an Italian aria, in addition to taking part in the operetta. Her hair was let down for the occasion, while she wore a costume in the Grecian style, surmounted by a red velvet cap. This was the only time my mother ever appeared in "stage costume," or suffered rouge to be applied to her face.

During this period Johannes Brahms was living in Baden-Baden, and Antoinette Sterling has left a description of an episode in connection with the friendship of the composer for Mme. Viardot :—

"Herr Brahms at this time looked almost a boy, rather short and thick, with a full round face and fair yellowish hair. In honour of Mme. Viardot's birthday"—(this was in the year 1869)—"he wrote

a small chorus for women's voices, and came himself
to conduct the rehearsals, all of which took place in
my rooms.   At five o'clock on the birthday morning,
we walked with Herr Brahms through the grassy
fields up to her house, and there, under her window,
sang the morning serenade.   When she came down
from her room, her face wreathed in smiles, every
student threw her a bouquet, a stipulated price
being given for each of these bunches of flowers,
so that none should be more gorgeous than the
rest."

We have seen the admiration which Pauline
Viardot had aroused in many composers besides
Brahms.   One may add to the list the name of
Robert Schumann, for he dedicated to her his
beautiful Liederkreis, op. 24.   Nor was Señor
Garcia's sister unknown as a writer of music, for
she has been responsible for many beautiful compo-
sitions.

After spending some five years in Baden-Baden,
Mme. Viardot was forced to leave the town on the
outbreak of the Franco-Prussian War, owing to her
husband being of French nationality.   They made
their way at once to London, where Manuel Garcia
was residing, and of the months which they spent
there I shall have something to say later, since
Mme. Noufflard, the daughter of Lady Hallé, has
given some interesting reminiscences of that period.
When things had become sufficiently quiet again
Mme. Viardot decided to settle in Paris, and there
she has resided ever since.

And what of her life in recent years, in her grand

retirement? The year 1905, which saw her brother celebrating his centenary, found her in splendid old age after many years of widowhood, approaching her eighty-fifth birthday; living in a handsome house in the Boulevard St Germain; strong, tall, and of dignified bearing, her hazel eyes still retaining their true Spanish brilliance; her voice clear and well-sustained; herself full of vivacity, and with a memory no less remarkable than that of her brother; full of enthusiasm for music and art, a grandmother, with the most charming smile and magnetic gaiety, and still able to add to the number of her musical compositions.

A true Garcia.

One might well be tempted to dwell still further on that wonderful personality, laying stress on her care as a teacher, on her beneficent work among the artists whom she instructed, after they had journeyed from all directions, from the New World as well as the Old, to place themselves in her hands. One longs to paint her amid her home surroundings, in an atmosphere vibrating with music, bathed in art; one longs to show that lovable serenity, that wonderful gaiety and prodigious activity, which perhaps strike one most of all.

This little sketch of her career will be brought to an end by a quotation from a letter, in which one may appreciate the exquisite turn which she gives to every phrase and thought :—

" . . . Mais où trouver le temps de faire ce qu'on voudrait? C'est à peine si on arrive à faire ce qu'on doit! En vieillissant, le temps passe de plus en plus vite et vous entraîne d'une course vertigineuse vers le *Grand Inconnu!* sans arrêt, sans repos, sans pitié.   Il y aura peut-être dans le ciel une immense bibliothèque, où les œuvres du génie seront rassemblées, et je me promets d'y faire de fameuses séances de lectures! . . ."

It is the letter of a moment, but the sentiments, which she expresses so beautifully, are those of an eternity.

Photo by W. & D. Downey

Yours sincerely
Jenny Goldschmidt

CHAPTER X.

JENNY LIND.

(1841–1842.)

THE year 1841 may be looked on as the most important in Manuel Garcia's career as a teacher of singing, for it saw the arrival of the soprano who was to become the greatest of all his pupils—Jenny Lind. For this reason it is my intention to devote a chapter to the events which led up to her coming to him for lessons, to the period of study which she spent under his guidance, and to the success which followed on the completion of this training. For much of the material I am indebted to the interesting memoir of the prima donna's career written by Canon Scott Holland, through whose courtesy I have been enabled to quote from the volume in question.

Born in Stockholm in 1820 of humble parentage, Jenny Lind, at the age of nine, was admitted to the school of singing attached to the Royal Theatre. Of the incident which brought about her removal and fixed for ever the lines of her future career, it is possible for us to read in her own words, as they were taken down by her son, to whom she told the story at Cannes in the spring of 1887.

" As a child," writes Canon Holland, " she would sing with every step she took : one of the forms which the perpetual song assumed was addressed to a blue-ribboned cat, of which she was very fond. Here is the rest of the story as Jenny Lind related it :—

" ' Her favourite seat was in the window of the steward's room, which looked out on the lively street leading up to the church of St Jacob.   Here she sat and sang to the cat ; and the people passing in the street used to hear and wonder.   Amongst others was the maid of Mdlle. Lundberg, a dancer at the Royal Opera House, and this girl on her return told her mistress that she had never heard such beautiful singing as that of this little one when she sang to her pet.

" ' Mdlle. Lundberg thereupon found out her name and sent a note to the mother, who was in Stockholm at the time, asking her to bring the child to sing to her ; and when she heard her voice, she cried, " The girl is a genius ! you must have her educated for the stage."   But Jenny's mother, as well as her grand-mother, had an old-fashioned prejudice against the stage, and would not hear of such a thing.   " Then you must, at any rate, have her taught singing," said the dancer ; and in this way the mother was persuaded to accept a letter of introduction to Herr Croelius, the Court secretary and Singing-master, at the Royal Theatre.

" ' Off with the letter they started ; but as they went up the broad steps of the Opera House, the parent was again troubled by her doubts and repugnance.   She had, no doubt, all the inherited dislike of the burgher families for the dramatic life. But little Jenny eagerly urged her to go on; and so they entered the room where the teacher sat. The child sang him something out of an opera composed by Winter. When he heard her, Croelius was moved to tears, and said that he must take her in to the Count Puke, the head of the Royal Theatre, and tell him what a treasure he had found.

" ' Having been admitted to the manager's sanctum, the first question asked was, " How old is she ? " and Croelius answered " Nine years." " Nine ! " exclaimed the Count ; " but this is not a *crêche*—it is the King's Theatre ; " and he would not look at her, she being, moreover, at that time what she herself has called " a small, ugly, broad-nosed, shy, gauche, under-grown girl." " Well," said the other, " if you will not hear her, then I will teach her gratuitously myself, and she will astonish you one day." With that Count Puke consented to hear her sing ; and when she sang he, too, was moved to tears. From that moment she was accepted, being taught to sing, educated, and brought up at the Government expense.' "

Thus did Jenny Lind tell the crucial event of her life in her own graphic manner.

At eighteen she came out as an opera singer, appearing as Agatha in " Der Freischütz," Alice in " Robert le Diable," and many other parts. During the two years that followed, she caused considerable damage to her voice, partly through overstrain, partly through ignorance of the true principles of voice-emission. As soon as she realised what had happened she determined to go to Paris, for she had been long convinced that there was one man alone from whom she could learn all those technicalities of the art of singing of which she knew so little and longed to know so much. And the name of that man was Manuel Garcia, whose fame as a teacher had, even at that early period of his career, already travelled to Sweden.

It was not long before her project was put into execution. On Thursday, July 1, 1841, Mdlle. Lind, now in her twenty-first year, embarked on the steamship *Gauthiod* for Lübeck.

After a few days of rest and enjoyment she proceeded to Hâvre by steamboat and thence by diligence to Paris.

Here we can take up the narrative as it is told by Canon Holland :—

" On leaving Sweden she had brought with her a letter of introduction to the Duchesse de Dalmatie (Madame la Maréchale Soult) from her relative, Queen Desideria, the wife of Maréchal Bernadotte, who had become King of Sweden and Norway in the year 1818, under the title of Karl XIV. Johann.

"As a result of the letter she received an invitation, soon after her arrival, for a reception at Madame Soult's house. It was understood that she would be asked to sing, and Signor Garcia was specially requested by the Duchess to be present that he might hear the new arrival.

"She gave some Swedish songs, accompanying herself on the pianoforte, but either through nervousness or fatigue she does not appear to have done herself justice, and her singing did not produce a very favourable effect upon the assembled guests.

Her voice was worn not only from over-exertion but from want of that careful management which can only be acquired by long training under a thoroughly competent master.

"Such training she had never had. She had formed her own ideal of the difficult *rôles* that had been entrusted to her at the Royal Theatre in Stockholm, and had tried to reach that ideal by the only means she knew of — very pernicious means indeed. The result was that the voice had been very cruelly injured. The mischief had been seriously aggravated by the fatigue consequent upon a long and arduous provincial tour ; and the effect was a chronic hoarseness, painful enough to produce marked symptoms of deterioration upon the fresh young voice which had never been taught either the proper method of singing or the cultivation of style necessary for the development of its natural charm.

"Manuel Garcia was not slow to perceive all this, and he afterwards told a lady who questioned him upon the subject that the Swedish soprano was at that time altogether wanting in the qualities needed for presentation before a highly cultivated audience.

"Soon after this Mademoiselle Lind called by appointment upon the maestro, who then occupied a pleasant *deuxième étage* in a large block of houses in the Square d'Orleans, near the Rue Saint Lazare. It was a handsome residence, built around a turfed courtyard, with a fountain in the centre and a large tree on each side.

"As on this occasion she formally requested the

great teacher to receive her as a pupil, he examined her voice more carefully than he had been able to do at Madame Soult's party.

" After making her sing through the usual scales and forming his own opinion of the power and compass of her organ, he asked her for the well-known scena from 'Lucia di Lammermoor'—'Perchè non ho.' In this, unhappily, she broke down completely—in all probability through nervousness, for she had appeared in the part of Lucia at the Stockholm Theatre no less than thirty-nine times only the year before, and the music must therefore have been familiar to her. However, let the cause have been what it might, the failure was complete, and upon the strength of it the maestro pronounced his terrible verdict : 'It would be useless to teach you, mademoiselle; you have no voice left.'

" It is necessary that these words should be distinctly recorded, for their misquotation in the newspapers and elsewhere has led to a false impression, equally unjust to master and pupil. The exact words were—'Vous n'avez plus de voix,' not 'Vous n'avez pas de voix.' Jenny Lind had once possessed a voice, as Garcia realised perfectly clearly, but it had been so strained by over-exertion and a faulty method of emission that for the time being scarcely a shred of it remained.

" The effect of this sentence of hopeless condemnation upon an organisation so highly strung as hers may be readily conceived. But her courage was equal to the occasion, though she told Mendelssohn, years afterwards, that the anguish of that moment exceeded all that she had ever suffered in

her whole life. Yet her faith in her own powers
never wavered for an instant. There was a fire
within her that no amount of discouragement could
quench. Instead, therefore, of accepting his verdict as a final one, she asked, with tears in her
eyes, what she was to do. Her trust in the
maestro's judgment was no less firm than that
which she felt in the reality of her own vocation.
In the full conviction that if she could only persuade him to advise her, his counsel would prove
invaluable, she did not hesitate to make the attempt, and the result fully justified the soundness
of her conclusions.

"Moved by her evident distress, he recommended
her to give her voice six weeks of perfect rest,—to
abstain during the whole of that time from singing
even so much as one single note, and to speak as
little as possible. Upon condition that she strictly
carried out these injunctions, he gave her permission to come to him again when the period of
probation was ended, in order that he might see
whether anything could be done for her. Intense
indeed must have been the relief when these six
weeks had at last expired.

"Once more Mdlle. Lind sought an interview
with the master, and this time her hopes were
crowned with success. Signor Garcia found the
voice so far re-established by rest that he was able
to give good hope of its complete restoration, provided that the faulty methods which had so nearly
resulted in its destruction were abandoned. With
the view of attaining this end he agreed to give
her two lessons of an hour each regularly every

week—an arrangement which set all her anxieties
at rest.

"The delight of the artist at being once more
permitted to sing may be readily imagined. Though
discouraged sometimes by the immense amount
she had to learn—and, with still greater difficulty,
to unlearn—she never lost heart; and so rapidly
did the vocal organs recover from the exhaustion
from which they had been suffering, that before long
she was able to practise her scales and exercises
daily for the fullest length of time which a singer
could manage without over-exerting the voice."

The lessons were commenced about the 25th of
August, and were continued without a break from
then until the month of July, 1842.

Jenny Lind thus describes her first introduction
to the new system in a letter to her friend, Fröken
Marie Ruckman :—

"PARIS, *Sept.* 10, 1841.

" I have already had five lessons from Signor
Garcia, the brother of Madame Malibran. I have
to begin again from the beginning, to sing scales up
and down slowly and with great care, then to
practise the shake—awfully slowly, and to try to
get rid of the hoarseness if possible. Moreover, he
is very particular about the breathing. I trust I
have made a happy choice. Anyhow, he is the
best master, and expensive enough—twenty francs
for an hour ! But what does that signify if only he
can teach me to sing ? "

A fortnight later she writes to Madame Lindblad :—

"I am well satisfied with my singing-master. With regard to my weak points especially, he is excellent. I think it very fortunate for me that there exists a Garcia. And I believe him also to be a very good màn. If he takes but little notice of us apart from his lessons, well — that cannot be helped; but I am very much pleased, nay, enchanted, with him as a teacher.

And again to Herr Forsberg :—

PARIS, *February* 1, 1842.

"Garcia's method is the best of our time, and the one which all here are striving to follow."

In a still later letter she writes :—

PARIS, *March* 7, 1842.

"To-day, four years ago, I made my *début* in 'Der Freischütz.'

"My singing is getting on quite satisfactorily now. I rejoice heartily in my voice,—it is clear and sonorous, with more firmness, and much greater agility. A great, great deal still remains to be done; but the worst is over. Garcia is satisfied with me."

The teaching she now received was evidently the exact thing she needed; for of the management of the breath, the emission of the voice, the blending of its registers, and other technical details upon which even the most perfect singers must depend in great measure for success, she knew nothing.

We have seen Jenny Lind's opinion of her
master : what of Garcia's opinion of his pupil ?
During my own lessons with him he would often
speak of the Swedish Nightingale, and hold her
up as an example in the most embarrassing way.
Among other things he remarked that he had
never heard her sing even a hair's-breadth out of
tune, so perfect was her natural ear. Moreover,
when she made a mistake, he only had to point
it out once, explain the cause of the error, and
show how it could be rectified : the fault would
never be repeated.

Mdlle. Lind's course of study under Garcia lasted
in all ten months, by 'which time she had learned
all that it was possible for any master to teach her.
After this period she had improved so wonderfully
under his magical tuition that, as he himself pic-
turesquely expressed it, she was able to look down
on her former efforts as from a mountain to a plain.
The result for which she had so ardently longed,
so patiently waited, so perseveringly laboured, was
attained at last.   Her voice, no longer suffering
from the effects of the cruel fatigue and the in-
ordinate amount of over - exertion which had so
lately endangered, not merely its wellbeing, but its
very existence, had now far more than recovered
its pristine vigour,—it had acquired a rich depth
of tone, a sympathetic sweetness, a bird-like charm
in the silvery clearness of its upper register, which
at once impresssed the listener with the feeling
that he had never before heard anything in the
least degree resembling it.

Few human organs are perfect.   It is quite possible that other voices may have possessed qualities which this did not—for voices of exceptional beauty are nearly always characterised by an individuality of expression which forms by no means the least potent of their attractions. But the listener never stopped to analyse the qualities of Mdlle. Lind's voice, the marked individuality of which set analysis at defiance. By turns full, sympathetic, tender, sad or brilliant, it adapted itself so perfectly to the artistic conception of the song it was interpreting, that singer, voice, and song were one.

"With such rare power at command, she was able, without effort, to give expression to every phase of the conception which she had originally formed by the exercise of innate genius alone. Her acting had grown up with her from infancy, and formed part of her inmost being. She had found no one in Paris capable of teaching her anything that could improve that, though she thought it necessary to take lessons in deportment. The rest she had studied for herself, though she had naturally gained experience by observation of others.

"She had acted to herself the part of Norma, which had been the last *rôle* she had undertaken in Stockholm before setting out for Paris, and calmly passed judgment upon her own performance. That she was satisfied with it one cannot doubt, for she had studied the difficult character of her heroine to such good purpose that she had reconciled all its apparent incongruities, and elevated it into a consistent whole, dramatic and musical, breathing poetry and romance from beginning to

end, yet as true to nature as she was herself, and
no longer fettered by the fatal technical weakness
which had so long stood between her ideal and its
perfect realisation. There was no weakness now.
The artist was complete."

When Jenny Lind was drawing near the close
of her studies under Garcia, the crucial question
arose, Should the finished artist make her *début*
in Paris? Or should she return at once to Sweden,
and reappear in all the glory of her newly acquired
powers in her beloved Stockholm? There were
arguments to be brought forward on both sides.
The problem was no new one. It had been frequently discussed, but her own feeling on the subject was very strong indeed. She could not recon-
cile herself to Paris. From the very first she had
suspected the hollowness of its social organisation.
In the September of 1841 she writes—

"There might be much to say about Paris, but
I put it off until I am better able to judge. This
much, however, I will say at once, that if good
is sometimes to be found, an immeasurable amount
of evil is to be found also. But I believe it to be
an excellent school for any one with discernment
enough to separate the rubbish from that which
is worth preserving—though this is no easy task.
To my mind the worst feature of Paris is its
dreadful selfishness, its greed for money. There
is nothing to which the people will not submit for
the sake of gain. Applause here is not always
given to talent, but often enough to vice, — to
any obscure person who can afford to pay for it.

Ugh! It is too dreadful to see the *claqueurs* sitting at the theatre, night after night, deciding the fate of those who are compelled to appear,—a terrible manifestation of original sin."

Six weeks later she writes: "All idea of appearing in public here has vanished. To begin with— I myself never relied upon it; but people said so many silly things about just one performance, that at last I began to feel as if I were in duty bound to try. But monstrous and unconquerable difficulties are in the way. In any case I want to go home again. But if I can arrange to sing at a concert before leaving, I will do so, in order that I may not return home without having at least done something."

All through the ensuing months she was still tortured by doubts as to the best course to pursue. In the following May she received from the directors of the Royal Theatre at Stockholm the offer of a definite and official engagement at the Opera House in which her early triumphs had been made, but this was not at once accepted.

At the end of June her studies with Garcia came to an end.

During this month it happened that Meyerbeer was in Paris on business connected with the production of "Le Prophète." Of the first performance of this opera Garcia retained a vivid memory, and, in speaking of it to me one day, recalled how, during the preliminary rehearsals, the singers all grumbled at its great length. Yet for the memorising and rehearsing of this, previous to its being

put on the stage, they were given only eighteen
days,—the same period as for that other lengthy
work, "William Tell."

On June 15 Herr Lindblad arranged an interview with Meyerbeer, and Jenny Lind sang for
him the aria from "Roberto" and from "Norma."
The composer was much pleased with her voice,
but seems to have entertained doubts as to whether
it was powerful enough to fill the auditorium of
the Grand Opera.

Garcia himself considered her voice still somewhat *fatiguée*, and not quite attained to the
quality of which in a few months it would be
capable.

It may have been this which Meyerbeer noticed.
At any rate, in order to satisfy himself upon the
point, he wished to hear her sing on the stage of
the theatre itself. Accordingly, on the 24th an
audition took place, in which she gave the three
grand scenes from "Der Freischütz, "Robert le
Diable," and "Norma." Meyerbeer was delighted,
and made such comments as, "Une voix chaste et
pure, pleine de grâce et de virginalité," while the
next day he spoke of her to Berlioz with the
greatest enthusiasm. He was anxious for her to
make her appearance in London soon. Garcia,
however, feared that the fame of Grisi would hinder
his pupil from receiving a real chance. He therefore prevented her from making her *début* there
till five years later, when she achieved a veritable
triumph.

On October 10, 1842, the prima donna opened
at the Stockholm theatre with a performance of

" Norma,"—the very opera in which she had closéd her appearances on June 19, 1841.

It must have been a direct challenge to the critical world of Stockholm, to recognise the change that had intervened between the two performances. What that change was we learn from an estimate supplied by a most competent and judicious critic, who sang with her often, both before and after her visit to Paris. He writes as follows :—

" When, during the years 1838-40, Jenny Lind enraptured her audience at Stockholm by her interpretation of the parts of Agathe, Pamina, Alice, Norma, or Lucia, she succeeded in doing so solely through her innate capacity for investing her performances, both musically and dramatically, with truthfulness, warmth, and poetry.

" The voice and its technical development were not, however, in sufficiently harmonious relation with her intentions.

" In proof of this it was noticed that the artist was not always able to control sustained notes in the upper register—such, for instance, as the A flat above the stave in Agathe's cavatina, ' Und ob die Wolke' — without perceptible difficulty ; and that she frequently found it necessary to simplify the *fioritura* and *cadenza* which abound in florid parts like those of Norma and Lucia.

" Nay, there were not wanting some who, though they had heard her in parts no more trying than that of Emilia in Weigl's ' Swiss Family,'—a *rôle* which, in many respects, she rendered delightfully, —went so far as to doubt the possibility of training the veiled and weak-toned voice in a wider sense.

"Yet, in spite of this, Jenny Lind, when resuming her sphere of action at the Stockholm theatre, proved not only to have acquired a soprano voice of great sonority and compass, capable of adapting itself with ease to every shade of expression, but to have gained also a technical command over it great enough to be regarded as unique in the history of the world. Her *messa di voce* stood alone —unrivalled by any other singer.

"In like manner, in her shake, her scales, her legato and staccato passages, she evoked astonishment and admiration no less from competent judges than from the general public; and the more so since it was evident that, in the exercise of her wise discrimination, the songstress made use of these ornaments only in so far as they were in perfect harmony with the inner meaning of the music.

"The incredibly rapid development of her voice and technique caused many people to question the value of the instruction she had originally received before going to Garcia. Such doubts, however, must be dismissed as unjustifiable. The true reason why Jenny Lind's singing before she went abroad could not be said to flow in the track which leads to perfection is undoubtedly to be found in the fact that she was a so-called *theatereler*—a pupil educated at the expense of the directors of the theatre itself—and, as such, was unable to escape from the necessity of appearing in public before her preparatory education was completed,—a proceeding no less disastrous to the pupil than contrary to the good sense of the teacher."

Such, then, was the transformation that had

come over her rendering of Norma. No wonder
that Stockholm went wild with enthusiasm, and
that from that time on her career was one long
crescendo of success.

Jenny Lind had the priceless power of taking
pains, added to which hers was a glorious voice,
properly developed under her master's tender care.
The combination of these gifts, mental and physical,
enabled her to overcome every obstacle which
crossed her path, and to reach the lofty position
which she retained up to the time of her retirement
from public life. Her career was the pride of her
fellow - countrymen, and the name by which she
became known, the Swedish Nightingale, acted as
a constant reminder of her nationality.

The Swedish people paid their tribute to Garcia
by making him a correspondent of the University
of Stockholm, while the Swedish king created him
"Chevalier de l'Ordre de Merite (Gustavus Vasa)."

But the thing which the maestro prized more
than all else was the undying gratitude of his
pupil.

CHAPTER XI.

SOME FAMOUS PUPILS.

(1842–1848.)

THE remaining six years which Señor Garcia spent in Paris before migrating to London were important for the musical world.

We have seen how at this point in his career he was able to claim as pupils a trio of world-renowned singers — Maria Malibran, Pauline Viardot, and Jenny Lind. During the period between 1842 and 1848 this number was greatly increased, for there passed through his hands a series of artists whose successes were a tribute to their master's method and powers of teaching, and to his right to be acknowledged by all the world as the foremost *maestro di canto* of his age. Henriette Nissen, Catherine Hayes, Mathilde Marchesi, Johanna Wagner, Julius Stockhausen, Barbot, Bussine, and Battaille,—these are the principal ones.

Even if his career had ended in '48, instead of being continued in England with no less triumphant results, he could well have claimed to have brought out a greater number of famous artists than any other teacher : only certainly he never *would* have claimed it, for he was ever the most modest of men, the most reticent on the subject of his own powers.

And now to say something concerning the career of the pupils whose names have been set down above.

Henriette Nissen (afterwards Mme. Siegfried Salomon) had commenced her vocal studies with Garcia in 1839, at the same time learning the piano under Chopin, and had made immense progress in her singing during the two years preceding the arrival of Jenny Lind. Being a favourite with the maestro, and a Swede by birth, it is not surprising that Garcia hastened to introduce her to Mdlle. Lind, and that she became her most intimate friend at this period. For the following details I am again indebted to Canon Holland :—

"The two would frequently sing together, and before long a feeling of generous rivalry sprang up between them, which must have been of infinite advantage to both. Mdlle. Lind makes frequent mention of her fellow - pupil in letters written during this period. 'I go to see her pretty often, and we sing together. She has a beautiful voice. In future we are going to have music together at Herr Blumm's.'"

These meetings at his house became quite an institution. Herr Blumm was a Swedish gentle-man of kindliest disposition and infinite *bonhomie,* who held the appointment of "Chancelier" to the Swedish legation in the Rue d'Anjou ; and he bestowed on the two young friends innumerable acts of courtesy and kindness during their study with Garcia.

"I am going to Herr Blumm's," she wrote again, "where Mdlle. Nissen is waiting for us, with an old relation of hers, and we four are going somewhere into the country for the day. She is a very sweet girl. The divine song draws us to each other."

A charming episode is recounted as having happened at the Christmas of 1841. When the festival drew near, Jenny Lind's heart was torn by yearnings for home.

"Ah! who will light the Christmas tree for my mother?" she wrote. "No one, no one! She has no child who can bring her the least pleasure. If you knew how she is ever before me! How constantly she is in my thoughts! How she gives me courage to work! How I love her, as I never loved before!"

In the midst of this cruel burst of home-sickness, good Mdlle. du Puget, in whose house she was staying, bethought her of an expedient, and the result was seen in the following letter :—

"Christmas Eve passed off better than I expected, for Mdlle. du Puget went to fetch the dear sweet Nissen, and all of a sudden, as I was standing in my room alone, she came creeping in to me. We sang duets together,—but my thoughts strayed homewards."

It was beautiful, as time progressed, to note the utter absence of jealousy which characterised this rare artistic friendship between two young students, each of whom had a reputation to ensure, and a name to render famous.

In the beginning of 1842, Garcia considered Mdlle. Nissen sufficiently advanced to make her appearance, and in April her *début* was made at the Italian Opera as Adalgisa in "Norma," this being followed by an immediate engagement for three years under the same management, commencing at a salary of from three to four hundred pounds for the first year. At the conclusion of this she toured Italy, Russia, Norway, Sweden, and England till 1849, when she appeared at Leipsic, and in the following years sang at most of the Gewandhaus concerts there, while in Berlin she almost rivalled Jenny Lind in popularity.

In the summer of 1842, the year of Nissen's *début*, Catherine Hayes came from Ireland, by the advice of Lablache, to place herself under Garcia, being at the time seventeen years of age. After four years' study she made her *début* at Marseilles in "I Puritani." Next year she appeared at Vienna, and in the following seasons sang in various parts of the Continent with success.

Her London *début* was made in 1849, and during that season she appeared at Covent Garden in the *rôles* of Lucia, Linda, and Amina. She soon became one of the most popular vocalists of her day in England, showing herself to be possessed of remarkable power, while her chief forte lay in the rendering of ballads.

The year 1844 saw the advent of three interesting pupils, the names of all curiously enough beginning with the same initial letter, — Barbot, Battaille, and Bussine.

Joseph Barbot came to Garcia at the Conservatoire at the age of twenty, and soon proved himself to be possessed of a remarkably fine tenor voice. At the completion of his training he was engaged at the Grand Opera, but soon left it for Italy, where he sang with great success. Perhaps the most noteworthy event of his career took place on March 19, 1859, for on that date he created the title part at the first performance of Gounod's "Faust" at the Théâtre Lyrique; while sixteen years later he was appointed to a professorship at the Conservatoire as successor to Mme. Viardot.

Charles Battaille appears to have commenced earning his livelihood as a doctor of medicine, the while he carried on his vocal studies. When he had brought these to a close he gave up his practice, and accepted an engagement as basso at the Opéra Comique. Here he remained for ten years, till an affliction of the larynx caused his retirement. From that time on he devoted his life to teaching, having already, in 1851, been appointed professor at the Conservatoire. In 1861 he published the first portion of a voluminous treatise entitled 'L'Enseignement du Chant,' containing some important results of his physiological study. His principal claim to fame, however, is the fact that he was chosen by Meyerbeer to create the bass *rôle* in "L'Etoile du Nord," while he won special renown in the "Seraglio," of Mozart.

As to Bussine, he was connected for some time with the Opéra Comique, and left it for an engagement as principal tenor at the Grand Opera in Paris. Moreover, he gave much time to teaching, one of his best known pupils being Duc.

The year 1845 saw the advent of one who ultimately became Garcia's greatest pupil in the field of teaching — Mathilde Marchesi, or, as she was at that time, Mdlle. Graumann.

Her father had been a wealthy merchant, but in 1843 he lost his fortune, and his daughter, being at this time seventeen years old, decided to adopt the musical profession. She went in the first place to study in Vienna, but in 1845 came to Paris to place herself under Garcia, who soon discovered in his new student a remarkable aptitude for teaching. Of her own recollections of studying under the maestro, Madame Marchesi has sent me the following details, some of which have already been narrated in her interesting book of reminiscences, published under the title, 'Marchesi and Music':—

"I need scarcely mention how the maestro's clear, intelligent, and thorough method furthered my artistic efforts. His ideas on the female voice and its development were a revelation to me, and they were the foundation of my future career. With Nicolai and Mendelssohn I had only studied classical music; now Garcia initiated me into the style of the Italian school, as at that time a florid execution was the principal aim of all good singers. The compositions of Rossini, Bellini, and Donizetti were the chief objects of study, and I was obliged, therefore, to work away at countless scales, arpeggios, &c., and, what was worse still, with the metronome, which sometimes rendered me almost desperate.

"Besides Garcia, Bordogni and Banderali were

also justly celebrated at this time, but he alone had made a thorough study of anatomy and physiology.

" All the maestro's pupils were enthusiastic about him, and patiently submitted to the necessity of waiting sometimes for hours in the anteroom, as he permitted no one to assist at his lessons. When at length the anxiously awaited moment had, as we thought, arrived, he often sent us home with the remark, 'I am tired, children; I will see you to - morrow.' Whenever this occurred we were terribly disappointed, but this wonderfully gifted man's next lesson made us soon oblivious of the previous day's deprivation.

" In the spring of 1847 Garcia fell from his horse and broke his right arm, which accident prevented him for a time from continuing his lessons. He therefore intrusted me with a number of his private pupils. I was very much flattered with this mark of distinction and the confidence thus placed in me, and as he had on various occasions already confided many of his beginners to me, I was not afraid of the responsibility, more especially as I was always able to go to him for advice in difficult cases."

Four years after Mdlle. Graumann had commenced her studies with the maestro, she followed him to London, and soon obtained high standing as a mezzo-soprano concert singer. In 1852 her marriage took place, and two years later she accepted the post of professor at the Vienna Conservatoire. From the first her attempts at carrying on the Garcia traditions of " Bel canto " singing met with the crown of success, and during the succeeding years Mme.

Marchesi turned out such pupils as Ilma de Murska, Fricci, and Kraus, to bring fresh fame to the already glorious banner of Manuel Garcia. 1861 saw her removal to Paris, where pupils came from all parts, while about this time her text-book, 'École du Chant,' was published.

In 1865 Mme. Marchesi went to teach at the Cologne Conservatoire, where Antoinette Sterling came to her for a few lessons; while three years later she returned to Vienna to resume her post at the Conservatoire. This was resigned in 1878, but she continued to teach there for a time, after which she returned to Paris, and took up her work there again.

In addition to those already mentioned, her pupils have included Suzanne Adams, d'Angri, Calvé, Ada Crossley, Eames, Evangeline Florence, Frau Gerster, Blanche Marchesi, Melba, Emma Nevada, Sybil Sanderson, Francis Saville, and Tremelli. Truly a wonderful record to add to the list of exponents of Manuel Garcia's method.

In 1847 an important pupil was coming to Señor Garcia's studio—one who was destined to do great things hereafter. This was Johanna Wagner, the niece of Richard Wagner. Her musical ability already began to make itself noticeable at the age of five, when her father and uncle were residing at Würzburg; for she used to sing everything she heard, and the composer in after years would often laugh as he quoted these childish versions.

In 1844, when Johanna was in her seventeenth year, her uncle obtained an engagement for her at the Royal Opera in Dresden, where he was preparing for the first performance of " Rienzi." Though of but tender years she had such success as Agathe in the " Freischütz," that she was engaged for three years by the management, and created Elisabeth in " Tannhäuser."

On October 21, 1845, fifteen months later, the King of Saxony, who had taken the greatest interest in her progress, sent her to France to study under Garcia. She arrived at the beginning of February, accompanied by her father, who had hitherto been her only instructor. Thanks to the assistance which she received from Garcia during her stay in Paris, she quickly made her mark.

On her return she went to Hamburg, creating Fides in the German version, and taking part in the first performance there of the " Prophète." In 1850 she left for Berlin, where she was permanently engaged by the management of the Royal Opera House. Whilst there Fräulein Wagner was a great favourite with the royal family, and frequently sang in private for Frederick William IV. and his Queen, being generally accompanied by Meyerbeer.

In 1856 the prima donna appeared in London at Her Majesty's Opera House in " Tancredi," " Lucrezia Borgia," and as Romeo. In 1859 she married Herr Jackmann ; two years later she lost her voice suddenly, and started on a second career as an actress, in which she made her name no less surely than as a singer. In this, Johanna Wagner resembled Geneviève Ward, for that famous tragédienne only entered upon a career of acting after having sung in opera under the name of Ginevra Guerrabella. With her, too, it was owing to loss of voice in consequence of overstrain that the change of career was adopted.

The training of Johanna Wagner by Garcia raises an interesting point in connection with German singing. Richard Wagner was so delighted upon hearing the improvement in his niece's voice on her return from Paris, that he wrote the maestro a letter full of the warmest recognition of the progress which she had made under his tuition.

But the gratitude did not end here : over twenty-five years later there came a very signal proof of the extent to which he had been impressed with Garcia's powers, for, when he was making the arrangements for the first Bayreuth Festival, he wrote to his old friend, asking whether he would undertake the training of the singers who were to take part in it. Garcia was so busy with his teaching in London at this time that he was unable to accept the offer; but the mere fact that he was asked to do this is a very material answer to those who would have it that Wagner's music is not supposed to be treated according to the Italian ideals, but should be rendered in the style of *Sprechgesang*, which has been a current German cry.

After the publication of his ' Mémoire sur la Voix,' Señor Garcia had continued to labour incessantly in perfecting his method, and in 1847 (the year in which Jenny Lind made her triumphant *début* in London as Alice in "Roberto," took the town by storm, and earned the name of the "Swedish Nightingale") this culminated in the publication of what is without question the most valuable contribution to the books upon the study of singing.

It was issued in two parts, under the title of 'Traité complet de l'Art du Chant,' and was dedicated to King Oscar I. of Sweden, as a tribute to the nationality of the greatest of the maestro's pupils.

The work was translated into various languages, and thereby gained a world-wide reputation. The 'Traité' was acknowledged on all sides to be invaluable, and it laid the foundations of all important subsequent investigations into the emission of the voice.

As to Garcia's treatment of his pupils, he exhibited ever the most untiring patience. The infinite pains he took with them never failed to win their affection as well as their admiration, and this undoubtedly contributed in some considerable degree to the progress which they made under his care. A story has been told by Jourdan, which gives a good illustration of the great master's care of his pupils.

One day, being upset and ruffled at some remarks made upon his singing by the maestro, Jourdan left the class in a temper, and did not return for the next lesson. Garcia, noticing his absence, went to his lodging, a small room on the fifth floor, and took the young student by the ear, saying, "Come along, *méchant garçon*, come and have your lesson."

And now we come to 1848, the year in which Manuel Garcia terminated his residence in Paris.

He did so in consequence of the Revolution, which flared up on February 24, and finally resulted in the flight of Louis Philippe. It was during these disturbances that the maestro was sought out by Julius Stockhausen, a lad of

twenty-two, who was eventually to become one of
Germany's greatest teachers and singers. Of this
period Herr Stockhausen sent me some reminiscences, and in reproducing them there is a pathetic
interest, owing to the fact that two days after
their arrival from Germany the lieder-singer passed
away in his eighty-first year.

"I first made the acquaintance of the maestro,"
writes Herr Stockhausen, "in 1848. The year had
begun with much unrest, and on February 24 the
Revolution broke out. Owing to the absence of the
friend under whose roof I was residing at the time,
I was obliged to enter the National Guard as a
substitute. As such I presented myself before
the maestro in full uniform. He received me very
kindly, for a relation of mine, Frau Reiter, who
had already been studying with him, had spoken a
few words of recommendation on my behalf.

"What struck me most at the first meeting were
the steadiness of his glance, the swiftness of his
movement, and the rhythm of his tread. He was
a man of middle age — forty-three years old, his
manner alert, his voice possessing a friendly ring.
When I timidly inquired his terms he replied,
'Combien voulez-vous me donner? je n'ai plus
d'élèves; ils ont tous fui la révolution.' But,
honoured master, you have just been trying a tenor
who has a powerful voice. 'True; but he has no
ear,' replied Garcia. 'When I asked him what his
occupation was, he replied, 'Je suis tourneur.' 'Eh
bien,' I answered, 'tournez, tournez encore; pas
d'oreille, pas de chanteur!'

"My position as a member of the National Guard

and a son of artistic parents seemed to interest the
maestro, and he asked me only ten francs a lesson.
After a few days studies were commenced, and I
used to attend in my regimentals.   Unhappily,
however, the hardships of bivouacking on those cold
winter nights proved very pernicious for my young
voice, so that after a few weeks I found myself
obliged to cease lessons temporarily.   For six weeks
I struggled against catarrh and sore throat; but at
the beginning of May there came a happy change.

"On the 26th of the same month I received an
invitation from Basle to sing in Mendelssohn's
'Elijah.'   Garcia raised no objections to my attempting the task, and went through the difficult
passages with me very carefully, showing me
further how I might commit the title-*rôle* to
memory in a short time without overtiring the
voice.   When in due course I sang the Elijah in
Basle, the audience had no idea how my voice had
suffered during those weeks of military hardship
and discipline in Paris."

Such is the characteristic description which Julius
Stockhausen gave of his first months under Garcia.

CHAPTER XII.

THE first revolution of 1848 broke out in February. The grand Reform banquet which had been announced was suddenly prohibited on the 21st of the month, the immediate consequence being that revolutionary tumults burst out, and the next day brought with it the impeachment and resignation of Guizot. This was quickly followed by the throwing up of barricades in the streets; the Tuileries were ransacked, the prisons opened, and the most frightful disorders committed. At this Louis Philippe completely lost his nerve, and abdicated on the 24th in favour of his infant grandson, the Comte de Paris, who was not, however, accepted by the populace. Upon this the royal family and ministers made their escape as best they could, and a week later the ex-king landed at Newhaven as "Mr Smith."

On February 26 a republic was proclaimed from the steps of the Hôtel de Ville; and this decisive measure was followed by a grand funeral procession in honour of the victims of the revolution.

The next three months passed by in comparative

quiet. The provisional government, which had
been formed in the great public commotion, resigned to an executive commission, elected by the
National Assembly of the French Republic, and
the perpetual banishment of Louis Philippe and
his family was decreed.

With June there came an outburst of still more
frightful disorder, owing to the reconstitution of the
National Guard of France, it being enlarged from
80,000 to 100,000. Among those who enrolled
themselves in this body of men was Manuel Garcia ;
and it is not surprising that he did so, for, as all
who knew him are well aware, he was a great lover
of law and order.

The precautionary measure acted as a lighted
fuse to a barrel of gunpowder. On June 23 the
red republicans rose up in arms against the troops
and the National Guard, more than three hundred
barricades were thrown up, and firing continued in
all parts of the capital during the night. Garcia
well remembered George Sand standing on the top
of a barricade surrounded by a band of students,
and shouting down to him, " N'est-ce pas que c'est
magnifique, n'est ce pas que c'est beau ! "

Next day the troops under Cardignac and Lamo-
ricière, after suffering immense loss, drove the insurgents from the left bank of the Seine. On the
25th Paris was declared in a state of siege, while
on the following day the Faubourg du Temple was
carried with cannon, the insurgents surrendered,
and the revolution was brought to an end.

But at what a cost had peace been restored ! The
national losses caused by the outbreak were esti-

mated at thirty million francs; while during the
four days of fighting no less than sixteen thousand
persons were killed and wounded, among the former
being the Archbishop of Paris, who lost his life
while tending the dying on the final day of conflict.

But for all its excitement and bloodshed this four
days' revolution failed to excite much enthusiasm in
the maestro. Perhaps it seemed poor fun after
those scenes of the Napoleonic Invasion and the
successive campaigns of the Peninsular War, which
he remembered from his childhood. He may even
have grown weary of such scenes, and considered
the whole affair badly managed after the other
revolutions he had been through. Certainly there
had been much less fuss when, eighteen years before, he had seen Charles X. driven out and Louis
Philippe made king. He had passed through too
many excitements already.

One can almost imagine the scene that must have
taken place in the July of 1846, when he was
informed by a breathless pupil at the beginning
of a lesson that an attempt had just been made on
the king's life by Henri. One can picture him
shaking his head reprovingly and replying, "Yes;
but it was not as exciting as some of the other
attempts on his life that I remember. Let me see,
it must have been—yes, it was in the July of 1835,
almost exactly thirteen years ago to the day, that
the first one took place. Now that really *was* a
fine one! Fieschi fired an infernal machine as the
king was riding down the Boulevard du Temple
along the lines of the National Guard. Louis
Philippe was accompanied by his three sons. They

all four escaped, but the Duke of Treviso was shot
dead, and forty persons were killed and wounded.
Now that's what I call something *like* an attempt!

"Then, next year, there was Louis Alibaud, who
fired at the king on his way to the Tuileries.
Pauvre garçon! He was guillotined for his trouble.

"There wasn't another attempt for some time,
but in 1840, again, Darmès fired at Louis Philippe:
that was the year before the attempt made to
assassinate one of the king's sons, the Duke of
Aumale; but there was no result. Much better
leave things to Providence. Why, it was only a
year later that the heir to the throne was killed
without bothering any one to risk his neck over it!
Yes, he had a fall from his carriage. Bless me! you
must remember that; it was only six years ago.
Then there was Lecompte, who had a try at his
unhappy majesty when he was going to Fontainebleau. How many people did you say were killed
to-day when Henri made the attempt? None?
Dear, dear. It's not like the old days. Well, let's
get on with the lesson. What songs have you
brought?"

If such a scene as this did *not* take place, it
certainly might well have done so.

However, what with revolutions, the driving out
of kings, and the general unrest during the twenty
years that followed his return from America as a
young man of twenty-three, the maestro came to
the conclusion that the French capital was getting
too unsettled to be suitable for the giving of singing
lessons. At the end of the month, therefore, he
shook the dust of Paris from his feet and set out for

London, where he had made up his mind to settle and establish himself as a teacher.

With this change of *locale* the second period in Manuel Garcia's life is brought to a close. Before leaving it, we will cast an eye over some of the figures prominent in the musical and artistic world of Paris during the twenty years in which the centenarian made it his home.

Rossini, as we have seen, was director both of the Théâtre Italien and of the French Opera when Garcia joined his sister in Paris at the close of 1827. During this time the composer adapted several of his works to French taste. Of these, " Moïse " and " Le Siège de Corinth " were the new titles given to " Mose in Egitto " and " Maometto Secondo," of which the original productions had taken place during the four years following Manuel's arrival from Naples as a lad of eleven. Rossini, however, only stayed in Paris for eighteen months, and left after the production there of his greatest work, " Guillaume Tell," in August 1822, nor did he return to settle down and become one of the most notable personalities of the city till a quarter of a century later.

Many interesting musical productions took place during Manuel Garcia's residence in Paris.

In 1828, the year of his arrival from Mexico, Liszt was a boy of sixteen, an infant prodigy, just returned from a visit to England, and beginning to teach pianoforte, owing to circumstances already referred to in speaking of the lessons which Mme. Viardot had from him.

Berlioz had been sent by his parents some little

time before to study medicine in the French capital.
Instead of doing so, however, he had devoted him-
self to music, and was at this time a pupil at the
Conservatoire.

Soon after Garcia's arrival there took place the
production of one of Auber's best known works,
"La Muette di Portici," or, as it is usually entitled,
"Masaniello." The next year, that in which
Schubert died, saw the completion of "Agnes von
Hohenstaufen," the greatest work of Spontini,
whose opera, "La Vestale," had been greeted with
enthusiasm and adjudged Napoleon's prize of 10,000
francs twenty-two years before.

In 1830 came Auber's "Fra Diavolo" and
Halévy's "Manon Lescaut."

The following year was an important one in many
ways, for there were produced not only Bellini's two
favourite operas, "Somnambula" and "Norma"
(the "Puritani" was given four years later), but
Hérold's "Zampa" and Meyerbeer's "Robert le
Diable." But this is not all, for it saw the advent
to Paris of Frédéric Chopin, a young man of twenty-
two. Here he quickly found fame, and became the
idol of the salons, giving lessons to a select *clientèle*
of pupils, and employing his leisure in composition. He rarely performed in public, though, in
Mendelssohn's judgment, he was "a truly perfect
virtuoso" as well as a thorough musician, with a
faculty for improvisation such as, perhaps, no other
pianist ever possessed.

In 1832, a date made memorable on the tablets
of literature by the death of Goethe and Sir Walter

Scott, there came Hérold's "Le Pré aux Clercs," while Berlioz obtained the first proper hearing for some of his compositions. Their complicated and peculiar nature, however, failed to win popular recognition, and he was driven to support himself and his wife by writing musical criticisms.

In the summer of 1833 the birth took place of a musician who was to become world-famous, Johannes Brahms; while the winter was rendered memorable in the artistic circles of Paris by the fatal journey which Alfred de Musset made to Italy with George Sand. In the following April he reappeared alone, broken in health and sunk in the deepest depression. A quarter of a century later, when Garcia had long been settled in London, he was to be reminded of the episode by reading the version of the events which George Sand gave to the world in the guise of a novel, 'Elle et Lui'; to which Paul de Musset at once retorted with 'Lui et Elle,' in which he asserted that she had been grossly unfaithful.

The year, which robbed the world of one musician and brought forth another,—for with the death of Bellini there came the birth of Saint-Saëns,—was one full of musical interest, for 1835 saw the completion of a perfect avalanche of new operas, including Auber's "Cheval de Bronze," Halévy's "La Juive" and "L'Etoile du Nord," Adolphe Adam's "Postillon de Longjumeau," and two operas by Donizetti, "Marino Faliero" and "Lucia di Lammermoor."

In 1836 the first performance took place of

Meyerbeer's great opera, the "Huguenots," given at the Académie Royale de Musique on February 29, with the following cast :—

Valentine	.	.	Mdlle. Falcon.
Marguerite	.	.	Mme. Doras-Gras.
Urbain	.	.	Mdlle. Flécheux.
Marcel	.	.	M. Levasseur.
Nevers	.	.	M. Dérivis.
Saint Bris	.	.	M. Serda.

The part of Raoul was played by the elder Garcia's famous pupil, Adolph Nourrit.

It is, moreover, the date of the commencement of a fresh episode in the life of George Sand (Madame Armandine Dudevant), this time with Chopin, who was introduced to her by Liszt.

The "Domino Noir" was produced in Paris in 1837, the year which saw the first performance of Mendelssohn's "St Paul" in England, to be followed three years later by the "Hymn of Praise," and in 1848, the year of Garcia's arrival in London, by the "Elijah."

In 1839 Flotow's "Le Naufrage de la Méduse" was produced; but the year is of far more interest to us from the fact that Richard Wagner, a young man, twenty-six years of age, first arrived in Paris, resolved to try his fortune there with "Rienzi," only to be forced to leave the city after a sore struggle of nearly three years, with his opera still unperformed.

In 1840, the year of Paganini's death, three operas of Donizetti saw light, " La Fille du Régiment," "Lucrezia Borgia," and "La Favorita."

In the next year Auber's "Les Diamants de la

Couronne" was performed; and a twelve-year-old musician, newly arrived from Moscow, was given an opportunity of playing the piano to Liszt, and of being patted on the head, while he listened to words of warm encouragement. And the name of the boy - pianist ? Anton Rubinstein, who died more than twelve years ago, at the age of sixty - five.

In 1842, the year in which Massenet was born, Meyerbeer's opera "Le Prophète" was finished, which was destined not to be produced at the Grand Opera House till seven years later.

In 1843 Donizetti's "Don Pasquale" was brought out, and in the following year Flotow's "Stradella" and Félicien David's grand ode-symphony "Désert." It saw, moreover, the completion by Richard Wagner of "Der Fliegende Holländer," as the next year, in which Tom Hood died, saw that of "Tannhäuser."

In 1847 the Parisian public witnessed for the first time Flotow's "Martha," while in the last year of Garcia's sojourn in the capital, Nicolai's "Merry Wives of Windsor" and Wagner's "Lohengrin" were finished; Offenbach was appointed *chef d'orchestre* at the Théâtre Français (this being long before "La Grande Duchesse" and "Madame Favart" had been set down on paper); Gounod was still in his twenties, and had not yet even composed his first opera, while "Faust" was not to be brought out for eleven, and "Roméo et Juliette" for just on twenty years. As for Bizet, he was a mere boy of ten.

Allusion has already been made to George Sand,

M

Henry Mürger, and Alfred de Musset. One must add to the literary circle of that time such personalities as these : Balzac, who first tasted success with the publication of 'Les Derniers Chouans,' about a year after Señor Garcia had arrived from Mexico, soon following this up with the earliest of his great works, 'La Peau de Chagrin'; Théophile Gautier, whose first long poem, 'Albertus,' was published about the same time, to be followed, in 1835, by the celebrated novel, 'Mademoiselle de Maupin,' with its defiant preface ; Alfred de Vigny, whom Manuel Garcia, as a young man of twenty-five, saw abandon for good in 1830 the publication of his exquisite poetry, and confine himself after that date to works in prose alone.

Then there were Alphonse de Lamartine, statesman, poet, and historian, who, in 1829, had declined the post of Foreign Secretary in the Polignac Ministry, and by his 'Harmonies Poétiques et Religieuses' achieved his unanimous election to the Academy ; Lamercier, one of the three chief exponents of the Romantic school, with some of his detached passages equal in beauty to anything in the language, and others so bizarre as to border on the ridiculous ; Delavigne, representative of the golden mean of French literature, the half-classic and half-romantic school ; Béranger, the "Horace" of French poetry, whose outspoken ballads achieved such immense popularity, that in turn Louis XVIII. and Charles X. threw him into prison because of his freedom of ideas,—for probably no poet has ever exercised such a power over the destiny of

a nation; Victor Hugo, engaged in bringing out
'Notre Dame de Paris,' 'Le Roi s'amuse,' 'Les
Voix Interieures,' in which the poet's diction is
held to have found its noblest expression, 'Ruy
Blas,' almost the most famous of his stage rhap-
sodies, and many another work of world - wide
fame; Eugène Sue, whose first hit was made in
1842 with the too famous 'Mystères de Paris,'
followed three years later by 'Le Juif Errant';
the elder Dumas, who, during these years, published such works as 'Monte Cristo,' 'Les Trois
Mousquetaires,' and 'Les Mémoires d'un Médecin';
while in the year of the maestro's departure for
London, Alexander Dumas the younger was bringing out his immortal 'La Dame aux Camélias.'
Nor must one forget Paul de Kock, Henri Roche-
fort, who was then only sixteen years old, Zola
half that age, and François Coppée a child of six.

When we turn to the painting world there is
an equal *embarras de richesse*. What can one
say to such a dazzling list of artists as Rosa
Bonheur, Horace Vernet, Paul Delaroche, the
founder of the modern "Eclectic School," Prud'hon,
Gericault, Delacroix, Gros, Scheffer, Decamps,
Corot, Rousseau, Troyon, Duprè, Diaz, Jean
François Millet (who took his place with Garcia
on the barricades during the Revolution of '48),
nay, even Meissonier himself, whose first contribution to the Salon in 1834, a water - colour
and an oil - picture, the centenarian remembered
to have seen, followed two years later by the
"Chess - Players," the precursor of that long
series of elaborate genre - pictures, in which he

depicted the civil and military life of the seventeenth, eighteenth, and nineteenth centuries.

Truly, had Manuel Garcia passed away· in the year of the Revolution, in accordance with the modern cry of "too old at forty," his career and experiences would have still been of surpassing interest. But with this year we only see the scene of his triumphs shifted from France to England, and have yet to watch him not only carrying through a further forty - seven years of work as teacher, but appearing in the new *rôle* of inventor, and then passing on to that last period, ten years of wonderful old age.

THIRD PERIOD

LONDON

(1848–1895)

CHAPTER XIII.

AT the close of June 1848 Manuel Garcia, at the age of forty-three, arrived in London, where he was to make a new home and spend the rest of his days.

What changes had taken place in the capital since he had last been there in the autumn of 1825! When he left George IV. was still king; when he returned William IV. had reigned and been succeeded by Queen Victoria, who had already been on the throne over ten years, while our present king, as Prince of Wales, was six years old.

Let us glance for a moment at the position of musical affairs in London, and at some of the artists who were in favour when Garcia arrived.

In the previous year (in which both Mendelssohn and Donizetti had died) an important event had taken place, for the Covent Garden Theatre was opened as an opera house, and a new period in its history begun.

The scheme had been originated by Signor Persiani, who took the lease of the place in partnership with Galletti; then, finding that they had embarked on an enterprise which was too much for them to carry through without assistance, they brought in Messrs Cramer, the music publishers, to help finance the undertaking.

As to the company which took part in the opening season, Signor Costa left Her Majesty's Theatre in order to fill the responsible post of conductor of an orchestra which had M. Prosper Sainton as principal violin; and of the artists themselves the stars were Grisi, Mario, Tamburini, and the Persianis, while Mdlle. Alboni made a triumphant *debut*, and proved herself another strong card to strengthen the hand of the new management.

With the launching of this enterprise a triangular duel was fought between Covent Garden, Drury Lane under Bunn, and Her Majesty's under Lumley, who, after the famous " Bunn Controversy," had been successful in securing a trumpcard with Garcia's now world-famous pupil, Jenny Lind.

Next let us conjure up the artistic circles of London, among which Señor Garcia found himself in 1848. What names of the past we find when we glance in turn at science and literature, the stage and music. In one and all it was an age of giants.

The scientific world could boast such lights as Brewster, Darwin, Faraday, Sir John Herschel, Huxley, Miller, Owen, and Tyndall.

Literature poured forth a veritable Niagara of Prose writers: Charlotte Brontë, Carlyle, Dickens, Disraeli, Grote, G. P. R. James, Douglas Jerrold,

Charles Kingsley, Charles Lever, Bulwer Lytton, Macaulay, Martineau, John Stuart Mill, Ruskin, and Thackeray ; while Poetry was scarcely less prominent with Arnold, P. Bayley, the Brownings, Clough, Tom Hood, Horner, Alexander Smith, Sir H. Taylor, and Tennyson.

En passant, we may note the following pieces of literary news, culled from newspapers published during the month in which Manual Garcia landed in England.

The Nestor of literary France died in Paris on Tuesday last, Monsieur de Chateaubriand.

* * *

Ralph Waldo Emerson will deliver a lecture at Exeter Hall on "Domestic Life."

* * *

Review of the last new Transatlantic poem, "Evangeline," by Longfellow.

* * *

Macaulay's 'History of England.' Volumes one and two. Just published.

* * *

"NEW HISTORICAL ROMANCE," by the Author of 'Rienzi.'

Now ready at all libraries. In three volumes.

'HAROLD.'

The Last of the Saxon Kings.

By Sir Edward Bulwer Lytton, Bart.

Of the Stage we get a strange glimpse from the advertisements in the papers of July 1848. Three things are specially noticeable in them. Practically all the theatres boast "a regal air," a large proportion are managed by ladies, and the bill of fare laid before the voracious public is, to put it mildly, somewhat of an *embarras de richesse*.

Opera seasons are, of course, running at Her Majesty's Theatre and the Royal Italian Opera, Covent Garden. Leaving these and other musical matters of 1848 for the moment, let us reproduce some of the advertisements from the papers of that July, for we shall obtain in this way the best insight into the places of amusement of that time.

THEATRE ROYAL, DRURY LANE.

BENEFIT OF Mr MACREADY.

His last appearance previous to his departure for America.

THEATRE ROYAL, HAYMARKET.

Mr B. WEBSTER (*Sole Lessee*).

"THE WIFE'S SECRET."

Sir Walter . . .	Mr Charles Kean.
Jabez	Mr Webster.
Neville . . .	Miss Reynolds.
Lady Eveline . .	Mrs Charles Kean.
Maude . . .	Mrs Keeley.

ROYAL LYCEUM THEATRE.

Under the Management of Mme. VESTRIS.

"The Captain of the Watch," after which "The Beggar's Opera," to conclude with "Anything for a Change."

THEATRE ROYAL, SADLER'S WELLS.

Under the Direction of Miss RAINFORTH.

Rossini's opera of "Cinderella," after which "No Song, no Supper."

THEATRE ROYAL, ADELPHI.

Under the Management of Mme. CELESTE.

" The Harvest Home," after which " Going to the Derby," to conclude with " The Married Bachelor."

THEATRE ROYAL, MARYLEBONE.

Under the Management of Mrs WARNER.

Macbeth	. . .	Mr Macready.
Lady Macbeth	. .	Mrs Warner.

After which " The Spoiled Child."

ROYAL SURREY THEATRE.

Shakspere's original version of " The Life and Death of King Richard Third," after which " A Grand Ballet," to conclude with Boz's " Oliver Twist."

ROYAL OLYMPIC THEATRE.

Mr H. Spicer's new play, " The Lords of Ellingham," to conclude with the Drama, " The Miller and His Men."

ST JAMES'S THEATRE.

(French Plays.)

" L'Almanach des 25,000 Addresses," concluding with " L'Enfant de Quelqu'un," with M. Grassot, M. Sainville, and M. Ravel.

To commence at 7.30.

PRINCESS'S THEATRE.

" La Vivandière," to conclude with the " Spirit of Gold," a Ballet, and other entertainments.

ROYAL GRECIAN SALOON.

An entirely new opera in three acts by Auber, " Le Chevalier d'Essone," with a Farce and a Divertissement.

Commencing at 6.30.

ASTLEY'S ROYAL AMPHITHEATRE.

An entirely new grand spectacle, entitled "Marmion; or the Battle of Flodden," with other entertainments in the Ring.

THE DIORAMA, REGENT'S PARK.

(New Exhibition.)

"Eruption of Mount Ætna."

COAL-HOLE TAVERN, STRAND.

(Opposite Exeter Hall.)

Chair taken by JOHN RHODES every Evening.

Glees, Duets, Solos, Catches, Comic Songs, &c., executed by the most numerous company of vocalists in the Metropolis, under the direction of Mr Warren, R.A.

MADAME WARTON'S WALHALLA.

(Leicester Square.)

"Tableaux Vivants."

CREMORNE GARDENS.

Grand Aquatic Tournament.

Magnificent Water Pageant.

The following paragraph appeared on July 29, and from it we get an insight into the aftermath which the months of revolutionary disturbance had bequeathed to the city Garcia had left only four weeks before.

" From a Paris Correspondent.

" The theatres here seem struggling to get on their legs again. The only speech that was listened to attentively during my visits to the Assembly was that by Victor Hugo, advocating an annual grant of 680,000 francs to the Paris theatres."

Let us now look at the musical events which were taking place during the first weeks after Manuel Garcia's arrival in London.

We find many interesting announcements in the concert world; and it is strange to note that practically none of the halls in which they were given survive at the present day. On June 23 M. Chopin gives his *matinée;* while the Philharmonic Society informs the " subscribers and the public " that their eighth concert will take place at the Hanover Square Rooms, on June 26, with the following programme :—

Sinfonia in A, No. 2, Mendelssohn ; overture, " Leonora," Beethoven ; sinfonia in C minor, Beethoven ; overture, " The Ruler of the Spirits," Weber.

Vocal performers.—Mme. Castellani and Signor Mario.

Conductor.—Mr Costa.

Tickets, £1, 1s. each.

On the same day there takes place in the Great Concert Room of Her Majesty's Theatre, Mr Benedict's Grand Annual Morning Concert, with the following artists :—

" Tadolini, Cruvelli, Vera, de Mendi, Schwartz, Sabatier, Mme. Lablache, Miss Dolby, the Misses Williams, Mme. Doras - Gras, Gordoni, Marras, Brizzi, Lablache, Caletti, Belletti, Ciabatta, Pischek, and John Parry."

Three days later Monsieur Berlioz gives a recital at the Hanover Square Rooms.

During the same week we find the Musical Union giving a Grand Matinée at Willis's Rooms, with vocal music, sung by Mme. Viardot-Garcia and Mdlle. de Mendi: instrumentalists, Molique, Sainton, Hermann, Deloffre, Hill, Mellon, and Piatti; pianist, Charles Hallé; accompanist, Benedict.

Soon after this Thalberg gives a recital; while "John Parry, the laughter-provoking and ingenious," holds his concert in the Hanover Square Rooms. "His new 'whimsy' (for he is the Hood of musicians in his amount of whim, and whim cannot exist without genius) is 'The Rehearsal of an Operetta.'"

There is also a notice of Exeter Hall: "Mr Hullah's choralists celebrated the anniversary of laying the first stone of their new music hall with the best miscellaneous English concert that one recollects. . . . Mr Sims Reeves, who seems wisely taking the tide at the flood, and by increased care justifying his increasing success, was an attraction, singing among other music Purcell's 'Come if you dare,' with spirit enough to 'rouse a shire.'"

Then there is a season of Promenade Concerts at the Royal Adelaide Gallery, Strand, not to mention "M. Jullien and his unrivalled band" at the Royal Surrey Gardens.

'Musical Gossip' of July 1848 contains some items, the first of which cannot fail to bring an ironical smile to the face of modern composers.

"We have year after year adverted to the unsatisfactory state of the law of musical copyright in this country."

"It is now stated that Mdlle. Lind has at last

declined to take an engagement at Norwich : the sum of £1000 was offered her."

" A correspondent at Florence writes : ' Old Rossini is here enjoying his well-earned *otium cum dignitate.*' "

Now let us turn to operatic matters in that far-off season of 1848.

Mr Delafield had undertaken to finance the Covent Garden venture, for which a bevy of great names had been secured. As in the preceding season Garcia's pupil, Jenny Lind, had been the principal star at Her Majesty's, so in this year another pupil, his sister, Pauline Viardot, was the star at the rival establishment. In addition to her there were Alboni, Persiani, Grisi, Mario, Ronconi, Marini, and Castellani. Unhappily, things did not run as smoothly as might have been wished : Michael Costa and Delafield were at loggerheads, and in July, soon after Garcia arrived from Paris, a financial crisis occurred which was only averted by the assistance of Gye.

On the 20th of the month the first important operatic event took place of the many which the maestro was to witness here during the last fifty-eight years of his life. As the " Huguenots " had been produced twelve years before in the original French version during his stay in Paris, so now, with his advent to London, Meyerbeer's masterpiece was given for the first time at Covent Garden in its Italian version, under the title " Gli Ugonotti," with the part of Urbain transposed for Alboni, and an additional cavatina written specially for her. The cast on this occasion was as follows :—

Valentine	.	.	Mme. Viardot-Garcia.
Marguerite	.	.	Mme. Castellani.
Urbain	.	.	Mdlle. Alboni.
Raoul	.	.	Signor Mario.
Marcel	.	.	Signor Marini.
Nevers	.	.	Signor Tagliafico.
Saint Bris	.	.	Signor Tamburini.

As to the rival operatic season at Her Majesty's Theatre, it will be sufficient if we quote a rather typical critique of one of the representations :—

" ' Poor Don Pasquale,' Donizetti's prettiest musical comedy (!), 'produced to fill an off-night,' was an exclamation there was no escaping from on Tuesday evening. Why was it produced at all? To us the performance was an execution in the Tyburn acceptation of the word.

" But a murder far more heinous has been committed at Her Majesty's this week. Poor M. Meyerbeer, how must his ears have tingled when his ' Roberto' was given with one principal character —involving two entire acts, the two principal soprano songs of the opera, and its only grand finale —coolly swept away ! By past musical performances we were apprised that neither Mr Lumley nor Mr Balfe recognises the difference between one of the flimsy Italian operas and those thoughtful works in which sequence, contrast, and stage effect have all been regarded by the composer. . . . If no prima donna equal to ' En vain j'espère' and ' Robert' be in the theatre, wherefore give the work at all, unless ' the Swedish lady' is *in extremis* for a new attraction ? Why not withdraw as superfluous all solos in Mdlle. Lind's operas save Mdlle. Lind's own ? Why not mount 'Don Juan' without Donna Anna's arias ? Rapacious as these propositions sound, they are as defensible as the liberties taken with Meyerbeer."

We find the first mention of Señor Garcia's arrival made in the 'Musical World' of July 1, in these words :—

"Manuel Garcia, the celebrated professor of singing in the Conservatoire of Paris, has arrived in London. He is brother to Malibran and Pauline Garcia, and was teacher of Jenny Lind."

On July 15 the 'Athenæum' gives further details : "We are informed that Monsieur Garcia meditates settling here as professor of singing."

With the publication of this news the maestro was besieged with applications from those who were desirous of becoming pupils. He was at once regarded as the foremost professor in the capital, and his house in George Street, Hanover Square, not only saw numbers of students anxious to enter the profession, but was equally sought out by the aristocracy and wealthy classes of society, as had been the case in Paris.

On November 10, 1848, he was appointed a member of the professional staff at the Royal Academy of Music.

The institution had only been founded twenty-five years previously, when Garcia was eighteen, receiving its charter of incorporation seven years later.

It was very different from the Academy as we

N

know it now. Up to the January of the year in which Garcia joined, it had had in all 767 pupils. It may be of interest to those who have been connected with it during recent years, to learn that the total number of new pupils admitted to the Academy during 1847 were forty, of which thirteen only were members of the sterner sex. Assuming that every pupil stayed at the Royal Academy of Music for a three years' course—the assumption is rather more than doubtful—we should find the average number of pupils per term during the first twenty-five years of its existence to have been exactly ninety. Compare that with the five hundred or more who attend at the present day.

The principal of the Academy at that time was Cipriani Potter, and we find some strangely bygone names upon the staff of professors. Sir Henry Bishop, Mons. Sainton, Moscheles, Goss, George Macfarren, Signor Crivelli, Sir George Smart, Mme. Dulcken, J. B. Cramer, Julius Benedict, Lindley, Chatterton, J. Thomas (the harpist), Signor Puzzi, and as an assistant professor of the pianoforte, Walter Macfarren. These were some of the colleagues with whom Garcia found himself associated when he commenced his work at the Academy.

At the beginning of 1849 there came a reminder of the scenes of revolution through which the maestro had passed a few months before, for Julius Stockhausen followed him to England, to pursue in the quieter atmosphere of London those studies which were so rudely broken up by the alarums and excursions of his duties with the French National Guard. Stockhausen continued to have

lessons from the maestro till 1851, and during this
period sang at various concerts, by means of which
appearances he quickly began to make his mark.
During the last year of his studies he sang for the
Philharmonic Society no less than three times.

The close of 1852 saw his first appearance on the
operatic stage at Mannheim; while between the
years 1857 and 1859 he was engaged at the Opéra
Comique in Paris, making especial success as the
Seneschal in "Jean de Paris." In 1862 he settled
in Hamburg as director of the Philharmonic Concerts
there and of the "Sing-akademie," a position which
he held till the end of the 'Sixties. During this
period he took many concert tours with Mme.
Schumann, Brahms, and Joseph. In 1870 he was
back in England, and stayed till the close of 1871,
singing once more at the Philharmonic, Crystal
Palace, and other leading concerts. Three years
after this he went to live in Berlin, to take direction
of the vocal society founded by Stern. Thence he
migrated to Frankfort as professor of the Conserv-
atorium, presided over at the time by Raff; and it
was in Frankfort that he spent the rest of his
days.

His principal pupils were van Rooy, Scheidemantel, and George Henschel; and as a teacher he
was generally acknowledged to be the foremost of
his time in Germany, as Mathilde Marchesi was in
France. It is therefore a matter of some note that
during the years in which Manuel Garcia was
himself the finest teacher in England, he should,
through these two pupils, have had his banner
thus upheld upon the Continent.

Among the most promising of Garcia's earliest pupils at the Royal Academy was Kate Crichton, who came to study under him at the commencement of 1849—the year in which Sims Reeves made his operatic *debut* and music-lovers mourned the death of Chopin.

Miss Crichton soon showed that the maestro had not left behind him in Paris his cunning in the training of voices. As the time approached at which the idea of her *début* was taking shape, the advice of Garcia upon the point was sought by her father. The letter in which was embodied his reply may be quoted as showing the deep interest and sound advice which was ever displayed in his relations with his pupils :—

MONSIEUR,—Veuillez avoir la bonté d'excuser le retard de ma réponse ; une indisposition en a été la cause.

Je regrette que le manque de courage tienne en échec les moyens de Mademoiselle Browne et comme Mr Hogarth je juge que l'exercice fréquent devant le public est le meilleur moyen de vaincre sa peur.

Mais aussi je pense que les premiers essays (*sic*) de Mademoiselle Browne vont être fort incomplets et par une sorte dans l'usage de procédés qu'elle ne domine pas encore complétement et par la terreur que bien a tort lui inspire le public.

Or pensez vous qu'il faille donner à ses premiers essays (*sic*) tout le rétentissement possible, ou ne trouvez vous pas qu'il serait plus prudent de les faire à petit bruit laissant à la débutante le temps d'acquerir l'applomb (*sic*) qui lui manque avant de lancer son nom à la grand publicité.

Je vous soumets ces réflexions en vous laissant d'ailleurs la faculté de faire usage de mon nom si vous le croyez utile aux interests de votre enfant.

J'ai l'honneur d'être, Monsieur, Votre trés humble Serviteur,   M. GARCIA.

At last her teacher thought her ready to make the trial. An engagement was secured under the management of Alfred Bunn, and on January 23, 1852, Kate Crichton made her *début* on the opening night of the Drury Lane season in "Robert le Diable." As to her success we may quote 'The Times' :—

"As Princess Isabelle, Miss Crichton (in whose person we recognised Miss Browne, the most promising pupil of the vocal art in the Royal Academy of Music) made her first appearance on any stage. She was successful to a degree which, since the *début* of Mr Sims Reeves in 1849, has had no parallel on the English stage."

Unhappily Miss Crichton's career, so brightly begun, was brought to a sudden close by her catching a malignant fever at Milan, resulting in the loss of her vocal powers. Had it not been for this, there is no doubt that she, too, would have been among that wonderful band of pupils who won fame in the operatic world for their maestro and themselves.

Miss Crichton, however, during her years of study seems to have caught the bacillus of old age from her master, for, upon ultimately regaining the beauty of her voice after many years of retirement, she continued to sing to her friends until within a few months of her death in her eightieth year. Among other eminent pupils who acquired from Garcia the bad habit of longevity, one may recall Stockhausen, who lived to pass his eightieth birthday; Charles Santley and Bessie Palmer, who are well on in the seventies; and Pauline Viardot, who is not so very far off her ninetieth year. Who will assert that old age is not catching?

1850 was a year interesting to musicians from the fact that Frederick Gye, the new manager of Covent Garden, produced Halévy's opera, "La Juive," while the great German basso, Herr Formes, made his English *début;* but the year was memorable for England at large, from the fact that it saw the death of two of her best-known men—Robert Peel and Wordsworth.

With the following year—in which Turner passed away—the subject of this memoir was included for the first time in the census of the United Kingdom. It affords a curious comparison with the numbers of the present day, when we note that the Return, taken a month before the opening of the Great Exhibition, gave the population as 27,637,761, the last figure of which shows the advent of the maestro with unmistakable clearness.

1852 again brought Garcia's name before the English public as it had in 1848. Just as in that year three rival opera companies in London had fought for the possession of his pupil Jenny Lind, so now the two managers—Gye and Lumley—strove for the possession of another of his pupils, Johanna Wagner, whose name was the only one rivalling that of the Swedish Nightingale in its magnetic hold upon the musical world.

The January of the following year, 1853, brought another pupil, Bessie Palmer, the contralto. She tells the story of her difficulties in becoming his pupil in her book of 'Musical Recollections':—

"By the advice of C. L. Gruneisen, the critic of

'The Morning Post,' I entered the Royal Academy of Music as a student. When I commenced studying in September 1851, Manuel Garcia's class, which I had chosen to enter, was full, so I was placed in Mr Frank Cox's class for six months. Then Signor Crivelli heard me at one of the Academy weekly concerts, and suggested that I should become his pupil next term. Imagine my surprise when the old man positively asserted that my voice was soprano, and made me learn many of Grisi's songs.

"After some months I found my voice becoming thin and scratchy and my throat in a constant state of irritation. At last, in January of 1853, I wrote to M. Cazalet, the superintendent, requesting that I should be placed in Signor Garcia's class, as Signor Crivelli had quite altered the tone and quality of my voice, and had made a mistake. M. Cazalet answered that the committee refused to permit me to go into Signor Garcia's class, and unless Signor Crivelli would kindly take me back as his pupil I could not return to the Academy. Of course I wrote at once and said I would *not* rejoin Crivelli's class, and certainly would not return at all.

"On leaving the Academy I went to Garcia's house and explained to him how my voice had been changed. He made me sing a few bars, and then told me I must rest entirely for some considerable time, not singing at all, and not talking too much, so as to give the throat, which was out of order, complete rest. After six months of quiet I went again to him, when he tried my voice and said I could now begin to practise. I therefore commenced lessons at once, and soon found it improving, thanks to the careful way in which he made me practise, bringing the voice back to its proper register, and giving me Italian contralto songs after many lessons."

With this episode we are brought to the year which medical men will consider the most important one in Manuel Garcia's life, as it was in 1854 that he perfected his great discovery.

MANUEL GARCIA.

(REPRODUCED FROM AN ORIGINAL SKETCH BY PAULINE VIARDOT
SOON AFTER THE INVENTION OF THE LARYNGOSCOPE.)

CHAPTER XIV.

THE LARYNGOSCOPE.

(1854–1857.)

IT was in 1854 (the year which saw the ultimatum
of England and France presented to St Petersburg,
the prelude to the Crimean War) that the important invention was made—or, as the maestro
with characteristic modesty described it, "the idea
dawned on him"—of the laryngoscope.

As to its lasting value to the world at large,
it will be sufficient to point out that since that
year, according to reliable estimates, 3 per cent of
the entire human race have been benefited by the
invention.

With regard to the history of the discovery, an
account of the earlier attempts which had been
made has been set down in the number of the
'British Medical Journal' published at the time of
the Garcia Centenary.

Before proceeding further, it may be well to warn
the reader that the next few pages are bound to
deal with a certain amount of technical detail which
it is impossible to avoid in relating this portion of
the maestro's career.

Although the dentist's mirror was in use among

the ancient Romans, the first trace of an attempt to examine the throat by means of reflected light is found about the middle of the eighteenth century.

In 1734 Levret, whose name is still held in honour among obstetricians, described a speculum, consisting of a plate of polished metal, which "reflected the luminous rays in the direction of the tumour," and received the image of the tumour on its reflecting surface. Levret seems to have used the mirror, not as a means of diagnosis, but as a guide in the application of ligatures to tumours in the throat. At any rate, his invention bore no fruit.

Half a century later Bozzini, of Frankfort-on-the-Main, devoted much attention to devising means of illuminating the main canals of the human body. In 1807 he published a description of an apparatus by which the throat and the posterior nares could be examined by reflected light. The official heads of the profession laughed away his invention, which, though cumbrous, deserved a better fate.

In 1825 Cagniard de Latour introduced a little mirror into the back of the throat, hoping with the aid of the sun's rays and a second mirror to be able to see the epiglottis, and even the glottis, but failed. In 1827 another unsuccessful attempt was made by Senn of Geneva; and two years later Benjamin Guy Babington exhibited at the Hunterian Society of London an instrument very like the laryngoscope now in use : he employed it in many cases, but for some reason seems to have left no record of them.

In 1832 Bennati of Paris stated that he could see the vocal cords by means of a double-tubed speculum, invented by a patient suffering from laryngeal phthisis. Trousseau, however, proved to his own satisfaction that the epiglottis must always make it impossible to see the inside of the larynx.

In 1838 Baumès of Lyons showed a mirror with which he said the larynx could be examined.

In 1844 Warden of Edinburgh reported two cases in which he said he had been able to make " satisfactory ocular inspection of diseases affecting the glottis," by using two prisms of flint glass. In the same year Avery of London devised a laryngoscope in which a laryngeal mirror was combined with a lamp and reflector : the apparatus embodied the essential features of the modern laryngoscope, but its clumsiness made its practical application difficult, and in many cases impossible.

Up to 1850, then, the different attempts had met with failure in varying degrees. When Garcia attacked the problem he was quite ignorant of the fact that others had been at work, and his reason for wishing to overcome the difficulty and catch a glimpse of the glottis was perfectly different from theirs. His was one connected entirely with his work as a teacher of singing. Ever since he had given attention to the scientific aspects of voice-emission, he had longed to see a healthy glottis in the very act of singing. The idea of employing mirrors for the purpose of studying the interior of the larynx came to him in 1854. The following is the story of the discovery as he related it one day :—

" During all the years of study and investigation of the problems of the voice - emission," he said, "one wish was ever uppermost in my mind—'if only I could see the glottis!'"

One day in the September of 1854, when on a visit to Paris, he was standing in the Palais Royal. Suddenly there came to him an idea. "Why should I not *try* to see it?" How must this be done? Why, obviously by some means of reflection. Then, like a flash, he seemed to see the two mirrors of the laryngoscope in their respective positions as though actually before his eyes. He went straight to Charrière, the surgical instrument maker, asked whether they happened to possess a small mirror with a long handle, and was at once supplied with a dentist's mirror, which had been one of the failures of the London Exhibition of 1851. He bought it for six francs.

Returning home, he placed against the uvula this little piece of glass, which he had heated with warm water and carefully dried. Then with a hand-mirror he flashed on to its surface a ray of sunlight. By good fortune he hit upon the proper angle at the very first attempt. There before his eyes appeared the glottis, wide open and so fully exposed that he could see a portion of the trachea. So dumfounded was he that he sat down aghast for several minutes. On recovering from his amazement he gazed intently for some time at the changes which were presented to his vision while the various tones were being emitted. From what he witnessed it was easy to conclude that his theory, attributing to the glottis alone the power of engendering sound, was confirmed, and thence it followed that the different positions taken by the larynx in the front of the throat had no action whatever in the formation of the sound. At last he tore himself away, and wrote a description of what he had seen.

Six months later, on March 22, 1855, his paper, "Physiological Observations on the Human Voice," was submitted to the Royal Society of London. In it was set down the scientific thesis of his discovery in language which would have done credit to expert anatomists and physiologists.

On May 24 this was read before the Society by Professor Sharpey at a meeting held under the presidency of Lord Wrottesley, and was duly published in the 'Proceedings of the Royal Society,' vol. vii.

Investigation shows that primarily it is an account of the oral cavity and of the physiology of the voice, exemplified by the mechanical contrivance of the author's own thoughtful invention, actually used in an autoscopic manner with the idea of elucidating the action of the larynx during vocal effort.

As far as Garcia was concerned, the laryngoscope ceased to be of any special use as soon as his first investigations were concluded. By his examination of the glottis he had had the satisfaction of proving that all his theories with regard to the emission of the voice were absolutely correct. Beyond that, he did not see that anything further was to be gained beyond satisfying the curiosity of those who might be interested to see for themselves the forms and changes which the inside of the larynx assumed during singing and speaking. The method of making scientific use of the voice is due to his discovery and ocular verification of the action of the vocal cords and of the glottis in the emission of sound.

As to the subsequent use of the laryngoscope in another sphere of investigation, and the far-reaching results which are due to it, it was nearly two years before the possibility of making practical use was seen. The medical profession was slow to realise what an invaluable instrument of observation the musician had provided, and at first it was treated by superior persons as nothing more than a physiological toy; in fact, as so often happens when a discovery is made by some one not belonging to the craft, Garcia's communication was originally received by the doctors with indifference, if not with incredulity.

It might have been expected that the uses to which the instrument could be put for diseases of the throat would forthwith have been perceived, and its value as a means of diagnosis appreciated. Yet, but for an accident, the paper might have lain buried in the dusty tomb of the 'Proceedings' of the Royal Society.

It is generally said that Türck of Vienna, coming by chance across it two years after the date of its presentation, was inspired to apply the invention to the examination of the upper air-passages. "This," says the 'British Medical Journal,' "is not accurate. Türck had been working independently on much the same lines as Garcia, and had even devised a laryngoscope. He showed the instrument to a friend, who at once informed him that the invention was not new, and directed his attention to the paper in question."

Türck continued his experiments for a time; and it was in this year, 1857, that the instrument was actually used for the first time for diagnostic purposes. He seems, however, to have given up his experiments later, owing to the want of sunlight in the winter.

Soon after this, Professor J. N. Czermak of Buda-Pesth, another great physiologist, visited Vienna, and was shown the instrument, in which he was keenly interested. With it he made the observations which he published. This fact gave rise to one of those bitter controversies as to priority, of which the history of science offers so many examples.

The famous dispute had the immediate effect of directing the attention of the whole world to the laryngoscope. As to the rights of the matter, it would appear that while there is no doubt that Czermak owed his knowledge of the method to Türck and indirectly to Garcia, he made the important modification of substituting artificial illumination for the uncertain light of the sun.

One thing is certain, and that is that to Czermak belongs the credit of making known to the world the laryngoscope, and to some extent the possibilities lying hidden in the little mirror. He visited the principal medical centres of Europe, and, luckily being gifted with a capacious and exceptionally tolerant throat, he was able to give convincing demonstrations of the value of the discovery, and

its scientific and practical possibilities. If Garcia
was the founder, Czermak was the apostle, of
laryngology.

As to the demonstrations with the instrument,
many amusing incidents have taken place. Two in
particular I remember hearing Garcia relate.

His pupil Charles Battaille, to whom reference
has been already made in an earlier chapter,
was most enthusiastic over it, and, having been
a medical student at one time, considered himself
well qualified to demonstrate its virtues. Hearing
that the Turkish Ambassador in Paris was going to
give a dinner to the most prominent French in-
ventors of that time, he obtained permission to show
off the uses of the new exhibit during the evening.
After pointing out that it would revolutionise the
scientific study of the throat, he proceeded to force
the instrument down the gullet of an unfortunate
Court official who had barely finished dinner. The
result was disastrous.

The other story was a comical experience of a
well-known specialist.

Like all very sensitive areas of the human body,
the organ of the voice is sometimes invaded by
special symptoms, notably in hysterical patients.

When the laryngoscope became a speciality, a
young lady who for two whole years had lost all
power of articulation was brought up to London by
her mother for advice and treatment. The experienced laryngologist to whom she was introduced
placed her in proper position before his lamp, while
the parent poured out the prolonged tale of affliction.
Without taking any apparent notice of the latter,

he placed the mirror in the girl's throat with the usual request, delivered in a cool and commanding tone, "Say 'aw,' please"; when the young lady snappishly drew back her head with, "How can I with that thing in my throat?"—followed by, "Oh, dear, I've spoken!" The specialist turned at once to the anxious parent, and told her she might take her daughter home cured,—as she proved to be.

In the present state of our knowledge of such matters, it is rather startling to remember that two and a half centuries ago the famous physician of Norwich, Sir Thomas Brown, thought it a part of his duty, as an advanced teacher of his contemporaries, to devote a chapter of one of his books to stating and proving that food and drink did not descend into the body by two separate tubes. It appears that at that date the majority of the British public actually believed that, as Nature had placed two pipes in the neck, solids were transmitted by one and fluids by the other during the ordinary act of swallowing.

Most people nowadays are aware that the vibrations of the elastic bands, of which there is one on each side beneath the membrane of the upper part of the larynx, produce the sounds of the voice by their effect on the air issuing from the lungs. Certain qualities of tone, and of course the pitch of a note, are determined by their length and tension, while the special characteristics which make the voice of each individual definitely recognisable are due to the varied forms of the several parts of the throat, nose, mouth, &c., above that level. Again, the "breaking" of the voice of a boy on reaching

o

the threshold of adolescence is due to the mechanical effect of the elongation of the elastic bands above referred to—so-called " vocal cords,"—produced by the forward growth of the cartilages of the larynx which determine the formation of the " Adam's apple." All these simple facts were absolute mysteries previously to the enlightening device of Manuel Garcia.

Though Czermak took up the laryngoscope and added to its general feasibility by the introduction of artificial light, it still had many obstacles to overcome, but in this it only shared the common fate of all innovations. A number of the men who bore the heat of the day in the early time of storm and stress are still alive, and must rejoice in the fulness of recognition which their speciality has gained.

Intralaryngeal medication and surgery soon followed the discovery of the diagnostic properties, and its principles were extended to the elucidation and treatment of diseases of the parts situated between the nose and throat.

Professor Osler has told us that if we take the sum of human achievement in science and the arts, and subtract the work of those above forty, "while we should miss great treasures, even priceless treasures, we should practically be where we are to-day." The achievement of Garcia supplies a striking comment on these hasty words. He was ten years over the limit fixed by the professor when by his invention he opened up a new world to scientific exploration. Subtract the laryngoscope from medicine, and what a gap is left in modern methods of diagnosis and treatment! Before its

invention threw light into places which had been
dark since the birth of the human race, the larynx
was an undiscovered country, and its diseases lay
beyond the limits of medical art.

" Had Garcia's work ended when he was forty, we
should still not improbably be powerless to deal with
functional aphonia, with laryngeal growths, with
tuberculosis of the larynx, and with many conditions
in the upper air-passages which can now be treated
satisfactorily, because they can be seen. What is
more important, we should be without a means of
diagnosis which has proved invaluable in the detec-
tion of unsuspected disease of the brain and in the
elucidation of obscure mediastinal affections. Ab-
ductor paralysis of a vocal cord is often the only
appreciable symptom in the early stage of tabes,
and it may give the key to the situation of a growth
in the fourth ventricle, the medulla, or the cere-
bellum. Faint appearances, discoverable only by
laryngosocopy, may furnish the first indication of
pulmonary tuberculosis before any physical signs
are present. The state of the larynx, in fact, is
often a danger-signal to those who can read its
meaning. The laryngoscope may also reveal the
presence of an aortic aneurism or a mediastinal
tumour. Its value in medicine is greater than that
of the ophthalmoscope, because its application is
wider, and the indications which it supplies are
often more definite."

While touching general medicine at many points,
laryngology is also to a large extent an autono-
mous territory in the great federation of the human
organism. The extensions of Garcia's discovery

which have been made in so many directions, have given it a field of usefulness vaster than was dreamt of by those who first applied the laryngoscope to medicine.

As to the development of the instrument, Manuel Garcia, the discoverer of the hidden land, attained his results by the most simple means. He merely placed the little dentist's mirror (previously heated) with a long handle against the uvula, holding it at an angle of 135 degrees, and then, by means of an ordinary hand-mirror, flashed a ray of sunlight upon its surface. Next Czermak and Türck took the matter up, and made certain improvements in the instrument, substituting artificial light so as to render it useful independently of the sun. The laryngoscope was illumined by a concave mirror fastened to the forehead of the observer. This mirror received the rays of a lamp situated close to the head of the subject, and focussed their concentrated light on to the laryngoscope. The position to be given to the patient was definitely fixed by these workers.

With the advent of electric light fresh perfections were introduced; while in 1896 Kirstein, of Berlin, discovered a novel method of laryngeal investigation which led to the establishment by Killian, in 1902, of a new method of "bronchoscopy," which permits of the direct exploration of the "bronchiæ."

But all these discoveries are only a continuation of that invention which assures to Garcia a glorious name in the history of medicine.

With the advent of March 17, 1905, which saw

not only Manuel Garcia's hundredth birthday, but the fiftieth anniversary of this discovery, the acorn which he had planted in the middle of the nineteenth century had grown to a stately and wide-branching oak-tree. We shall see later, when we come to the description of this event, how medical representatives from every part of the world combined to do honour to him as the author of a most fruitful addition to the resources of medical art and as the initiator of a great advance in medical science. It must have brought the centenarian a great and justifiable pride when on that day he looked on the representatives of the Laryngological societies encircling the world, who united to call him Father.

CHAPTER XV.

CHARLES SANTLEY AND ANTOINETTE STERLING.

(1857–1873.)

1841 became a memorable date in the earlier period of Manuel Garcia's career as a teacher, as bringing Jenny Lind to his studio in Paris. In the same way, 1857 stood out in the later portion, as bringing to him the first pupil in London who was to achieve a world-wide reputation, Sir Charles Santley. In making this statement I leave out of account Julius Stockhausen, since his lessons had been commenced in Paris.

The circumstances which brought about the advent of Santley are related in his 'Reminiscences':—

"One morning in the autumn of 1857 I received a message to go round to Chorley's house immediately, as he had something of importance to communicate. It was to the effect that Hullah was going to perform the 'Creation': he could not offer me any terms, but if I was satisfied with this opportunity of making an appearance in public, he would be pleased to accept my services to sing the part of Adam."

Santley accepted at once, having only a few

weeks before returned from Italy, where he had
been studying under Nava.

"I went to try over the duet with the lady
who was to represent my *malheureuse cotelette*,
and found someone seated in the drawing - room,
who made me a distant bow on my entrance.
After a few moments' hesitation I ventured to remark, 'Miss ——, I presume.' 'No,' she replied,
'I am Miss Messent, and I understand I am to
have the pleasure of singing the duets in the last
part of the "Creation" with you. Miss —— was
to have sung them, but for some unexplained
reason has given up the engagement.'"

The reason the baritone only learned some years
after. Miss —— had made a small reputation
already, which she declined jeopardising by singing duets with a young man fresh from Italy.

"I dined with Chorley on the evening of the
concert, and met Manuel Garcia, who accompanied
us to St Martin's Hall.

"I succeeded better than I had dared to hope.
When I walked home with Chorley and Garcia
after the performance, the latter expressed himself
as pleased, but pointed out certain defects to be
overcome, at the same time offering to render me
any assistance in his power."

It was an offer of which Santley promptly
availed himself, and he commenced lessons forthwith, the maestro being at the time in his fifty-
third year, his pupil a lad of twenty-three. The
profit which was received during those lessons the
baritone has never forgotten. As to his personal
memories of the maestro,—"It would require a

whole book to say what I should be bound to say," he wrote to me in a letter during the preparation of the present memoir.

The feelings with which the world - renowned baritone regards his old master may best be summed up in the words inscribed on the photograph which used to stand on the grand piano in Señor Garcia's home: "To the King of Masters." Moreover, I remember his remarking one day, while I was studying under the maestro, "You are learning from the greatest teacher the world has ever known." Nor is he less ardent in his admiration for Mme. Viardot-Garcia. "No woman in my day has ever approached her as a dramatic singer," he once said; "she was perfect, as far as it is possible to attain perfection, both as vocalist and actress."

Santley is himself remarkable as a man no less than as an artist. After having made a name which will ever be honoured and reverenced throughout the musical world for high ideals nobly sustained, he is, though over seventy, still able to make before the public occasional appearances, in which he shows how the old Italian method, coupled with a fine intellect and dramatic instinct, can triumph over mere weight of years. As one listens it seems impossible to believe that a man who sings to-day with all the fire, vigour, and passion of youth, can have been before the public for anything like so long a period as half a century. Up to the present time Sir Charles Santley remains unquestionably the greatest baritone this country has produced.

Al rey de los maestros
de canto" Don Manuel Garcia
de su afectisimo discipulo y amigo

Cando
1903

Photo by   Chancellor, Dublin.

Shortly after Santley had commenced lessons under the renowned teacher, he received an invitation to a party at Chorley's to meet a pupil of Garcia, Gertrude Kemble, who was about to make her *début* at St Martin's Hall in the Christmas performance of the "Messiah."

"I would have much preferred staying at home with a book," he writes. "I had made my first appearance at the Crystal Palace in the afternoon, and felt depressed with the poor impression I had made. The party, which had been arranged to give Miss Kemble an opportunity of singing before a small assembly previously to confronting the larger audience at St Martin's Hall, included the famous Adelaide Kemble, Virginia Gabriel, John Hullah, Mr and Mrs Henry Leslie, and others.

"I felt great sympathy for the poor trembling girl who was about to undergo an ordeal for which she was not physically prepared. I learned afterwards her voice had been much strained by an incompetent professor during her long residence in Hanover. Manuel Garcia had done wonders with it since her return to England, but she still had great difficulty in controlling the upper register, which naturally added considerably to her nervousness. Nevertheless she sang exceedingly well and with great intelligence.

"This party," he concludes, "which I would willingly have shirked, proved a very important event for me,—in less than eighteen months Miss Kemble became my wife."

The year 1859 was memorable for the fine work of Garcia's two pupils—Pauline Viardot and Bat-

taille.   The former revived Orphée, and achieved
so great a success in the part that it stood out
afterwards as one of her most famous *rôles*.   The
latter brought out a book on singing which reflected the greatest credit not only on himself but
on the maestro from whom he had received inspiration and knowledge.

The next year, which saw the capture of Pekin
in far - off China, brought with it a strange coincidence.   As we have seen, some improvements in
the laryngoscope had followed its invention, due to
the labours of Türck and the experimental skill and
acumen of Czermak, and in due course questions of
priority became a bone of contention, as they had
done nearly two decades previously in connection
with Señor Garcia's 'Mémoire sur la Voix humaine.'

For the annual prize awarded in 1860 by the
Paris Academy of Sciences, under the Montyon
foundation, Türck and Czermak submitted contributions on the art of laryngoscopy.   But nice points
of priority were brushed aside by the Academy, and
to each there was awarded a " mention honorable,"
accompanied by a gift of money.

This action seems to have prompted Garcia to
put forward a claim for the prize in Experimental
Physiology to be awarded for the year 1861.
Accordingly he presented a memoir, in which he
recapitulated his pioneer work, and expressed the
hope that the favours meted out to the before-
mentioned authors might be extended to himself.
The matter does not, however, appear to have gone
any further.

In this year another of his famous pupils, Mathilde Marchesi, brought out a book on singing, 'L'École du Chant,' founded on her master's teaching, and with it achieved notable success.

With 1862 there came the first tardy recognition which Manuel Garcia received from the medical world for the inestimable boon which he had conferred on them by his invention : the diploma of Doctor of Medicine, *honoris causa*, was bestowed on him by the University of Königsberg. But as the year brought in its train this pleasure, so, too, it had its compensating sorrow, for on the 10th of May, at Saint-Josse-ten-Noode in Belgium, his mother passed away at the ripe old age of eighty-four.

1868, in which Disraeli assumed the helm of State as Prime Minister, saw the advent of Antoinette Sterling, who came on to Garcia from Cologne, where she had been studying under Mathilde Marchesi.

The letter which the maestro sent to Signor Marchesi, after hearing the contralto, I am able to quote :—

Translation.

LONDON, *July* 17, 1864.

To Signor S. de C. MARCHESI, Professor at the Conservatoire of Music, Cologne.

MOST ESTEEMED SIGNOR MARCHESI,—Miss Sterling, whom I have already heard several times, possesses a beautiful voice, but she is still a beginner. In every way I will do what little I can to continue the very excellent direction given to the studies of the young lady by your wife, to whom I beg you to present my most distinguished salutations. Pray accept the same yourself from your sincere friend,

MANUEL GARCIA.

I am very grateful for the recommendation. Farewell.

Antoinette Sterling ever regarded Señor Garcia with the greatest affection and esteem, and used to delight in recalling the following memories of the days when she had studied with him. I have set them down before in the little memoir of her career already published.

When Miss Sterling, as she then was, went to the maestro for lessons, he was so carried away with the voice of his new pupil that he could not bring himself to keep her to exercises, as was his custom in the case of others. Almost at once he began taking her through all the Italian operatic *rôles*. One day she was struggling to execute a particularly difficult phrase, and at last burst out crying, "You ought not to give me these songs until I have mastered the exercises properly." "You're quite right," he answered, and took her back to the exercises once more.

Until Antoinette Sterling commenced her training under him she used the full extent of her voice, singing from the D below middle C to the top soprano C sharp—a range of three octaves. She sang all the contralto arias from opera and oratorio, and at the same time felt equally at home with the soprano *rôles*.

The first thing her new master did on hearing her was to make the remark, "If you continue as you have been doing, do you know what will happen? Look at this piece of elastic. I take it firmly at the two ends and stretch it. What is the result? It becomes thin in the middle. If I were to continue to do this constantly, it would get weaker and weaker, until finally it would break.

Photo by   Elliott & Fry, Baker Street, London, W.

It is thus with the human voice. Cultivate an extended range, and keep on singing big notes at both extremes, and the same thing will occur which we have seen with the elastic. Your voice will gradually weaken in the middle. If you persist in this course long enough, it will break, and the organ be rendered useless." For this reason he strongly advised her to abandon the higher notes, confining herself to genuine contralto music. Moreover, with the reduced range, he told her strictly to avoid practising on the extremes, to use them as little as possible, and build up her voice by exercising the middle portion of it. It is an invaluable hint for all singers. His pupil realised the wisdom of what he said, and from that time onwards ceased to use the top half octave of her voice.

After a return to America, during which she was engaged to sing at Dr Ward Beecher's church, she came over to England again to make her *debut*. Señor Garcia heard of the forthcoming appearance of his old pupil, and tried to find out her address. She in her turn had lost that of the maestro. In consequence of this they did not have an opportunity of meeting again till the eventful evening had passed, and all London was ringing with the new contralto's praises. He had, of course, been present at Covent Garden, and at the end of her first song went round to the door of the artist's room to congratulate her. The attendant met him with the stereotyped reply, " We cannot let any one in." " But I insist—I *must* see her. She is my pupil." The request, however, was met with stolid indifference, and he was obliged to return to his seat.

When, finally, they did meet again, she at once recommenced her lessons, and these were continued, as regularly as engagements would permit, until seven years after her *début*.

On July 5, 1869, Manuel Garcia was elected a member of the Committee of Management at the Royal Academy of Music, with which he had now been connected for twenty years.

Twelve months later he was brought to a sudden realisation of the catastrophe that shook Europe, for July saw the commencement of the Franco-Prussian War, all the French being ordered to leave German territory. In consequence of this edict Mme. Viardot was obliged to move from Baden-Baden, where she had been teaching ; and, like many others, she made her way to England. On her arrival there with her husband she settled down in London near her brother, till the march of events rendered it possible for her to return to the Continent.

Of this period Mme. Noufflard, daughter of Lady Hallé, has given some recollections.

"While Mme. Viardot was taking refuge in London, her house was the rendezvous of every talent ; and I well remember one evening, when serious music had given way to fun, Saint-Saëns sitting at the pianoforte to improvise the 'rising of the sun in a mountainous country.' In the twinkling of an eye Manuel Garcia cut out a large halo from a newspaper, and was seen slowly emerging from behind a high-backed chair, his full face, with its paper decoration, disclosing itself at the top, as the last triumphant chord was struck.

CHARLES HALLÉ AND MANUEL GARCIA PLAYING CHESS.

(REPRODUCED FROM AN ORIGINAL SKETCH BY RICHARD DOYLE.)

"I recollect him also as the talented and patient teacher, always full of interest even in those whose efforts were feeble. To his musical talents was added the charm of courtly manner, never-failing wit, and love of fun. The last he gave a fresh proof of but two or three years ago, when in answer to the pleasure shown by some friend, who had not seen him for some little time, in meeting him again at a *soirée*, he replied with the characteristic foreign shrug of the shoulders, ' Que voulez-vous? Je suis trop occupé pour avoir le temps de mourir.' "

Mme. Noufflard also tells how the maestro used to visit her parents at Greenhays in Manchester :—

"I was too young at the time to remember any details of those very interesting days; but my earliest recollections of Signor Garcia are those of the delight with which we children always greeted him, as he was ever ready to enter into our pursuits and to enjoy a romp. I remember, as quite a child, having undertaken to teach him German, and the solemnity with which he took his so-called lesson each day, although the teacher knew far less of the language than did the pupil. As we grew older he would often take us to his rooms near Manchester Square, and explain the invention and uses of his laryngoscope with as much care and precision as if we were the whole College of Surgeons listening to him."

What need to recapitulate the events which followed on the outbreak of the Franco - Prussian War? In less than three months Paris was besieged, a calamity followed in October by the pitiful surrender of Metz.

With the January of 1871 came the capitulation of Paris, followed by the conclusion of peace in February, the revolt of the Commune, and the second siege of the capital in March.

Señor Garcia must have been glad indeed that he had come to England nearly a quarter of a century before, and was thus able quietly to pursue his work as a teacher, instead of remaining in Paris to be upset once more, as he had been with the Revolution of '48.

CHAPTER XVI.

TWENTY YEARS OF MUSIC.

(1853–1873.)

AT this point it may be of interest to recall the principal musical events which took place during the earlier years of Manuel Garcia's residence in London.

The year of the invention of the laryngoscope is principally of interest to musicians from the fact that Gye was able to secure for his opera company a valuable aid in that greatest basso of any time, Luigi Lablache, then sixty years of age.

The following year brought the London *première* of "L'Etoile du Nord," and of Verdi's new opera, "Il Trovatore"; it is additionally memorable for the advent of Cerito, on whom the mantle of Taglioni and Vestris had fallen as a *première danseuse*.

1856 brought in its train a series of catastrophes to music-lovers. During the twelve months there died not only the veteran tenor, Henry Braham, in his eightieth year, but, what was a far greater loss, the immortal Robert Schumann, after two years spent in a private asylum near Bonn; moreover, a further blow was dealt by the burning down of Covent Garden for the second time, the

P

ruins being visited next day by her Majesty, Prince Albert, and the Princess Royal.

The Opera House was rebuilt and opened once more in 1858, the year in which Lablache died. The Covent Garden season commenced on May 15 with a notable body of artists, which included Grisi, Didiée, Parepa, Victoire, Mario, Formes, Rossi, Tamberlik, and Costa; while in the early autumn the Birmingham Festival was held, with Pauline Viardot amd Sims Reeves as the stars.

In the last month of '58 we find the Pyne-Harrison Company giving a season of English opera, with W. Harrison, George Honey, Weiss, and Louisa Pyne as the leading attractions, and Alfred Mellon in the conductor's seat.

The next year (1859) brings the production in Italian of Meyerbeer's new opera, "Dinorah," at Covent Garden; while in the autumn the Pyne-Harrison Company give it in an English version provided by Chorley, with Charles Santley making his operatic *début* as Haël. This is followed at Christmas by Hallé's production at Manchester of an English version of Gluck's "Iphigénie en Tauride," in which two of Garcia's pupils take part—Catherine Hayes and Charles Santley.

In the following February Wallace's "Lurline" was produced, and later in the year Flotow's "Stradella." March 29 is an interesting date, for it gives us a sight of the theatrical names which were prominently before the public at this time. On that day a monster benefit was organised, at which the following stars took part: Webster, Phelps, T. P. Cooke, Toole, Mrs Mellon, Miss Glyn,

Louisa Pyne, Charles Mathews, Catherine Hayes, W. Harrison, and Buckstone.

A few weeks later, during the Italian opera season, came the first appearance in England of Faure, as Haël, a part which Meyerbeer had specially written for him in "Dinorah."

One may perhaps be allowed to note in passing that 1859 brought with it the first appearance of Henry Irving on the London stage. In the winter season of 1860 Her Majesty's was running English opera with a fine cast, which included Lemmens-Sherrington, Mdlle. Parepa, Reeves, Santley, George Honey, J. G. Patey, and Chas. Hallé as conductor.

With 1861 we come to the English *début* of the greatest star of the last half of the nineteenth century, for on May 14 Adelina Patti made her first appearance at Covent Garden, as Amina in "La Somnambula," amid such enthusiasm as to ensure her the premier place among the operatic artists of her day. And indeed after this memorable date the *diva* continued to appear for no less than twenty-five consecutive seasons at Covent Garden, her name proving an infallible draw, no matter in what opera she chose to appear.

During the same season Grisi gave a series of eight farewell performances, creating an enormous *furore;* moreover, Delle Sedie came over for Mapleson's season at the Lyceum, being afterwards engaged for Covent Garden. At the latter house the autumn season opened with "Ruy Blas," followed later by "Robin Hood," with a cast including Mme. Guerrabella (Geneviève Ward), Haigh,

Honey, and Santley, and this in turn gave way to the production of Balfe's new opera, "The Puritan's Daughter," which had a run of no less than fifty-seven performances.

The following February, 1862, saw the production of another of Balfe's operas, the "Lily of Killarney," the plot being that of the "Colleen Bawn," which had just had a huge success at the Adelphi Theatre.

The artists engaged for the Covent Garden season of Italian opera included such names as Patti, Tamberlik, Mario, Faure, Formes, and Gordoni; while in the autumn of the year Mapleson gave a season of opera with Tietjens, Alboni, Giuglini, and Santley.

For 1863 may be writ large the five letters FAUST. Mapleson tells the story of its production in his memoirs. Thomas Chappell had bought the English rights for £40, after seeing it at the Théâtre Lyrique. The music of an opera is worth nothing until the opera itself has become known, and Messrs Chappell opened negotiations with Mr Frederick Gye for its production during the Royal Italian Opera season.

The work had not, however, made much impression at the Lyrique, and Gye, on his return from Paris, assured his stage-manager, Augustus Harris, that there was nothing in it but the "Soldier's Chorus," and refused to have anything to do with it. Mapleson on hearing it felt convinced it would be an immense success; and Chappells were ready to pay £200 towards the cost of its production, and to give £200 more after four representations. He therefore engaged his company, and put it into rehearsal at Her Majesty's.

A few days before the date fixed for the production, he found that only £30 worth of seats had been taken. Then came a Napoleonic scheme. He announced at once four successive performances, and gave the astounding instructions at the office that for the first three out of these four not one place was to be sold beyond those already taken. The rest of the tickets he took home in a carpet-bag and distributed far and wide over a gigantic free list. At the same time he advertised in ' The Times ' that, in consequence of a death in the family, two stalls for the first representation of " Faust " —the opera which was exciting so much interest that all places for the first three representations had been bought up—could be had at 25s. each.

Meanwhile demands had been made at the box-office for places, and the would-be purchasers were told that everything had gone up to the fourth night : this they repeated to their friends, and the opera began to be seriously talked of. The first performance was received with applause, the second still more warmly, and the third gained additional favour. No further device was necessary for stimulating curiosity : the paying public flocked, and it was given for ten nights in succession, after which it was constantly repeated until the termination of the season.

The following was the cast of the *première* at Her Majesty's :—

Marguerite	Tietjens.
Siebel	Trebelli.
Faust	Giuglini.
Mephistopheles . . .	Gassier.
Valentine	Santley.

Not to be outdone, Gye at once produced his own version at Covent Garden, with Carvallo as *Marguerite*, her old part in the original Paris production, Didier as *Siebel*, Faure as *Mephistopheles*, Graziani as *Valentine*, and Tamberlik as *Faust*.

The year is also noteworthy for the fact that Pauline Lucca made her *début* as Valentine in the "Hugenots," while Mdlle. Artot, the pupil of Mme. Viardot, also made her first appearance here.

With 1864 (in which Meyerbeer passes away) we find the Italian Opera Company including Patti, Lucca, Tamberlik, Faure, Graziani, Mario, and, of course, Costa, with an interesting addition at the organ in Arthur Sullivan; while to the younger generation, at any rate, a strange realisation of those bygone days is given by the announcement of a gala performance to Garibaldi.

At Her Majesty's there is an interesting *première*, the first performance of " Faust " in English, with the following cast :—

Marguerite . .	Mme. Lemmens-Sherrington.
Siebel . . .	Mme. Lucia.
Mephistopheles .	M. Marchesi.
Valentine . .	Mr Santley.
Faust . . .	Mr Sims Reeves.

The next year brings the production of Meyerbeer's " L'Africaine " at Covent Garden, and of Gounod's

" Mock Doctor " by the Royal English Opera Company. At Her Majesty's, moreover, Ilma di Murska makes her first appearance as Lucia, and Giuglini is obliged to give up the season there through illness; while among the operatic stars of the year we find Wachtel, Graziani, Ronconi, and Mario.

1866 sees the *début* at Covent Garden of Carlotta Patti, coming with a considerable reputation as a concert singer; while among the artists of the season are Naudin, and Nicolini, who afterwards married Adelina Patti. At Her Majesty's, the company includes Gordoni, Santley, Gassier, Tietjens, and Grisi, who is announced for a limited number of performances; while the Irish basso, Foley, makes a hit in "Il Seraglio" under the Italianised nomenclature, "Signor Foli."

Next year, in which the death of Sir George Smart is chronicled, Covent Garden announces—on July 11—the first production of Gounod's "Romeo et Juliette" in an Italian version, with Mario and Patti in the title-*rôles*. At the rival house Mapleson has collected a fine company in Tietjens, Sinico, Gassier, Santley, Gordoni, Mongini, and two *débutantes*, Clara Kellogg, fresh from her American triumphs, and Christine Nillson, who makes her first appearance in "Traviata."

On December 6 a terrible calamity occurred in the London musical world, with the burning down of Her Majesty's Theatre. At the beginning of the month, during a rehearsal of "Fidelio," Mapleson's insurance-agent called to complete the insurance of the house. Colonel Mapleson agreed to insure for £30,000; but as the costumier's list was not at hand, and the costumier himself was out at dinner, the agent suggested that the manager should give him £10 " on account," and thus keep the matter open till the following Monday, when he—the agent —would call again.   Mapleson replied, jokingly, " There is no fear," and the agent left without the advance.

At half-past eleven the same evening Mapleson, who was dining in St John's Wood, was called by an excited servant to look out of the window, and saw the sky red in the distance.   Her Majesty's Theatre was on fire !   The manager hurried to the scene of the conflagration, and found the house in full blaze.   Without a moment's delay he despatched Mr Jarrett, his acting-manager, to Mr F. B. Chatterton, then the lessee of Drury Lane, to endeavour to secure that theatre from March till the end of July.   It was of great importance that the emissary should reach Chatterton, who lived at Clapham, before that astute manager could learn of the fire ; for had he been aware of Mapleson's extremity, he would, of course, have raised his terms accordingly.

On arriving at Chatterton's house early in the morning, the first thing Jarrett saw, lying on a table in the hall, was a copy of that day's ' Times.' On this he threw his overcoat, in order to hide the paper from view, and waited for the manager of Drury Lane to descend and receive him.   Without appearing at all anxious, Mr Jarrett quietly concluded an agreement by which Mapleson secured the use of Drury Lane Theatre for the following spring and summer seasons, with a right to renew the occupation for future years.   This document was in Mapleson's hands by nine o'clock, and it was not till half-past ten that Chatterton learnt of the fire.

The Monday after, the insurance-agent called on Mapleson and offered him his sympathy, since, if the manager had paid down the £10 on account of the proposed insurance, he would have received a cheque for £30,000 ! Mapleson replied that he was exceedingly glad that he had *not* paid the deposit, as he certainly would have been suspected of setting the theatre on fire, and would never again have been able to set himself right with the public.

In 1868 (the year of Rossini's death), the date is rendered memorable by the *début* of Minnie Hauk and the discovery of Mme. Scalchi, who was singing at the time in a building that was little more than a circus ; while Costa resigned his position as conductor, owing to a quarrel.   His place was taken by Arditi and Vianesi, who shared the duties of conductor.

In 1869 Mapleson and Gye resolved to join forces, the result being a probably unexampled collection of stars.   Ambroise Thomas's " Hamlet " was given for the first time in England with Christine Nillson as Ophelia, and " Don Giovanni " was performed with the following extraordinary cast, which has never been equalled in brilliancy :—

Donna Anna	Tietjens.
Donna Elvina	Nillson.
Zerlina	Patti.
Don Ottavio	Mario.
Don Giovanni	Faure.

But these do not by any means exhaust the list of stars who took part in the season under the joint management. To the above quintette we must add Lucca, Scalchi, Ilma di Murska, Sinico, Tamberlik, Foli, Santley, and Mongini, while Costa and Arditi alternated the conducting. The season is probably unexampled in the whole annals of opera.

The next year, 1870 (in which Balfe died), saw the production of Verdi's " Macbeth " and of Ambroise Thomas's " Mignon," with Christine Nillson and Faure in the leading *rôles*, under the Gye-Mapleson management. During this year, moreover, a brilliant benefit was given to Charles Mathews, and from the list of star performers we can obtain some further idea as to the rise and fall of the theatrical artists which Garcia witnessed as he passed through life.

Charles Mathews, of course, took part himself, and was assisted by Barry Sullivan, Lionel Brough, Mrs Mathews, Mrs Chippendale, Ben Webster, Mrs Mellon, Mme. Celeste, together with the Bancrofts.

With 1871 (the year in which Auber died) Mario bade farewell to Covent Garden audiences, before whom he had appeared for no less than twenty-three out of the twenty-four seasons the Royal Italian Opera had been in existence.

The Italian tenor was a great friend of Garcia, and the latter used to tell many anecdotes of him. One of these I will quote. When in London once, Mario and his wife, Grisi, decided upon giving a wonderful luncheon to a large party of their friends, among the number being Señor Garcia. The total cost may be imagined from the fact that they paid £80 for some dessert and other light delicacies for the table, sent specially over from Paris. After all had assembled Grisi suddenly exclaimed, "It is far too hot to eat anything here. Let us drive out to Richmond for lunch. It will be far pleasanter." No sooner said than done, and carriages sufficient to accommodate the entire party were at once ordered. A telegram was sent on in advance, so that on their arrival at Richmond another magnificent lunch was awaiting them. Mario, without a thought, left behind at his own house the two-hundred guinea luncheon to waste its sweetness on the servants' hall.

It was in this year that the terrors of the Franco-Prussian War, to which we have already alluded, drove to London large numbers of refugees, many of them celebrities connected with the leading musical and dramatic institutions of Paris. It was a golden opportunity for music-lovers. At Covent Garden there were Adelina Patti, Lucca, Scalchi, Tamberlik, Mario, Bettini, Faure, Cotogni, Tagliafico; at Her Majesty's, Christine Nillson, Tietjens, Trebelli, Marimon, Ilma di Murska, Mongini, Gardoni, Capoul, Wachtel, Agnesi, Rota, Santley, Foli, and Carl Formes. In the concert - room there were to be heard the still marvellous voices of Alboni, Carlotta Patti, and Sims Reeves ; or the glorious playing of Sivori, Vieuxtemps, Wieniawski, Neruda, Joachim, Clara Schumann, and Alfredo Piatti.

Then among the French refugees were the members of the Comédie Française, and these gave a memorable series of representations at one of the London theatres, selecting for it most of the gems of their matchless repertoire, with casts that included such artists as Got, Delauny, Mounet-Sully, Worms, Febvre, the Coquelins, Sarah Bernhardt (who during this season was making her London *début*), Blanche Pierson, Bartet, Barretta, Reichemberg, and Samary.

The following year, 1872, saw the *début* at Covent Garden of Albani. Later in the year, after the close of the opera season, a "fantastical spectacle" by Dion Boucicault and Planché was produced at the Opera House, under the title of "Babil and Bijou," in which took part Mrs Howard Paul, Lionel Brough, and Joseph Maas.

Finally, in 1873, Gye gathered round him a bevy of stars which included Patti, Lucca, and Albani; Scalchi, Sinico, and Monbelli, Nicolini, Bettini, Graziani, Cotogni, Maurel, and Faure.

CHAPTER XVII.

THREE-SCORE YEARS AND TEN.

(1874–1890.)

"EVERY year a man lives, he is worth less." This is what Manuel Garcia used to assert when he was drawing near to the completion of those three-score years and ten which have been set down as the natural span of human life. As far as his own career was concerned, however, the statement was singularly lacking in truth. His mode of living at the age of seventy has been well described by Hermann Klein, his pupil, friend, and collaborator in the final text-book, ' Hints on Singing,' published some twenty years later, when the veteran musician was over ninety years of age.

Mr Klein has been kind enough to send over from New York some interesting reminiscences for insertion in this chapter.

In the year 1874 Mr Klein's parents occupied a large house at the corner of Bentinck Street and Welbeck Street, Cavendish Square, and I will leave the sometime musical critic of ' The Sunday Times' to tell the story of the next few months.

"I find by a letter of my mother's," he writes, " that Señor Garcia first called to see her at 1

Bentinck Street in November 1873, and took the
rooms on the ground floor on a yearly agreement
from the following March. He moved in punctually on Lady Day 1874, bringing with him his
trusty Erard grand piano (which had even then
seen considerable wear, but continued to serve him
faithfully at 'Mon Abri' to the last); also the
noble bust of Beethoven, which used to stand upon
a marble ledge or shelf fixed permanently to the
wall between the two windows. The piano stood
in the middle of the room, and he always took care
to place his pupils so that the light fell full upon
their faces. I recollect my mother asking him if
he would like another mirror besides the one over
the mantelpiece. He replied, 'No, it is not necessary. I don't want my pupils to be looking at
themselves all the time. They have to look at me.'

"His lunch invariably consisted of the same
simple fare—some sponge-cakes and a pint of milk,
which would be fetched from a baker close by by
my younger brother Charles. I asked Señor Garcia
once if he did not feel hungry long before dinner,
teaching as he did all day on such slender diet.
'No,' he answered, 'I don't feel half the discomfort
from waiting that I should if I took a hearty meal
in the middle of the day and then tried to teach
immediately afterwards. Besides, I don't really
need it. Most singers and teachers of singing eat
more than they should. A man with moderate
teeth, such as I have, can grow old on sponge-cake
and milk!' And he lived for more than thirty years
after that to prove the truth of his remark.

"At this time he had entered on his seventieth

To M. Sterling Mackinlay Esq
with Kindest regards of
            Hermann Klein

        New York, October /06

year, but in appearance was not past fifty. He had a light buoyant step, always walked quickly, and had a keen observant eye, which, when he spoke, would light up with all the fire and animation of youth. His dark complexion and habit of rapid gesticulation bespoke his southern origin. He was at home in Spanish, Italian, English, and French, but preferred the last. His modesty was remarkable. He could rarely be induced to talk of himself, but was firm in his opinions. In argument he was a close reasoner, and would be either a doughty opponent or a warm advocate: the middle line never attracted.

" His activity during the Bentinck Street period was amazing. Except on his Academy days he taught at the house from morning till night, and never seemed to know the meaning of the word fatigue. As to relaxation or recreation, I never knew him to indulge in any, save on the extremely rare occasions when I could persuade him to attend an operatic performance or some special concert, such as one at the Crystal Palace, when Anton Rubinstein conducted his own endless ' Ocean ' symphony. His criticisms on these events were a delight to listen to. He was, I remember, immensely enthusiastic over Rubinstein's performance of his concerto in D minor; but the symphony bored him terribly, and he would gladly have left before the end came. The only concerts that he attended regularly were the Philharmonic (to which he was for many years a subscriber) and those of the Royal Academy students, at which some pupil of his own almost invariably appeared. At the

latter concerts I used often to sit beside him, and
it was wonderful to watch his animated face as,
with suppressed energy, his hand moved in response
to the rhythm of the music. He seemed to be
trying to infuse into the singer some of the mag-
netism of his own irresistible spirit.

" Manuel Garcia was one of the most inspiring
teachers that ever lived. All of his distinguished
pupils, from Jenny Lind downwards, have dwelt
upon his extraordinary faculty for diving deep into
the nature of those who worked with him, and
arousing their temperamental qualities to the
highest degree of activity. His profound knowledge of his art, his familiarity with all the great
traditions, and the absolute authority with which
he spoke, combined to awaken a measure of confidence and admiration such as no other *maestro
di canto* could possibly command.

" Even when annoyed he was seldom abrupt or
impatient. His voice had gone, but he would
employ its *beaux restes* to impart an idea for the
proper emission of a note or phrasing of a passage.
His sounds never failed to convey the desired
suggestion. Though his own voice trembled with
the weight of years, he never brought out a pupil
with the slightest tremolo : moreover, he was never
guilty of forcing a voice. His first rule was ever
to repress the breathing power, and to bring it into
proper proportion with the resisting force of the
throat and larynx.

" Among the aspirants who came to study at
Bentinck Street were several whose names yet
enjoy universal reputation.

" He always played his own accompaniments for teaching, and in the ' Seventies' was a very fair pianist. He had at that time a Russian pupil, an excellent baritone, with whom he was fond of taking part in duets for four hands. They used to play Schubert's marches, &c., whenever the master could find time (which was not very often); and at the end of a delightful half-hour of this recreation he would exclaim, ' What fine practice for my stiff old fingers ! How I wish I could get more of it !'

" One of his most intimate friends at that period was Joseph Joachim, for whom, alike as a man and a musician, he cherished the warmest admiration and regard. When the great violinist received the honorary degree of Mus. Doc. in 1877, Señor Garcia paid him the highest compliment in his power, by making the journey to Cambridge especially, in order to be present at the ceremony and to attend the concert given by the University Musical Society. I had the privilege of accompanying him on that occasion, and sat beside him both at the rehearsal and the concert, Mr (now Sir) Villiers Stanford being the conductor. How he revelled in Joachim's performance of the Beethoven concerto ! Every note of that masterpiece, as it issued from the fingers of its noblest interpreter, seemed to afford him most exquisite delight. He was also impressed by the first symphony of Brahms (given as the ' exercise ' for his doctor's degree, conferred *in absentiâ*), and considered it not only a fine work, but a remarkable example of reticence in a composer whose powers had attained maturity long before. We returned to town after the concert, but in spite of the fatigue involved by this lengthy 'outing,' the maestro was at his làbours at the usual hour next morning, and feeling, as he expressed it, 'Frais comme un jeune lion.'

"At Bentinck Street Señor Garcia taught several budding Jewish vocalists, entrusted to his care by members of the Rothschild family, who showed their love of music by defraying the cost of teaching (and sometimes of maintaining) the youthful singers. One of these pupils, who subsequently became a prominent member of an English Opera Company, was an especial *protégée* of Baroness Lionel de Rothschild ; and one day the kind lady, accompanied by her daughter (afterwards the Countess of Rosebery), called to inquire how the girl was progressing. The maestro's reply was characteristic. 'Madame la Baronne, she has all the musical talent of her race, but little of its industriousness or perseverance. Still, as in spite of that she accomplishes in a week what takes most other girls a month, I hope sometime to make a singer of her.'"

Here I will abandon Mr Klein's narrative, to resume it later in describing the preparation of Garcia's last text-book, 'Hints on Singing.'

During the next few years a number of pupils passed through his hands at the Royal Academy of Music, who were afterwards to take an important place in their profession.

In 1875 Miss Orridge came to place herself under the maestro. The years which she spent at the Academy brought victory after victory. She gained in turn the Llewellyn Davies Bronze and Gold Medals for declamatory singing, the Parepa-Rosa Medal, and the Christine Nillson's Second Prize. While still a student at the Royal Academy of Music, Miss Orridge made her *début* at the St James's Hall Ballad Concerts, and also went on a successful tour with Sims Reeves. From that time she continued to make rapid strides in her professional status, and gave promise of being one of the best contralto concert singers of her time, when her career was brought to a sudden close by an untimely death, when she had been before the public scarcely six years.

At the commencement of 1876 Garcia received the letter from Wagner to which attention has been already called, embodying the offer for him to train the singers for the first Bayreuth Festival. This, however, he was obliged to refuse, owing to his large *clientèle* in London.

On July 14, 1877, the inventor of the Laryngoscope received his second recognition for the services which he had rendered to the medical profession, fifteen years having elapsed since the degree of Mus. Doc. had been conferred on him, *honoris causa*, by the University of Königsberg.

An influential meeting assembled to give their support at the ceremony of presenting him with a service of plate.

Professor Huxley presided, and in his speech bore strong testimony to the great services that Manuel Garcia had rendered alike to science and humanity by his important discovery. It was unnecessary, Huxley said, to do more than remind the physician that in the laryngoscope he had gained a new ally against disease, and a remarkable and most valuable addition to that series of instruments, all of which, from the stethoscope onwards, had come into use within the memory of living men, and had effected a revolution in the practice of medicine. They owed this instrument to Signor Garcia.

The following year brought fresh honours at the Royal Academy of Music. As previously the maestro had been elected a member of the Committee of Management after twenty years' connection with the institution, so now, after thirty years, he received a further mark of distinction by being made one of the Directors of the Academy.

With 1879 Charlotte Thudicum entered the Royal Academy of Music as his pupil. Success soon came to her, for after a year's tuition she won the Parepa-Rosa scholarship, and two years later the Westmoreland. On leaving his hands the young soprano went over to Paris to study opera with his sister, Mme. Viardot, and upon her return in 1883 was at once secured for the "Pops," Crystal Palace Saturday Concerts, and other important engagements, while in the following season she sang with the Birmingham Festival Choral Society.

In due course she secured fresh laurels by taking part in "Ivanhoe" at the Royal English Opera House, in which opera she played Rebecca on alternative nights with another of Garcia's pupils, Margaret Macintyre.

1881 brought Garcia's third recognition for his invention.

The International Medical Congress was to hold its seventh session in London from the 2nd to the 9th of August, Dr de Havilland Hall, Dr (now Sir) Felix Semon, and Dr Thomas J. Walker being appointed honorary secretaries of the section devoted to "Diseases of the Throat," which was to meet with Dr George Johnson, F.R.S., in the chair.

At the suggestion of the late Sir James Paget, Señor Garcia received an invitation to read a paper before the Congress, describing his work in connection with his invention. The invitation was gladly accepted. He attended, and was introduced to the assembled doctors in the most flattering terms during the inaugural address by the chairman, who was one of the vice-presidents of the medical section.

In connection with the friendship which existed between Manuel Garcia and Sir Felix Semon, one may recall an amusing anecdote recounted in the latter's short memoir, published for Garcia's 100th birthday.

"On a certain occasion," the doctor writes, " I delivered a lecture at the Royal Institution of Great Britain on the culture of the singing voice. In the course of my remarks I attacked the dogmatic way in which the question of the registers was treated by different authorities, and showed there and then, by the aid of some excellent photographs of the larynx during the emission of tone, that the mechanism of the registers, even in relation to the same kind of voice, may in some cases be totally different from others.

"The lecture had a humorous sequel, for among my audience were a number of the best known singing teachers in London. When I had finished, one of these, well known for his obstinate dogmas, came up to me in a state of visible annoyance and said, 'You should not speak on things that you know nothing about.' A second expressed his recognition of the fact that I had taken up arms against the theorists, and then proceeded to describe an entirely new theory on the register formation discovered by himself.

"But, last of all, Garcia came up to me with a smile, and remarked, 'Good heavens, how much I must have taught during my life that is wrong!'"

In 1882 Margaret Macintyre and Marie Tempest commenced studying under the maestro.

The former, a daughter of General Macintyre, was to be the best known of Garcia's pupils at Dr Wyld's London Academy of Music, where he taught for some twenty years. The prima donna during her training there carried off in turn the Bronze, Silver, and Gold Medals of the Academy. During the last year she had the honour of singing the soprano *rôle* in the performance of Liszt's oratorio "St Elizabeth," given at the London Academy Concert in the St James's Hall in honour of the composer's presence in London. Two years later she appeared as Michaela in "Carmen," winning instant success. Moreover, as we have already seen, she shared with Miss Thudicum the *rôle* of

Rebecca in the production of "Ivanhoe," while shortly afterwards she took part in the Handel Festival of 1891.   After this she sang with the greatest success as prima donna in the Grand Opera seasons at Milan, Moscow, and St Petersburg.

Marie Tempest arrived at the Royal Academy of Music in the Easter term of 1882, and remained there three years under Garcia, carrying off the Bronze, Silver, and Gold Medals of the Institution. The Academy was specially prolific of talent at this time, for among the students during these years were Eleanor Rees, Miss Thudicum, Edward German, Courtice Pounds, and several others who were to attain wide fame in the musical world.

Of her studies under Garcia Miss Tempest told me a couple of very characteristic anecdotes.

When Miss Etherington, as she was in those days, came for her first interview with the maestro (having arrived from a convent in France only a few days before), she was wearing a very tight-fitting dress of Stuart tartan, cut in the Princess style, which showed off her figure to advantage and drew attention to the nineteen-inch waist of which she was the proud possessor.

Garcia raised his eyebrows when he saw his prospective pupil step forward from the group of girls who were waiting their turn to be heard. However, nothing was said until her song, an Italian " aria," had been brought to a close.   Then came a pause, while Marie Tempest tremblingly awaited the verdict on her voice.   At last the oracle spoke.   " Thank you, Miss Etherington ; will you please go home at once, take off that dress, rip off those stays, and let your waist out to at least twenty-five inches! When you have done so you may come back and sing to me, and I will tell you whether you have any voice."

The assembled girls tittered audibly, and the unfortunate victim slunk out of the room with flaming cheeks.

"He was quite right, though," Miss Tempest concluded; "no one can sing when laced in as tightly as that. I went home, and — well, I've never had a nineteen-inch waist since."

The other episode concerned the Academy weekly concerts. Garcia generally had a pupil singing at these, and would sit in front, nodding, waving his hand, and generally doing his best to establish telepathic communication with the vocalists, that he might inspire them with his spirit. At one of these Marie Tempest was due to sing with orchestra an air from "Ernani," which had been carefully studied under her master.

The conductor waved his hand and the aria was commenced. After a few bars Manuel Garcia began to fidget in his seat, then to frown, and to beat time with his feet. At last the veteran could stand it no longer. He rose from his seat, leapt on to the platform — approaching his eightieth year as he was,—and seized the baton from the conductor's hand, exclaiming, "Mon Dieu! you are ruining my pupil's song. I will conduct it myself."

Shortly after this episode Miss Tempest, as a member of the operatic class, took part in a mixed performance which included an act from "Carmen" and another from the "Mock Doctor."

Alberto Randegger was present at this, and came up to her afterwards, saying, " Miss Etherington, you must undoubtedly go on the stage."

" After that," said Miss Tempest, " I seemed to be on the boards before I knew where I was."

" The first piece in which I appeared was ' Boccacio,' at the Comedy Theatre ; from that I went to the Opéra Comique for ' Fay o' Fire,' and then came ' Dorothy,' and—the rest." What a record it has been, that series of triumphs in light opera, concert, and comedy, thus dismissed with a smile and a characteristic shrug of the shoulders as—" the rest " !

Another pupil of Garcia at the Academy about this time was Madame Agnes Larkcom.

Arthur Oswald, now a professor at the Royal Academy of Music, tells me that at one of his lessons he was stopped by Señor Garcia with the word " wrong ! " He was surprised, because he felt sure that he had sung the right notes in time and tune, and with careful attention to the words and vocal phrasing. " I will give you five minutes to find out," said Garcia to the puzzled pupil when he asked to be told the fault. At the end of that time the master said, " Voix blanche, voix ouverte, voix horrible."

Mr Oswald recounted another episode which was very typical. His friend William Nicholl, after studying under various Continental and English masters, was anxious to have an interview with Garcia to make sure that he had assimilated correct ideas. A meeting was accordingly arranged, and he went up to "Mon Abri," expecting to be put through some sort of catechism as to the human voice and

the principle of singing.   Instead of this, Garcia, on
learning that his visitor wished to teach, motioned
him to the piano-stool. "Will you sit down, please?
Merci.   Now, you are the master, I am the pupil.
I know absolutely nothing.   Give me my first
lesson."

Nicholl commenced to carry out this very practical test of his powers to the best of his ability.
All went well till in an unlucky moment he mentioned the phrase "voice - production," which was
the maestro's pet aversion.   In an instant Garcia
leapt to his feet and banged his fist on the piano.
"Mon Dieu!   How can you *produce* a voice?   Can
you show it to me and say, 'See, here it is.   Examine it?'   Non!   Can you pour it out like molten
lead into the sand?   Non!   There is no such thing
as voice - production.   Perhaps you mean, voice-
emission. You do?   Eh, bien!   Then say so, please."

"Through the good offices of a friend," says
another pupil, "I found myself one day in Garcia's
room at the London Academy of Music.   He was
just finishing a lesson, and I was struck at once by
the extreme courtesy and patience with which he
taught, the charm of his manner, the directness,
the common-sense, and uncommon penetration of
his remarks.

"He welcomed me with a few graceful words,
scrutinising me with a keen but friendly glance.
Thus I sang to him with much confidence, losing all
the nervousness with which I had looked forward
to the examination by so famous a judge.   He accompanied me gently, yet with firmness and rhythmical decision.   When I had finished he looked

straight at me, and to my utter astonishment remarked, 'You are a philosopher, are you not?'

"'Oh, I have studied philosophy to some extent,' I replied.

"'What do you think of your performance?'

"'But I should like to know your opinion,' I blurted out.

"'No, no,' he answered. 'Tell me what you think of it?'

"So I told him that I thought I had a voice and an ear, but I was afraid I did not succeed in making a strong appeal, and I was sure I did not know how to sing. He laughed. 'Quite right, quite right; you do not sing,' he said."

"Manuel Garcia's science and cleverness," writes another, "enabled him to know at once whether he had to deal with a pupil of promise or not, and unlikely aspirants were not allowed to waste his time and theirs.

"I remember a notable case in point. A very rich lady offered the master any price if he would only teach her daughter. He refused, knowing well he could never obtain serious work from her; but as the mother persisted he hit upon a compromise. He asked the ladies to be present during a lesson, and he undertook to teach her, if the girl still wished to learn singing after hearing it taught. The lesson began. The pupil—who seemed to the listeners an already finished singer—had to repeat passage after passage of the most difficult exercises before the master was satisfied; he insisted upon the minutest attention to every detail of execution. Mother and daughter exchanged

horrified glances, and looked on pityingly. The
lesson was finished, the master bowed the ladies
out, and in passing the pupil the young girl whis-
pered to her, 'It would kill me!' Señor Garcia,
returning from the door, said contentedly, 'They
will not come again. Thank you, mon enfant, you
sang well.'

"He was always careful to avoid making his
pupils self-conscious by too many explanations. In
one case he found a simple way of teaching chest-
voice to a girl. 'Do you know how a duck speaks?'
Señor Garcia asked her. 'Imitate it, please.'

"With much giggling, to which he listened
patiently, she tried to obey, 'Quack, quack.'

"'Good! Now turn this into a singing note;
sing one tone lower in the same manner, and one
more.'"

A simple enough device, which spared him and
his pupil much vexation.

His knowledge of the human voice and his
power of detecting its faults were equally marvellous. He had a pupil who, by singing higher
than her natural range, had strained her voice,
and it was necessary that she should avoid singing anything in a high register. Once only she
disobeyed him, and on entering his room the next
day she was greatly surprised that the master's
face was flushed with anger. At once he re-
proached her for having sung soprano. She
pleaded guilty. "But how did you know?"

"I heard you speak, that is quite enough," he
said; and he told her that in ten years not a note

would be left of her brilliant voice. However, on
her promising not to disobey his instructions again,
Garcia made up his mind to help the girl to
come out under his auspices as an oratorio singer.
"But," he told her, "you will need one year's
uninterrupted study before appearing in public."

The pupil's singing was much admired, for few
besides herself and her master could detect that
anything was amiss with her voice. She was
not inclined, therefore, to realise the importance of
his decision, and after a few months' work she
cheerfully accepted an invitation to spend the
winter abroad. When she informed him of this
he bade her farewell, saying that it would be
perfectly useless for her to come back to him,
because, when accepting her as a pupil, his condition was—"One year's uninterrupted study."

Thinking it would be an easy matter to talk
him over, she came back to him on her return.
But she had not reckoned with the iron will of
the maestro. He refused to give her any more
lessons. For over an hour she sat in his room,
and as one lesson after another was given, she
could not keep back her tears. The situation became intense, but the teacher did not lose control.
He was pained to see her sorrow, and at last rose
from his seat and led her gently away, saying,
"Never in my life have I wavered over a decision
once made; I cannot do so now. You must make
the best of what you know already; you will probably get engagements, but do not base your future
on singing."

Time has proved that he was right. After a few years she began to lose her high notes rapidly, and soon her voice was completely gone.

I have already alluded to the maestro's hatred of the tremolo. In this connection an old pupil has sent me the following note :—

"I was going through the various exercises in the book, 'Hints on Singing,' and one day, after I had been studying some little time, there came the usual query, 'What is the next exercise we come to?' 'The shake,' I replied promptly, and added, 'Shall I take that?' The maestro gave a quiet smile as he answered, 'Well, no, I think not. You shake quite enough for the present. We will pass on to the following one. With this gentle rebuke at the tremolo, of which I had not as yet been able to get rid, he went on to tell me how he had been at the opera a few nights before, 'and, Mon Dieu, what tremolo! I could have howled like a dog as I listened.'"

Not only had Manuel Garcia a remarkably accurate ear, but he possessed the gift of "absolute pitch," a fact shown by the following anecdote. A friend called to see him one afternoon, and the conversation turned upon the question of pitch. Garcia shook his head reproachfully when the visitor, who was some seventy years his junior, stated that he could not tell what a note was by ear.

"No sooner had I said this," writes this friend in describing the incident, "than the old maestro rose from his seat, stood with his back to the piano, and told me to strike any note I liked and he would name it. As rapidly as possible I struck the notes, and instantaneously he called out what they were. I must have sounded upwards of two dozen, one after the other, so rapidly that he was never left time to consider. Without a moment's hesitation he named each in turn without a single mistake."

CHAPTER XVIII.

THE five years preceding the celebration of Manuel Garcia's ninetieth birthday are principally noteworthy for two episodes, which I will leave Mr Hermann Klein to relate, since he was intimately connected with both.

The first took place during the summer of 1892.

"In the midst of this abnormally busy season, M. Maurel elected to deliver a lecture at the Lyceum Theatre on 'The Application of Science to the Arts of Speech and Song.' This duly came off, and its main feature proved to be an exceedingly virulent tirade against the *coup de la glotte.* This would not have mattered much had it not happened that Manuel Garcia himself was present, and had to 'possess his soul in patience,' while M. Maurel executed some ridiculous imitations of what he considered to be the indispensable vocal concomitants of the *coup de la glotte,*— a term derided only by certain Paris teachers who have misunderstood and misdirected its use.

"Age and dignity alike compelled Signor

Garcia to sit still and treat with silent contempt this ill-timed and unjustifiable attack upon his method.

"When the lecture was over, however, I offered him the columns of 'The Sunday Times' as a medium for replying to M. Maurel's assertions.

"On the spur of the moment he accepted, and sent a short account of the lecture, written in his own terse and trenchant manner. Then thinking better of it, he decided not to take any personal part in the discussion, and requested me not to print his copy.

"This threw the onus of reply upon me, and the answer proved so far effectual that M. Maurel was moved to make a protest in other London papers against any contradiction of his 'scientific argumentation,' save by M. Garcia himself, and not even then unless supported by something beyond 'simple denial.'

"Accordingly, the maestro then consented to write a letter to 'The Sunday Times,' confirming the statement that he had found M. Maurel's illustrations of the *coup de la glotte* 'extremely exaggerated,' but declining that gentleman's invitation to discuss the subject-matter of his lecture, and adding that it would be utterly impossible to argue upon theories which still remain to be revealed."

The second episode took place shortly after the maestro had entered his ninetieth year,—an event which was celebrated at the Royal Academy of Music by the gift of a silver tea service, subscribed to by the professors of the R.A.M., the actual

R

presentation being made by Walter Macfarren, as *doyen* of the teaching staff.

Some two months after this—that is to say, in the May of 1894—Hermann Klein received a letter from the veteran teacher, who a few days before had attended a dinner given at his house in honour of Paderewski, the other invited guests being Sir Arthur Sullivan, Sir Joseph Barnby, Sir A. C. Mackenzie, Signor Piatti, and other prominent musicians. The maestro, it may be mentioned, had never heard Paderewski play in private before, and was so enchanted when the latter sat down at the piano, that he remained listening to the music till past midnight. "A worthy successor to Rubinstein." This was his criticism of Paderewski's genius.

The letter ran as follows :—

"MON ABRI," CRICKLEWOOD.

DEAR MR KLEIN,—I want to know the cost of printing music, and in this connection would ask you to write answers to the four questions contained in the enclosed card. I suppose that in England or in France the ream consists of 500 sheets ?

Excuse my troubling you, and believe me your very sincere   M. GARCIA.

Your evening was charming !

Hermann Klein answered the questions in person, and thus quickly discovered the nature of the scheme that was afoot.

Manuel Garcia in his ninetieth year intended to bring out another text-book on Singing. His old pupil at once offered to assist in the editing and arrangement of the MS., and the maestro readily

accepted the proffered help. I will leave Mr Klein
to continue the story.

"For several weeks in succession I went to
'Mon Abri' regularly, to aid him in the work. On
two points he insisted—namely, the 'catechism'
form of the text, and the title, 'Hints on Singing,'
which I candidly confessed I did not care for.
Otherwise any little suggestion that I made was
cordially agreed to. He was very careful about the
signing of the contract with the publishers (Messrs
Ascherberg), and on this point wrote as follows:—

Translation.

'MON ABRI,' *Monday, May* 7.

DEAR MR KLEIN,—I have thought that at the reading of
the contract between Mr Ascherberg and myself, if it were to
be immediately followed by the signing, we should not have
time completely to understand the clauses. As these doubtless will contain the details regarding the Colonial, American,
and foreign rights, it is preferable that we should know in
advance what the terms are, and we should be very much
obliged to Mr Ascherberg if he would be so kind as to send
us on a copy of the contract. We will send it back to him
any day that may suit you.—Mille amitiés!

M. GARCIA.

"Three months later the printing was finished,
and early in September the proofs began to come
to hand. We were both away from London when
I received this missive:—

Translation.

GALE HOUSE, LAKE ROAD,
AMBLESIDE, WESTMORELAND,
September 7.

MY DEAR FRIEND,—Are you in town?
I have been working *like a little nigger* correcting, trans-
posing, suppressing, &c., the proofs. I will send you my

first corrected proof, and will you please forward it to Ascherberg for the printers? but I do not wish to do this until I know that you are in town.—Amitiés!

M. GARCIA.

"The question of a preface now came up. The maestro was somewhat averse to providing one, but ultimately he yielded to the desire of the publisher, who was naturally anxious that the 'Hints' should contain everything calculated to arouse attention. He wrote only a few lines, however, and I had to persuade him to add more. He also decided to include a reproduction of the well-known woodcut of himself using the laryngoscope by the light of an oil-lamp, and a couple of laryngoscopic mirrors (half-size), which by some mistake nearly came to being omitted. With the proofs he took infinite pains, and wrote me several notes about them, of which the following deserve quotation :—

Translation.

DEAR FRIEND,—Among some corrections which I have been making at the printer's, I have eliminated pages Nos. ——— (I have forgotten the numbers). I asked to see the whole of the proofs, and they have sent me only those which were uncorrected. If I can get them immediately (the newly-corrected lot) you will doubtless have the whole set without delay.

In the preface they have taken out the two little mirrors : now one—the smaller—would be necessary, and sufficient to explain the laryngoscope.

As to the preface, I will see what I can add. It seems to me, if I am not mistaken, that Mr Ascherberg has the intention of adding an editorial preface to the work, with the idea of increasing the sale. That, I think, would be a mistake.

Praise, if the book merits it, must come from without, unless one wishes to turn it into blame.

Send me, not those proofs which I have, but the corrected pages, including those in which I have corrected the accompaniments, and the whole shall be returned to you without delay. We shall be back again on the 18th (September), and if you care to come to me on the 19th we will prepare the index.—Bien à vous, M. GARCIA.

" By the middle of October the work was complete and ready for the press. However, a delay occurred, in consequence of the necessity for waiting until an American edition had been printed and published in accordance with copyright requirements. The dear old master grew a trifle impatient, although he knew the cause :—

Translation.

DEAR FRIEND,—Business having called me back to town, I paid you a visit at your house, but did not find you at home. No other cause led me to do this than the simple curiosity to know what has become of the 'Hints.' I suppose Mr Ascherberg is having them prepared for publication in America? If you have time, send me a line.—Mes amitiés ! M. GARCIA.

"Eventually the 'Hints on Singing' were published in the last week of January 1895. The reception of the book generally afforded pleasure to its venerable author, and he was particularly gratified by the long notice of it which appeared in 'The Sunday Times.' Hence the note here appended. The one that follows it was elicited by some remarks concerning the 'real' inventor of the laryngoscope, which I, in due course, answered in the columns of my journal.

Translation.

'Mon Abri,' Cricklewood.

My dear Mr Klein,—I owe you double thanks, first, for the cordial congratulations brought by your telegram, and again for the flattering article in 'The Sunday Times': two friendly emanations which have been greatly appreciated by the inhabitants of 'Mon Abri.' I trust your family are all well. Here we are in the best of health, and unite in warmest regards to you and yours, wishing you all the prosperity that you can desire!—Tout à vous de cœur,   M. Garcia.

Translation.

My dear Friend,—Since you wish to come to the aid of the artistic reputation of the 'maestro di bel canto,' be good enough also to favour his scientific reputation by saying that he invented the laryngoscope, and that the Laryngological Society of London created him an honorary member.

Ascherberg would like me to do something to push the sale of the 'Hints.' What can I do?

This little book has given you more trouble than it deserves, and I am sorry on your account.—Tout à vous cordialement,

M. Garcia.

" Acknowledging another notice of the book :—

Translation.

'Mon Abri,' Cricklewood.

Dear Mr Klein,—Thanks a hundred times for the exceedingly flattering article you sent me. Let us hope, for the sake of the sale, that the public will accept your point of view. If Mr Ascherberg should think of bringing out a new edition (when need arises), I will point out two or three errors which still exist, even in the 'corrected' copies I have received. I had already altered them in proof, but they were inadvertently left in.

What frightful weather! I dare not go out any more. I hope you and your family are well.—Tout à vous,

                                        M. GARCIA."

Here Mr Klein's contribution ends.

Two months after the publication of 'Hints on Singing' the subject of our memoir completed his ninetieth year, and with this the feeling was borne in upon him that at last he might enter on a less strenuous life.

Accordingly in the following September he relinquished his professorship, and membership on the Committee of Management at the Royal Academy of Music, and thereby severed a connection of nearly half a century. Already a middle-aged man when he first took up his work at the Academy under Cipriani Potter, he saw him succeeded as Principal in turn by Charles Lucas, Sterndale Bennett, Sir George Macfarren, and finally Sir Alexander Mackenzie, who was holding the position at the time of his retirement. Allowing for a possible break of a month or two, Señor Manuel Garcia was actively engaged in teaching singing at Tenterden Street for the long period of forty-seven years. The Chevalier Alberto Randegger, who was his colleague on the staff for the greater part of this time, sent me the following letter :—

"Although Señor Garcia and myself have been good colleagues for many years at the R.A.M., he was, as you know, so reserved, modest, and retiring that very, very few people were by him allowed to approach or frequent his society on very intimate terms."

What of musical London during the twenty years

preceding Garcia's retirement from the Academy ?
Let us recall some of the artists who were most
prominently before the public, and the more important musical events which were taking place in
the operatic field.   The glance need only be a brief
one, for with the last quarter of the nineteenth
century we are among events which are within
the ken of most people.

With 1875, the year after Sarasate's *début*, we
find three events worthy of note.   There took place
the first performance in London of " Lohengrin," with
Albani as Elsa, Cotogni as Telramund, and Nicolini
in the title part.   Then in the following September
the Carl Rosa Opera Company appeared in the
capital for the first time at the Princess's Theatre.
Lastly, during the season there was heard at Drury
Lane a young Polish singer, who met with emphatic
success in baritone parts such as Don Giovanni,
Nevers, Valentine, and Almaviva. He appeared then
under the name of "De Reschi": eventually he was to
return and take the town by storm as Jean de Rezké.

Two years later we hear of the *début* of Gerster,
and of Gazarré, a Spanish tenor, who bridges over
the interval between the retirement of Mario and
the advent of his famous successor.

In this year, moreover, Richard Wagner came to
England to take part in the series of Wagner
Festival concerts, which had been arranged with
a view to paying off the debt on the new theatre
at Bayreuth.

1878, in which the deaths of Charles Mathews and
Frederick Gye are chronicled, is important for the
London production of Bizet's " Carmen " on June

22.   Hermann Klein went to this *première* in the company of Garcia, and in his reminiscences has set down an interesting description of the evening.   On the distributing of the parts for "Carmen," Campanini returned the *rôle* of Don José, stating that he could not undertake a part where he had no romance and no love duet except with the seconda donna.   Shortly afterwards Del Puente, the baritone, declined the part of Escamillo, saying it must have been intended for one of the chorus; while Mdlle. Valleria suggested Michaela should also be given to one of the chorus.   For some time things were at a standstill, till at length the principals were, by persuasions and threats, induced to attend a rehearsal, and all began to take a fancy to their *rôles*, and in due course the opera was announced.

The receipts for the first two or three nights were miserable, and Mapleson had to resort to the same sort of expedients as in "Faust" for securing an enthusiastic reception, knowing that after a few nights it would be sure to become a favourite.

"It was no easy matter for a performance at the opera to satisfy the maestro in these days," writes Hermann Klein; "the singing rarely pleased him in comparison with the part.   Upon my reminding him that 'Carmen' had been nearly a failure at the Opéra Comique in Paris three years before — 'I know,' he replied; 'and the poor composer died of a broken heart three months later.   That is the way France generally treats rising talent, including her own. I place little value on the opinion of Paris about a new work.'

"Garcia was enthusiastic over the opera.   The

subject and treatment appealed to him to a singular degree, while the story he thought intensely dramatic, and was astonished and delighted at the Spanish colour in the music."

During the same year the Gatti brothers gave a series of Promenade Concerts at Covent Garden, with Sullivan conducting.

We may note here a piece of theatrical news. In December Ellen Terry first appeared at the Lyceum under Irving's management, taking the part of Ophelia in that memorable production of "Hamlet." 1879 sees the Italian Opera season given under Ernest Gye (whose father had died from the effects of a gun accident in the previous December), and the superb Jean Lassalle is added to the company. Concert-goers find an interesting fact in this year in the establishment of the famous Richter Concerts. These were the outcome of the Wagner Festival of two years before, and were announced for this preliminary season as a series of three "Orchestral Festival Concerts."

With 1880 comes the *début* of the great basso, Edouard de Rezké, as Indra in "Le Roi de Lahore."

Next year Anton Rubinstein was in London for the production of his opera, "The Demon."

In 1882 (bringing with it the death of Wagner), we may examine the list of stars at the Opera House once more, so as to note what names have disappeared, and by whom the gaps have been filled. Among the fair sex we find Patti, Albani, Trebelli, Sembrich, Valleria, and Lucca, who had returned after ten years' absence; while the men include Gazaré, Mierzwinski, Faure, Maurel, Nicolini, Soulacroix, and Lassalle. 1882 was further noteworthy as London's great Wagner year, for details of which I am once more indebted to Mr Klein.

"Early in the year a troupe had been formed by Herr Neumann for the purpose of performing 'Der Ring des Nibelungen' in the leading cities of Germany, Austria, Holland, England, and Italy. The months of May and June were chosen for the London visit, and Her Majesty's Theatre was engaged. In all, four cycles of the tetralogy were given. The casts included not a few of the famous artists who had taken part in the initial perform-ance of the 'Ring' at Bayreuth in 1876—among them Niemann, Unger, the Vogls, Hill, Schlosser, and Lilli Lehman (who sang 'Woglinde,' 'Helm-wige,' and the 'Bird' music); with Reicher-Kindermann as *Brunhilde*, while Anton Seidl conducted."

During the same month Herr Pollini arranged with Augustus Harris for a series of performances at Drury Lane, by the entire troupe of the Ham-burg Opera House, and with the very popular Viennese *chef d'orchestre*, Hans Richter, as conductor.

The Hamburg artists comprised at the time several who were to earn world-wide reputations.

"Imagine the advantage of hearing 'Tristan und Isolde' and 'Die Meistersinger' for the first time," writes Mr Klein, "with such a noble singer and actress as Rosa Sucher, as 'Isolde' and 'Eva'; with such a glorious 'Tristan' and 'Walther' as

Brangaene, with that fine baritone, Gura, as 'König Marke' and 'Hans Sachs!'"

In 1883 there are two new productions at Covent Garden, Boito's "Mefistofele" and Ponchielli's "La Gioconda." Then, again, Joseph Maas makes his *début* in Grand Opera as Lohengrin, while Carl Rosa inaugurates his first season at Drury Lane, and brings to a hearing two new operas by English composers,—the "Esmeralda" of Goring Thomas and the "Colomba" of Sir Alexander Mackenzie.

In 1884, the year of Sir Michael Costa's death, the great names are Patti, Albani, Lucca, Trebelli, and Edouard de Rezké.

In the next year Mapleson is once more in command, and the season closes with the presentation of a diamond bracelet to Adelina Patti, in commemoration of her twenty-fifth consecutive season at Covent Garden.

In 1886 Ella Russell made her *début*, while both the Abbé Liszt and Rubinstein paid their last visits to England. It was on this visit that Rubinstein gave that wonderful series of seven historical concerts at the St James's Hall, which realised no less than £6000 gross receipts.

The Jubilee year is noteworthy for the advent of Augustus Harris into operatic management, for we find him giving a season at Drury Lane for which he has secured a new tenor, Jean de Rezké, then practically unknown to London audiences. The artist opened in "Aïda," and obtained a complete triumph.

With 1888, Harris becomes lessee and operative director of Covent Garden, with a strong social

Nellie Melba 1906

Photo by
M. Shadwell Clerke.

support and subscription to grand tier boxes, and commences work with Melba and the two de Rezkés, Albani, Trebelli, Arnoldson, Zélie de Lussan, Ella Russell, Lassalle, and Margaret Macintyre, Garcia's pupil.

In 1889, the year of Carl Rosa's death, we have two important events. "Romeo et Juliette" is given in French, instead of Italian, with a superb cast, of which the star parts are taken as follows :—

Juliette	.	.	Melba.
Romeo .	.	.	Jean de Rezké.
Friar Laurent	.	.	Edouard de Rezké.

Moreover, in July, Jean de Rezké takes part for the first time in an Italian version of "Die Meistersinger," with this cast :—

Ena .	.	.	Madame Albani.
Magdalena	.	.	Mdlle. Bauermeister.
Walther .	.	.	M. Jean de Rezké.
Hans Sachs	.	.	M. Lassalle.
Beckmesser	.	.	M. Isnardon.
David	.	.	M. Montariol.
Pogner	.	.	Signor Abramoff.
Kothner	.	.	M. Winogradon.

The early summer of 1890 witnessed the London *début* of the successor to Liszt and Rubinstein, of the greatest of the *fin de siècle* group of great pianists — Ignace de Paderewski. He was announced for a series of four recitals at the St James's Hall. The first of these was given on May 9 before a meagre and coldly critical audience, the second to a better audience, which improved

again with the remaining ones.   But it was not until
the following season that the conquest was completed, and the meagre attendance became a thing of
the past.   In fact, his Chopin Recital at St James's
Hall, in the July of 1891, drew the largest crowd
and the highest receipts recorded since the final
visit of Rubinstein.   The early months of this year,
moreover, witnessed an operatic experiment which
was destined to mark the climax of the modern
development of English Opera.   D'Oyly Carte built
the "Royal English Opera House," engaged a
double company, and opened it with a repertory
of one work, "Ivanhoe."   The cast on the opening night of Sir Arthur Sullivan's work was as
follows :—

Rebecca	Marguerite Macintyre
	(Garcia's pupil).
Rowena	Esther Palliser.
Ivanhoe	Ben Davies.
Richard Cœur de Lion .	Norman Salmond.
Cedric	Ffrangçon Davies.
Friar Tuck . . .	Avon Saxon.
Isaac of York . .	Charles Copland.
and	
The Templar . . .	Eugene Oudin.

While the alternative group of artists included Miss
Thudicum (Garcia's pupil), Lucile Hill, Franklin
Clive, Joseph O'Mara, and Richard Green.   It ran
from January 31 till the end of July ; then in
November the house reopened with " La Basoche,"
in which David Bispham made his *début* on the
London stage.   With the autumn, however, all
went wrong, the public stayed away, and finally,

on January 16, 1892, the Royal English Opera House was finally closed, to be reopened later as the Palace Theatre of Varieties.

Before leaving 1891 we must note the Covent Garden season, where a very remarkable collection of artists appeared, who must have compared favourably with those whom Garcia had heard half a century before. The new-comers included Emma Eames, Sybil Sanderson, Van Dyck, and Plançon; while in the company were the de Rezkés, Lassalle, Maurel, Ravelli, and Montarid; Melba, Nordica, Albani, Zélie de Lussan, Rolla, Bauermeister, Giulia Ravogli, and Mme. Richard.

Nor must one pass over Signor Lago's venture of an Italian season, embarked on during the autumn of 1891 at the Shaftesbury Theatre. It was notable chiefly for the first production in England of Pietro Mascagni's " Cavalleria Rusticana." In the *première*, which was conducted by Arditi, Marie Brema made her *début* in opera as Lola, while the cast was made up with—

Santuzza	Adelaide Musiani.
Lucia	Grace Damian.
Alfio	Brombara.
Turiddu	Francesco Vignas.

In 1892 comes the *début* in London of Calvé, while Harris engages the great Wagner singers from Bayreuth, to appear for a season of German opera on Wednesday evenings at Covent Garden, with Rosa Sucher as Brunhilde, and Alvary as Siegfried. One must also note the *début* of

Clara Butt in "Orfeo" at the Royal College of Music.

In 1893, the year of Gounod's death, opera lovers at Covent Garden made the acquaintance of the younger school of Italian composers in Mascagni and Leoncavallo. The former first appeared at Covent Garden on June 19, when he conducted "L'Amico Fritz" with Calvè, De Lucia, Pauline Joran, and Dufriche. "Pagliacci" was given, with Melba as Nedda and De Lucia as Canio, while Ancona gave a magnificent rendering of the famous prologue.

The works of two English composers were also produced during the season,—Isidore de Lara's "Amy Robsart" and Villiers Stanford's "Veiled Prophet."

With 1894 there are two novelties added to the repertoire,—Verdi's "Falstaff" and Puccini's "Manon Lescaut"; while the English Jubilee is celebrated of Joseph Joachim and Alfredo Piatti.

With 1895, the year in which Manuel Garcia concludes his ninetieth year, Adelina Patti returns to Covent Garden for a few more performances, and Jean de Rezké makes a temporary absence during the season, for the first time for eight years.

The following year saw the death of Sir Augustus Harris, and with the event the present *régime* came into existence, the formation of the Covent Garden Syndicate, with Earl de Grey at its head, Higgins as director, and Neil Forsyth, secretary. Here we will abandon the narration of the trend of operatic events in London, for those which took place in the last ten years of Manuel Garcia's life are probably in the memories of all. Those which took place during the first forty years of the maestro's life in England seemed sufficiently remote to be worth recalling, for by them we obtain at any rate a bird's-eye view of the great names and events of the, operatic world during Garcia's active career as a teacher.

FOURTH PERIOD

RETIREMENT

(1895–1906)

CHAPTER XIX.

A NONAGENARIAN TEACHER.

(1895–1905).

IN commencing this chapter I must apologise for the personal tone, which is almost unavoidable, since I am giving purely personal reminiscences of the years of study that I spent under Manuel Garcia.

It was early in the May of 1895 that my mother (Antoinette Sterling) took me up to see her old master, in order that he might give his decision as to the advisability of my entering the musical profession.

When we had driven out to his house on Shoot-up-hill, we rang the bell, and a maid came to the door. "Is Señor Garcia well enough to see us? If he is sleeping, do not disturb him. We can wait till he is rested." The servant raised her eyebrows in slight wonderment. "Mr Garcia is out gardening, Madame. I will tell him of your arrival."

This astonishing information was uttered in the most ordinary tone, as though such a thing were a mere episode of everyday life. We were ushered into the drawing-room, but were not kept waiting

long, for in a few minutes the door opened and
Manuel Garcia entered. With a genial smile and
an exclamation of pleasure he came rapidly across
the room, taking short, quick steps, and was
shaking hands with his old pupil almost before
she had time to rise from her seat. The next
quarter of an hour passed swiftly enough. A
stream of questions fell from the lips of the
wonderful nonagenarian as to what she had been
doing, where she had been, what were her latest
songs, what she thought of the pianist who had
recently come out, what of the political situation,
when could she come to lunch,—and so on.

He was short of stature, a little bent with age,
frail-looking perhaps, but wiry. His eyes were
bright and piercing, his profile clear-cut and distinguished. He had an olive complexion, a gift
of his native Spain which fifty years of London
fog and de-oxygenised air had been unable to
take from him.

His white hair was partially covered by a red
skull-cap, and his moustache was closely cut. He
spoke in rapid tones, yet with absolute distinct-
ness of clear enunciation.

Every word gave proof of that keen interest
which he felt in all that was going on around
him. In expression, voice, and gesture there was
an amazing alertness, vigour, and mental activity
which few men of seventy could equal, fewer still
surpass. His conversation gave evidence of the
fire of youth, tempered with the tolerance of
old age.

A more intimate acquaintance with the great

Mon Abri
Cricklewood

Dear Mr Mackinlay,

The Day I had the pleasure
of seeing your mother, I fancy
She said that you would
communicate with me about
your lessons. At any rate in
compliance with her wishes,
I will fix a time to receive
you when you are ready to
come
    Present my respects To your
mother and believe
            Truly yours
                M. Garcia

FACSIMILE OF A LETTER WRITTEN BY MANUEL GARCIA
AT THE AGE OF NINETY-ONE.

teacher revealed further qualities which made him loved, nay, worshipped, by all his pupils. Loyal and staunch, he had an old-world courtesy, a charm of manner, and a patience which was quite remarkable.

When Manuel Garcia had heard me sing he asked a few penetrating questions. Then he turned to my mother and said that he would take me as a pupil: he thought, however, that it would be better for me to wait a year before starting work.

There was something almost uncanny in being told by a man ninety years of age to come back in twelve months and commence singing-lessons. But seeing and hearing him, one could not doubt that he would be ready and waiting at the appointed time.

Nor was the supposition wrong. In the first week of April of the following year, when he was approaching his ninety-second birthday, the first lesson took place. From that time on, my studies continued under his care and guidance until April 1900, when he was in his ninety-sixth year. In this I had the honour of being the last pupil to be regularly trained by him for the musical profession with the full four-years' course of tuition.

That he should have been able to continue teaching at all at such an age is sufficiently astonishing. That during those years he should have postponed lessons through indisposition upon only some three or four occasions gives a still keener insight into the extraordinary life led by him as a nonagenarian.

What a wonderful experience those lessons

proved, lasting sometimes nearly two hours! When
he was interested in explaining certain effects in
singing or in recounting stories of artists and operas
apropos of the work in hand, time ceased to exist.
The luncheon-bell would ring three or four times
without having any apparent effect, so engrossed
was he in his subject. At the end of the lesson he
would, with the old courtliness of his youth, insist
on seeing one out himself. If one opened the door
and stood aside for him to pass, the manœuvre
proved perfectly useless. With a delightful gesture
he insisted on his guest preceding him, saying, "Ici
je suis chez moi." Then he would skilfully slip
along the hall and open the front door. There he
would stand—oblivious, and apparently impervious,
to draughts and cold—chatting for several minutes
or giving some parting advice before holding out his
hand and wishing one *au revoir*.

Almost more surprising is it that he should have
continued to carry on his correspondence. Many a
long letter was received from him during those
years; while on one occasion he actually wrote out
the entire music of an Italian aria, "Liete voci,"
giving his own elaborations of the original melody.

During the lessons he would remain seated at
the piano, undertaking all accompaniments himself.
These would be given quietly, but with a firm,
rhythmical precision. In the case of the old Italian
arie, they would generally be played from memory.
His white expressive hands would weave elaborate
preludes and harmonies into the music, and as one
sang he would sit with closed eyes as though his
thoughts were far away. But they were not, they

" Did you not hear ?   No ?   Then I will tell you how I did it.   Throughout the music I sang the least shade flat.   The result you observed."

And now a few words as to Manuel Garcia's Method of Teaching.

He always impressed on singers and teachers alike that the Art of Singing was not voice-*production*, a term which he loathed, but guidance in voice-*emission*.

His Method may be perhaps summed up in the doctrine that it was *not* a method—in the sense that he had no hard and fast rules,—his object always being to make each pupil sing in the way most natural and involving the least effort.   He was careful to impress on one the fact that any visible effort took away from the charm of the singer.   If one gave too free play to the lungs, and sang beyond oneself, he would remark, " You must not forget the advice my father gave me : ' Do not let anybody see the bottom of your purse ; never spend all you possess, nor have it noticed that you are at your last resource.' "

The first lesson for all pupils would be practically a chat on the singer's aims and on the instrument at his disposal : he would explain in clear language the different parts of the instrument, and show that the lungs had to be properly filled ; then in the first attempt at emission a steady gentle stream was to be sent out, while one guarded against the natural tendency to empty the lungs quickly.   At the larynx the air in passing through the little lips of the glottis received pitch, which varied according to the rapidity with which these opened and allowed puffs of air to pass through; then in passing through the passage from the larynx to the front of the mouth they received timbre and vowel-tone, which varied according to the shape of the pharynx and the height of the soft palate.

The tone was then to be directed to the front of the mouth, and here the consonants were made, but these latter were not to interfere with the flow of sound or cause any jerkiness. When a phrase was commenced the tone was to flow on evenly, smoothly, steadily, with greater or less sustaining power as desired, until the end was reached. He would further explain something of the theory of registers, and the causes of various kinds of tones, good and bad. Finally, before telling the pupil to make his first tones, he would impress on him this: "If you do not understand anything perfectly, ask me at once, and I will endeavour to clear up the point and show you how to get over the difficulty. And remember that we must have the knowledge to guide the emission of the voice with our brains. When the tone has once been emitted it is to late to correct a fault. We must be aware beforehand exactly what we are going to do. We must know what is right and how to do it. That is the secret."

After this preliminary explanation the first step invariably consisted in the emission of a steady tone, deep breathing being insisted on for the purpose. At the first sign of unsteadiness in the tone the pupil was directed to stop and begin again. In the intervals of rest the physiology of the voice was clearly and carefully explained, and the proper position of the various parts of the body and throat, and the management of the vocal cords necessary for the emission of resonant tone, were the first laws laid down. When once the pupil could sing a scale slowly and steadily, the way was open to the practice of exercises; and very often in the case of a voice of promise these exercises constituted the whole course of study for a considerable period.

The famous *coup de la glotte*, or shock of the glottis, with which his name is associated, has often been misapplied from ignorance of its real object, which was to secure that the vocal cords were closed at the commencement of the tone, and that there was consequently no preliminary escape of the breath. How far his methods, which also included the imparting of a remarkable grasp of every phase of vocal expression, were successful, is to be gathered from the list of his direct or indirect pupils, which, as we have seen, includes a great many of the most prominent representatives in the world of song.

At the lessons the maestro did not, as a rule, offer either praise or blame. He was, however, always encouraging, and treated pupils according to their individual powers. He seemed to know instinctively what they could manage and what was beyond them. His remarks might be made in English, French, or Italian, so that the pupil had to keep his wits about him. In them there was a directness and penetration which filled one with implicit confidence in his keen mind and extraordinary experience. Hardly a lesson passed in which he did not, during the intervals for rest, tell some anecdotes of the most engrossing interest. These would have as their subject the elder Garcia, Malibran, Jenny Lind, Meyerbeer, Rossini, Mario, Pasta, or some other of the great musicians of the past. Often, too, he would speak of his memories of Spain, of the Peninsular War, the French Revolution, the first New York season of Italian opera, his tour in Mexico, the discovery of the laryngoscope, or other memories of his long career. But though related with delightful readiness, these stories always displayed extreme modesty in reference to the part played by himself in the various episodes.

It was in the same spirit, too, that he would speak of his efforts as a teacher. " I only tell you how to sing, what tone is good, what faults are to be avoided, what is artistic, what inartistic. I try to awaken your intelligence, so that you may be able to criticise your own singing as severely as I do. I want you to listen to your voice, and use your brain. If you find a difficulty, do not shirk it. Make up your mind to master it. So many singers give up what they find hard. They think they are better off by leaving it, and turning their attention to other things which come more easily. Do not be like them.

" In Paris once a number of boys were set some problems whilst competing for a prize at the Gymnase. One of them was seen to cry, and on being asked why he did so, replied that the problems were too easy. He was afraid that all the others would be able to do them as well as himself, so that he would be prevented from carrying off the prize. The master smiled, and told him to answer the questions by a more difficult method, if he knew one. He did so, and gained the first place.

"Many singers do the opposite. They burst into tears because they find a thing too hard. Do not be afraid to face a difficulty. Make up your mind to conquer it. I only direct you. If you do a thing badly, it is your fault, not mine. If you do it well, all praise to you, not to me. I show pupils how to sing, and the proper way to study. Suppose some one meets me out of doors and says, 'Can you tell me the way to Hampstead Heath?' I answer, 'I will walk there with you.' We set out, and I keep by his side, saying, 'This is the street we have to pass through. Do not turn down there. That goes in the wrong direction. Follow my instruction, and you will arrive at your destination. I know the road well.' If he takes the wrong turning, that is his fault, not mine. I cannot prevent him from going off into the slums. I can only say 'Do not go there — that is wrong.' He must follow my advice or not, as he chooses. Again, if we come to a very steep hill, and he says, 'I can't climb that. It is too difficult. Let us not go up—I am tired'; I can only reply, 'If you wish to reach the Heath, you *must* climb it. There is no other way of getting to your destination.' But if he is lazy, and will not mount it by his own endeavour, I cannot lift him and carry him upon my shoulders."

How characteristic it was of the master's innate modesty to speak of his work in this simple way!

How he ignored the times when he pulled the pupils back by main force from that wrong path; when he cheered them on, should they get discouraged; when he described in concise terms the easiest way of climbing up that hill! If they failed to mount the ascent on the first occasion, he explained the reason for their failure. Then he bade them be of good courage and try again. If they failed ten times, he would once more carefully repeat exactly what had to be done, and seek for fresh illustrations which might perhaps put the matter in a clearer light. Truly, if he did not actually carry them up the steep path, he came very near doing so. He was like a friend offering assistance rather than a teacher paid to instruct. Ah, dear maestro! never shall I forget the infinite patience and gentleness which you displayed in those hours of study.

When a difficulty had been overcome, he would smile and say, "That was as I wish. Do it again. Good! Now try and impress upon your mind exactly what you did. Sing it once again. C'est ça! Do not let the old mistake occur again." If one *did* allow it to reappear, he would shake his head sorrowfully and say, "Jenny Lind would have cut her throat sooner than have given me reason to say, 'We corrected that mistake last time.'" It seemed at first strange, to say the least, to hear these comparisons made between oneself and a pupil who had studied under the same master fifty years previously. However, after studying for three years, I grew used to hearing him speak of musicians who had been dead forty years or more;

of a sister who, after a brilliant career, had died in 1836 ; of a father who had come into the world a hundred and twenty years previously; and of his first singing-master, Ansani, who was born early in the eighteenth century. At any rate, during the last year of study I was able to hear such casual remarks as "Ah, yes, I remember teaching this song to Stockhausen for his *début*" (the great German vocalist being at the time somewhere about seventy years of age), without evincing more than a momentary surprise.

Wagner's compositions never attracted Manuel Garcia. The heavy orchestration of the German music did not appeal to him, though he raised no objection to going through Wolfram's song, "O Star of Eve," in the Italian version, "O tu bel astro incantator." "Tannhäuser" was written in a lyrical style : one shudders to think what he would have said to anything like Wotan's "Abschied."

He did not believe in "vocalises," such as are used by most teachers in earlier lessons. Instead of these, he preferred to give simple Italian arias. He pointed out that with them one began at once to learn the value of articulation and expression. Exercises he looked on as the foundations of all good singing. They would take the form of sustained and swelled notes, scales, passages of combined intervals, arpeggios, chromatics, and shakes. The acquirement of agility in execution, he used to say, required *at least* two years' study, the result being that the voice became flexible, even mellow and strong. In the elucidation of difficulties he used to make use of many similes and illustrations, which

T

threw a vivid and illuminating light upon the matter in hand. These, together with the various maxims of artistic singing which he would impart, I used to write down in a book after each lesson, and as a teacher of singing I have found them of the most inestimable value and assistance.

When one day I told the maestro that I had decided to devote my whole attention in the future to teaching, he at once sat down and wrote a letter of recommendation, though in his ninety - eighth year, — a typical example of his kindness and thought for the benefit of others.

It was an inestimable advantage to hear him teach singers of various capacities. During the period I was under him I had the privilege of hearing him give many lessons ; for though I was the last pupil to receive the full four years' training, he was still teaching a few specially favoured amateurs,—in most cases the children or grandchildren of former pupils.

His ear was most accurate and unerring, while he was exceedingly quick of observation, and equally ready with a helpful remark, given in precise terms, a simile, a little anecdote, or even a slight gesture or a look.

In his lessons he was ever ready to give the most interesting information on any scientific questions or theories, and would discuss a point with the greatest animation. He was particularly annoyed at the way the *coup de la glotte* was misunderstood and exaggerated beyond all recognition by many musicians. In his 'Hints on Singing' he defines the *coup* as the neat articulation of the glottis that gives a precise and clear start to a sound. In reality, as taught by him, it simply meant that he wished one to get straight on to a note, without any uncertainty or feeling about for it, instead of slurring up to it (a very common fault), or taking it too sharp and having to sink to the proper pitch.

His works mark an epoch in a branch of human knowledge which one day may be called a science. They deserve to be most carefully studied by any one who wishes to gain a clear insight into that interesting subject—the human voice. They are the fruit of a great mind and of wonderful experience, written in a very lucid style, simple and terse, full of interest to the musician as well as to the voice trainer.

He expounds his views fearlessly but modestly, with logical cogency. Nearly every page bears evidence how cautious, discerning, and progressive a teacher he was.

As showing the importance which Manuel Garcia attached to poetic interpretation of all vocal music, I give three quotations from his 'Hints on Singing,' the extracts being taken from the section headed "Preparation of a piece."

"The pupil must read the words of the piece again and again till each finest shadow of meaning has been mastered. He must next recite them with perfect simplicity and self-abandonment. The accent of truth apparent in the voice when speaking naturally is the basis of expression in singing. Light and shade, accent, sentiment, all become eloquent and persuasive. The imitation of instinctive impulse must, therefore, be the object of this special preparation."

" A powerful means of exciting the mind to a vivid conception of the subject is to imagine the personage as standing before one, and let the phantom sing and act, criticising closely both efforts; then, when satisfied with the results, to imitate them exactly. By faithfully reproducing the impressions suggested by this creature of fancy, the artist will obtain more striking effects than at once rendering a piece."

"Another way is to recall some analogous situation in a work of art: for example, if we have to study the scene of Desdemona in the second act of Rossini's 'Otello,' 'L'error d'un infelice,' one of the fine paintings of the Magdalene at the feet of Christ might occur to the mind. Grief and repentance could not assume a more pathetic form."

He was always careful to secure the proper use of the registers on the part of the pupil, for, as he would point out, more female voices have been ruined by carrying the chest register too high (that is to say, beyond the E or F above middle C) than by anything else.

He had a wonderful insight into the capabilities of those whom he taught. Indeed, I remember his saying once that throughout his career he had very rarely failed in reading from the eyes of an intending pupil the prophecy as to his or her future success in the profession of music. He disliked, he said, to be associated with failures, and the moment he found that he had made a mistake in his estimate of a pupil's capacities, he at once disillusioned him and declined to continue his training.

His mannerisms while playing accompaniments were quite characteristic of the man. He would strike the chords with the greatest vivacity, and almost leap into the air from his piano-stool in his excitement at any wrong trick of vocalisation; or again, he would make a dash for the metronome, snatch it up and set it to time, and for the space of perhaps ten minutes compel one to go on counting mentally, or beating time with the hand in unison with the rhythmic movements of the guiding instrument, until the time difficulty had been mastered. When he had succeeded in preparing the voice for use like a beautifully toned instrument, his teaching spread over the whole extension of every style of music,—opera, oratorio, and song.

To his charm of courtly manners was added a never-failing wit and love of fun : of this he gave constant proof. For instance, an old pupil recounts how one day Manuel Garcia was seized with a fit of coughing. "Ah, maestro, I'm afraid it's the spring," he commiserated, and was met with the half-laughing, half-pathetic retort, "No, no; it is too many springs."

A further illustration of his keen sense of humour, even in extreme old age, is found in a letter which, as a nonagenarian, he wrote to a friend some seventy years his junior.

The young man was famous among his acquaintances for a rather eccentric handwriting, and no one was fonder of twitting him about it than the maestro. The chaff on one occasion took the form of a letter, which I am enabled to reproduce in facsimile. Señor Garcia wished to convey the following information :—

"I will remain here sometime longer, and when in town I will write to you.

"Hoping to find you in good health and voice,— I remain, yours truly, M. GARCIA."

Remembering, however, to whom he was writing, he took the trouble to make his communication as bewildering as possible by dividing the words thus :—

"Iw ill remain he re so—m—eti—me long er an d wheni n tow nIw il lw rite t oyo u.

"Ho ping to fin d you ing oo d hel than dv oic e, I rem ain y our strul y MGARCI A."

Often at the close of a lesson he used to ask me to stay to tea, and in the summer we would adjourn to the garden, where the table would be spread beneath the inviting shadow of the trees. Those would be red-letter days indeed.

On these occasions the maestro would leave thoughts of singing behind him, and show his wide interests and deep insight into all the questions of the day. Once when conversation had turned upon violin-playing, there came up the name of Kubelik, who had come out in London a few weeks previously. After four years' pupilage, I was not surprised to learn that he had already been to hear the new instrumentalist. I must, however, confess

29 September 1904
Ennerdale
Sutton
Surrey

Dear Mr Wat[son],

Iw ill remain he
re so—m—eti—me
long er an d Wheni
n tow ndw il lwr
rite t oyo u.

Ho piing to fin d you
my oo d hel than Ju
oic e,
I rim ain
y oir truly
M Garcia

FACSIMILE OF A LETTER WRITTEN BY MANUEL GARCIA
AT THE AGE OF NINETY-NINE.

to having been somewhat startled when, with the greatest *sangfroid*, he began comparing the execution with that of Paganini. At other times he would speak of Joseph Chamberlain and the newest developments of Fiscalities, the building of sky-scrapers in New York, the drama of the day, or the Spanish War. One day he even showed himself quite ready to discuss the pros and cons of Christian science.

My lessons came to a close in April of 1900, when the maestro was in his ninety-sixth year.

When in due course the time came for making my first provincial tour, he wrote several letters on the subject, of which I quote three, as being typical of the trouble which he was ever ready to take, and the wisdom of the advice which he would give.

"Mon Abri," Cricklewood.

I am a very bad maker of programmes. If I had to deal with that sort of work, I should have to take the advice of an expert who could tell what sort of music would meet the taste of every individual public. Your mother might be your best adviser.

Wishing you every success. M. Garcia.

Again he writes :—

Before you commence your tour you ought to give a *complete* rest to your voice. Prepare for work only a week before you begin.

Do not sing or study the "Elijah" nor any other music written for a baritone. For your organ the use of low notes is resting, therefore necessary.

Do not indulge in exaggerated display of power. Too much ambition in that respect is fatal.

A third runs as follows :—

> You will do well not to limit yourself to singing easy
> songs, but also to attempt upon occasion such pieces as
> require the full use of your means. This will be an excel-
> lent preparation for your appearance in London, and it will
> give you the confidence in your powers and the facilities in
> using them necessary to enable you to take a place among
> the best of the profession. It will always give me pleasure
> to hear of your successes. Give my kindest regards to your
> mother.

After this I continued to see the maestro fairly
often, and was not surprised to hear of his setting
off in his ninety-seventh year to spend the winter
in Egypt, or of his staying with his sister in Paris
for a few days on his way home.

In the early winter of 1903 my mother was taken
seriously ill, and Manuel Garcia on hearing of this
at once wrote a sympathetic letter.

On January 10, 1904, the end came, and with
the announcement in the papers, one of the first
tokens of sympathy was a beautiful wreath from
the maestro, followed by a telegram expressing
his desire to be present at the closing scene in the
career of his old pupil. Despite the distance, for
the service was held at Golder's Hill, the maestro
drove over, stayed for the entire service, and remained behind afterwards to offer a few simple
but never-to-be-forgotten words of sympathy.

Two months after this he entered his 100th
year. To celebrate the occasion, an address of
congratulation was presented to him, signed by
127 professors of the Royal College and Royal
Academy of Music.

Dear Mr. MacKinlay,

Before you commence your tour you ought to give a complete rest to your voice - Prepare for work only a week before you begin

Do not sing or study the Elijah nor any other music written for a Baryton - For your organ the use of low notes is resting therefore necessary.

Do not indulge in exagerated display of power. Too much ambition in that respect is fatal.

Wishing you success I remain
Truly yours
M. Garcia

FACSIMILE OF A LETTER WRITTEN BY MANUEL GARCIA
AT THE AGE OF NINETY-FOUR.

At the end of the year it was suggested by the editor of 'The Strand Magazine' that I should prepare an article on "Manuel Garcia and his Friends" for publication in the month of his centenary. On my communicating with the maestro, he wrote at once offering to render assistance, and asked me to bring the MS. up when ready. Accordingly, in the January, two months before his 100th birthday, I spent the afternoon with him, and was requested to read aloud the proofs of the article.

It was astonishing how memory enabled him to correct immediately any mistake. He would suddenly stop and say, "No, no; it was in 1827, not 1825." Again, in the case of a story in which some details were wrong, he said, "No, that is not right. I will tell it you again"; with which words he recounted in French the tale of how his sister, Malibran, came to make her *début* at Paris. And so the afternoon passed, until finally, after signing a photo, he insisted on coming to the door to see me out. This experience served to prepare me for the astonishing ease and energy with which, a few weeks later, he went through the Centenary festivities.

CHAPTER XX.

THE CENTENARY HONOURS.

(1905.)

Upon St Patrick's Day, 1905, Manuel Garcia entered on the "second century of his immortality," as Professor Fränkel felicitously put it. That 17th of March has become red-lettered in the annals of music by reason of its international character, and the fact that the two professions of music and medicine joined hands with the royalty of three countries, England, Spain, and Germany, in paying honour to whom honour was due.

Sir George Cornewall Lewis was a firm disbeliever in centenarians, but his scepticism must have suffered a severe shock could he have been present at the celebrations. He would then have seen not merely a man whose years beyond all question numbered a century, but one who at that great age showed no sign of senility, and could still take an active part in a series of trying ceremonies, and bear with dignity, if not altogether without fatigue, a load of honours and congratulations, a flood of speeches like the rushing of great waters, and repeated thunderstorms of applause that would were very much present. If a mistake were made the music would cease, the error be pointed out, and a suggestion given for its correction. This would take the form either of some helpful little observation, made in clear, precise terms, or of personal illustration, given in English, or more often French. Though over ninety years old, he was quite equal to showing how he wanted notes taken or an effect given by singing the passage himself. On one memorable occasion he sang two entire octaves, commencing at the low A flat, and ending with a high baritone G sharp. It sounds an almost incredible *tour de force*, but is an absolute fact. The voice naturally trembled with age, though in a surprisingly slight degree. But the timbre, enunciation, and dramatic power were still there, while every phrase revealed the extraordinary fire of his Spanish temperament.

When he had been singing thus one day he laughed and said, " I cannot sing any more. You see how the voice trembles. That, you must not imitate. The tremolo is an abomination—it is execrable. Never allow it to appear, even for a moment, in your voice. It blurs the tone and gives a false effect. Many French singers cultivate it, and I will tell you why."

There had been at one time, he said, an eminent vocalist worshipped by the Parisian public. His voice was beautiful in quality, faultless in intonation, and absolutely steady in emission. At last, however, he began to grow old. With increasing years the voice commenced to shake. But he was a great artist. Realising that the tremolo was a fault, but one which could not then be avoided, he brought his mind to bear upon the problem before him. As a result, he adopted a style of song in which he had to display intense emotion throughout. Since in life the voice trembles at such moments, he was able to hide his failing in this way by a quality of voice which appeared natural to the situation. The Parisians did not grasp the workings of his brain, and the clever way in which he had hidden his fault. They only heard that in every song which he sang his voice trembled. At once, therefore, they concluded that if so fine an effect could be obtained, it was evidently something to be imitated. Hence the singers deliberately began to cultivate a tremolo. The custom grew and grew until it became almost a canon in French singing.

The maestro told another story to illustrate the strange way in which effects were sometimes produced by the old vocalists. A certain artist was singing Secchi's "Lungi dal caro." Something in his voice gripped the audience from the first bar. There was an indefinable quality which they had never experienced before, something which thrilled and stirred them with an inexpressible weirdness, something which almost made the blood run cold. When the music ceased, every one drew a deep breath and remained silent for a few moments. Then came a burst of rapturous applause. Later on, a fellow musician went up to the singer, congratulated him, and then said, "Tell me how you were able to produce that effect upon your audience."

have overwhelmed many men in the full vigour of
life. Manuel Garcia went through the trying
ordeal without apparently feeling any ill effect, and
seemed thoroughly to enjoy the whole thing. It
was difficult indeed to believe that the venerable
figure on the right of the chairman at the banquet,
whom one saw light a cigarette and smoke it with
relish in defiance of the Anti-Tobacco League, was
born seven months before the battle of Trafalgar !
It was passing strange, as one saw him giving
the lie in every point to Shakespeare's picture of
extreme age, to think that he might not only have
" seen Shelley plain," but have been one of the
students who modelled their collars and their scowls
on those of Byron ; that he had finished his education before Pasteur was born, and had come to man's
estate before Lister saw the light ; that he had made
his name known on two continents while Scott and
Goethe were still alive, and Darwin was at school ;
and that he had made the discovery that will make
his name immortal while many of those whose
names are now illustrious were yet unborn. How
quick were his senses and how alert his intelligence
was shown in many ways, trifling, perhaps, but
significant, in the course of what must have been
the most trying day of his long life. His extraordinary vitality was put to a very severe test in
the functions held in honour of the occasion, but
he passed through them with the most wonderful
fortitude and genial courtliness.

When the King heard of the approaching birthday, he made inquiries as to whether the aged
maestro could stand the strain of personal investi-

ture of the honour which his Majesty had already decided to bestow. The answer came back that he was quite ready, and anxious to show his gratitude for this royal compliment by going to the palace.

An interview was accordingly arranged, and Señor Garcia, having risen between nine and ten o'clock on the morning of that day of days, was driven to Buckingham Palace, where he was ushered without delay into the King's presence. His Majesty entered into conversation with the old musician, showing his acquaintance with his long record of fame, and, ever interested in aged people, questioned him as to his health with the most sympathetic solicitude, being absolutely amazed at the vitality displayed. The King expressed to the maestro his congratulations and his recognition of all that he had done for medicine and music, and finally invested him with the insignia of a Commander of the Royal Victorian Order, at the same time signifying a wish to be personally represented at the banquet which was to take place in the evening. Needless to say that this characteristic kind-heartedness of King Edward, shown towards the hero of the day, acted as a splendid tonic to the Centenary celebrations.

From the Palace Señor Garcia drove to the rooms of the Royal Medical and Chirurgical Society in Hanover Square, where by noon the fine saloon was thronged by his old pupils and various deputations, representative of many departments of learning and research.

The reception-room had been decorated for the occasion with palms and foliage plants. In the centre of a carpeted dais at one end of the apart-

ment had been placed a high-backed chair, up-
holstered in crimson, and on the extreme left was
the still veiled portrait of the centenarian, which
had been painted by Sargent. In front of the seat
there were some beautiful floral tributes. The
largest bore on its ribbons the inscription, "À leur
cher et venéré Professeur, Manuel Garcia—Salvatore
et Mathilde Marchesi, Paris, Mars 17, 1905." Another came from Blanche Marchesi, and was addressed "To the Christopher Columbus of the
Larynx"; while yet another had been sent by the
Glasgow Society of Physicians.

Punctually at twelve o'clock, amid volleys of
applause, Manuel Garcia, looking amazingly bright
and hale, entered the room with short, quick steps,
wearing the insignia of the Royal Victorian Order,
conferred an hour before, and walked unaided to
the dais. This he mounted with agility, and took
his seat upon the crimson throne, a magnificent
basket of flowers on either side. There he sat
for an hour, upright and smiling, in full view of
the spectators, during the proceedings which-
ensued.

It fell naturally to the lot of Sir Felix Semon,
both as Physician Extraordinary to the King and
chairman of the Garcia Committee, to convey the
intelligence of the earlier ceremony which had
taken place that morning.

"Ladies and Gentlemen," Sir Felix said, "the
auspicious proceedings of to-day's memorable occasion could not have been more joyously opened than
they have just been. His Majesty the King, with

the kindness of heart which endears him to us all, has just been pleased to receive Señor Garcia at Buckingham Palace, in order to express to him his congratulations and his recognition of all that Señor Garcia has done for medicine and music. At the same time the King has conferred upon him the honorary Commandership of the Royal Victorian Order. His Majesty, at the conclusion of the interview, expressed a wish to be personally represented at the banquet to-night, and said that he would desire his Lord-in-Waiting, Lord Suffield, to attend as his representative. I feel quite sure that this whole assembly has already shown by its applause that it recognises in this act a new token of the King's invariable kindness and his appreciation of all that is good and high."

Next came the Spanish Chargé d'Affaires, the Marquis de Villalobar, who delivered a special message of congratulation from King Alfonso.

" I have been honoured by his Majesty the King, Don Alphonse XIII., with his august representation to congratulate you on the day of your centenary, and in the presence of the learned men who have assembled in this great metropolis for its celebration. In obeying the King's command, in which his Government and the Spanish people join, I honour myself, investing you, in the name of his Majesty and your motherland, with the Royal Order of Alphonse XII., as a high reward to your merits and the services rendered to mankind through your science and your labour. I feel it is also my duty to avail myself of this opportunity in order to make public the sentiments of my beloved Sovereign and of his Government, conveying sincere thanks, first to his Majesty King Edward VII., who I have just learned has most graciously conferred upon our compatriot a high distinction of this noble and hospitable country, and also to all the representatives of England and those of the learned societies here assembled to commemorate this centenary. Hearty gratefulness on behalf of Spain to all who have come and are represented here to - day to honour Don Manuel Garcia as a glory to modern science."

The Marquis de Villalobar then invested Señor Garcia with the Order, amid loud cheers. After this glowing tribute came Professor Fränkel, who said that they were assembled to honour one who had devoted his best days to the teaching of singing,—had not been content with attempting to discover the secrets of voice-culture by sound alone, but had proceeded in a thoroughly scientific way. Through his genius he had thrown light on the hitherto dark places of the larynx and the source of the living human voice. He had thereby laid the sure foundations of the physiology of the voice.

In recognition of his merits the German Emperor had conferred on him the Great Gold Medal for Science. The Minister for Public Instruction had requested him (Dr Fränkel) to present that rarely awarded distinction to Señor Garcia that day when he completed the first century of his immortality. He did so with the greatest pleasure, as one who owed a very great debt of gratitude to the method of laryngoscopy invented by their honoured friend.

An address from the Royal Society was then presented by Sir Archibald Geikie (principal secretary), Professor Francis Darwin (foreign secretary), and Professor Halliburton, F.R.S. The address, which was read by Professor Halliburton, was as follows :—

The Royal Society of London join very cordially in congratulating Manuel Garcia on the celebration of his 100th birthday.

The President and Council recall with much pleasure the circumstance that the Royal Society afforded in their 'Proceedings' the medium for publishing to the scientific world the memorable paper in which Señor Garcia laid the foundation of the experimental study of voice-production, and at the same time, through the laryngoscope, provided the starting-point for a new department of practical medical science.

The Royal Society trust that Señor Garcia may still continue for years to come to enjoy in good health the esteem which his scientific achievement and his high personal character have brought him.

Signed and sealed on behalf of the Royal Society for Promoting Natural Knowledge,

WILLIAM HUGGINS, *President.*

Sir Archibald Geikie (as a corresponding member of the Prussian Academy of Sciences) read the following telegram from that Academy :—

To the first investigator of the human voice by a new method which for all time has bestowed a signal service on art, on science, and on suffering humanity, the Royal Prussian Academy of Sciences sends on his 100th birthday its most respectful congratulations. WALDEYER, *Secretary.*

An address was next read from the University of Königsberg, which in 1862 had conferred on Señor Garcia the honorary degree of Doctor of Medicine. A hope was expressed that he would live to receive the fresh diploma which it is the custom to confer on doctors of fifty years' standing.

The next address was from the Victoria University of Manchester, presented by Professor Stirling, F.R.S., Dr Milligan, and Dr S. Moritz, followed by one from the Medical Faculty of Heidelberg.

The address from his old pupils was read by Mr Ballin. In offering their sincere congratulations they said : " The services you have rendered to the art of singing are very great, and the large number of your pupils who have become famous is incontestable proof of your genius." Madame Blanche Marchesi spoke in the name of her parents, who were unavoidably absent, expressing their gratitude for everything he had done for them. Their method and their success were due to Señor Garcia, who had laid the basis of their artistic career.

Mr Otto Goldschmidt, the husband of Jenny Lind, said that his late wife, to the end of her days, continued to have respect, regard, and veneration for Señor Garcia, who helped her to take the position in the musical world which she attained ; and he was very happy indeed to be able to make that statement, and to congratulate the old master on what he had done for the great art of singing.

An address from the Royal Academy of Music was followed by one from the Royal College of Music.

U

Addresses and messages from Laryngological societies and associations were then read, the following being among the bodies represented: The American Laryngological Association; the Belgian Society of Oto - Rhino - Laryngology (Dr Delsaux, Dr Goris, Dr Broeckkaert); the Berlin Laryngological Society (Dr Landgraf, Professor Kuttner, Professor Gluck); the British Laryngo-Oto-Rhinological Association (Mr Chichele Nourse, Dr Percy Jakins, Mr Stuart - Low, Mr Dennis Vinrace, Dr Andrew Wyld); the Danish Laryngological Society; the French Laryngo - Rhino - Otological Society (Dr Moure, Dr Lermoyez, Dr Toxier, Dr Molinié); the Italian Laryngo-Rhino-Otological Society and Neapolitan School of Laryngology (Sir Felix Semon, hon. member, Professor Poli); the London Laryngological Society (Mr Charters Symonds, Mr de Santi, Dr Davis, and Mr H. B. Robinson); the Netherlands Laryngo - Oto - Rhinological Society (Dr Moll, Dr Burger, Dr Kan, Dr Zaalberg); the New York Academy of Medicine, Section of Laryngology (Dr Harman Smith); the Paris Laryngological Society (Dr C. J. Koenig, Dr Mahu); the Rhenish - Westphalian Laryngological Society (Dr Hirschland); the St Petersburg Laryngological Society; the South - German Laryngological Society (Dr Avelis); the Spanish Laryngo - Oto - Rhinological Society and Academy of Medicine and Surgery (Dr Botella, Dr Tapia); the Vienna Laryngological Society (Professor Chiari); the Warsaw Laryngological Society; the West - German Laryngological Society (Dr Fackeldey, Dr Lieven); and the Hungarian

Laryngological Society. Congratulatory telegrams were received from the Laryngological Societies of Sweden, Moscow, and Cracow; from the Amsterdam Medical Society; from the Medical Society of Japan; from Professor Moritz Schmidt, as President of the New German Laryngological Society; from Dr Birkett of Montreal, in the name of the students of M'Gill University; from Dr French, of Brooklyn, and hundreds of others.

The next speech brought a touching note to the scene, for in it Dr Botella, of Madrid, as the official delegate of the Spanish Government and of the Spanish Laryngological Society, addressed the maestro in his mother-tongue. A new light came into the centenarian's eyes, and he bent forward in an attitude of the closest attention, as if he feared to lose a single note of the beloved speech, whose sound on such an occasion must have carried him back over that great gulf of years to the far-off days of his childhood.

Dr Botella said that before the discovery of the laryngoscope the sense of touch was the only means of knowing of the existence of tumorous growths in the larynx. The invention of the laryngoscope had opened immense horizons to science, had put within its range many diseases the existence of which could never have been suspected, had made possible their treatment, and had saved from suffering and death numberless lives. The Spanish Government sent Señor Garcia its enthusiastic congratulations, and the Spanish Laryngological Society begged his acceptance of the diploma of " President of Honour." He brought a kind greeting from Spain to England, from Señor Garcia's native land to his adopted one. If the former gave him birth, the latter gave him shelter, and on that occasion both felt equally proud to have him as a son.

The following was the address of the Laryngological Society of London :—

DEAR AND REVERED MASTER, — Amongst the many friends assembled to - day to lay a tribute of gratitude and admiration at your feet, and a greater number far away who are celebrating to-day's unique event in spirit, there can be none whose congratulations are more sincere or more cordial than those of the members of the Laryngological Society of London. We yield to none in our gratitude for your precious invention, the Laryngoscope, which will keep your memory green through all ages. We, with the rest of mankind, admire in you the distinguished physiologist, the great musician, the teacher of so many celebrated singers : and we, amongst whom you have dwelt for so many years, have in addition had the great privilege of seeing you, our oldest honorary member, with us on many occasions, and have learned to appreciate in you the true friend, the courteous gentleman, the charming speaker. You have been permitted to retain all your brilliant faculties to patriarchal age, and to-day to celebrate your 100th birthday in undiminished vigour of mind and body. That this happy state may continue for many years to come, and that we may. often have the pleasure and privilege of seeing the venerable father of laryngoscope amongst us, is the sincere wish of your devoted friends, the members of the Laryngological Society of London.

CHARTERS J. SYMONDS (*President*).
PHILIP R. W. DE SANTI (*Secretary*).

Sir F. Semon said there was a large number of telegrams of congratulation, and that in the midst of the great strife which was going on between two great nations, neither of them had forgotten a great benefactor. In addition to the congratulations from St Petersburg and Warsaw, already announced, telegrams had been received from the Moscow Laryngological Society and from the Medical Society of Japan.

Several of the foreign societies, including the Netherlands and the Vienna societies, announced that they had conferred their honorary membership upon Señor Garcia.

The programme was brought to a conclusion by the presentation to Señor Garcia of his portrait, painted by Mr Sargent, R.A., and subscribed for by international contributions of the friends and admirers of the centenarian. The members of the Garcia Centenary Celebration Committee came forward to make the presentation. They were Sir F. Semon (chairman); Mr E. Furniss Potter, M.D., and Mr P. de Santi, F.R.C.S. (hon. secretaries); Mr E. Cresswell Baber, M.D., Mr J. Barry Ball, M.D., Mr J. S. Ballin, Mr A. Bowlby, F.R.C.S., Mr H. T. Butlin, F.R.C.S., Mr H. J. Davis, M.B., Mr J. Donelan, M.B., Mr J. Walker Downie, M.B., Mr F. de Havilland Hall, M.D., Mr W. Hill, M.D., Mr Percy Kidd, M.D., Mr L. A. Lawrence, F.R.C.S., Mr P. M'Bride, M.D., Mr W. Milligan, M.D., Mr L. H. Pegler, M.D., Mr W. Permewan, M.D., Mr H. B. Robinson, F.R.C.S., Mr C. J. Symonds, F.R.C.S., Mr St Clair Thomson, M.D., and Mr F. Willcocks, M.D. Mr W. R. H. Stewart, F.R.C.S. (Ed.), the hon. treasurer, was prevented by illness from attending.

Sir F. Semon made the presentation, and announced that the album containing the names of the subscribers would be handed to Señor Garcia subsequently. About twenty laryngological societies and about 800 persons had united to offer that testimonial.

The portrait was then unveiled amid loud cheers, which were renewed when the aged maestro rose to return thanks. His voice trembled with emotion, for he had been deeply touched by all this loyal recognition and affection. His opening words were addressed to the Spanish Chargé d'Affaires.

"Sir, will you tell my king for me how deeply grateful I am to him for thus remembering that in this country, which has sheltered me so long, he has a loyal and a loving subject? Will you express, what I am not able to say in fitting words, my overwhelming sense of this great honour, and convey to him my reverent—if a subject may be so bold—my loving thanks. You, sir [addressing Professor Fränkel], will undertake of your great courtesy to make known to his Majesty the German Emperor my deep sense of the honour he has conferred on a stranger, and you will ask him to accept my grateful thanks. You, sir [Sir A. Geikie], who represent the illustrious English society that first gave me a hearing [the Royal Society]; you [Professor Stirling], by whom the learning of England's second capital [the Manchester University] sends me greeting." At this point Señor Garcia handed the MS. of his reply to Sir Felix Semon, requesting him to finish reading it. "You who have come from distant Königsberg to recall the grateful memory of those who gave the unknown man a place among them. You, who represent the world-renowned Academy of Sciences of Berlin, among the members of which are some I count dear friends. And you, dear sir, who bring me the greeting of a city of youth whose very name seems to set joy-bells ringing; you, sir, from Heidelberg, how shall I thank you all, if your goodwill should fail to interpret my poor faltering words? But that goodwill is my most trusty staff. You, doctors, laryngologists, dear friends, to whom the little instrument to which such kind allusion has been made owes all its power for good. You, representatives of the great music schools of London, in one of which I passed so many years, working happily beside brother musicians, and to the other of which I have so often come to mark with pride our own great art of music prospering beyond belief under the care of a beloved chief and genial staff. You, too, my pupils, among whom it rejoices me so keenly to welcome faces missed for many years and found again to-day, while others have been with me, near and dear. To you all, thanks, from an old heart that did not know what youth it still possessed till it expanded to embrace you all. This portrait, from the hand of this great master, which grew in happy hours too few for me since they passed so rapidly in his companionship, shall be my pride and joy in the days to come."

When Sir Felix hesitated at this point because he saw that he was coming to a passage about himself,

Señor Garcia at once cried, " Yes, yes ! read that ! "
Then, as the Chairman of the Committee looked
somewhat embarrassed, the centenarian said with
great vivacity, " Well, give it to me ; I will read
it." With these words he took over the paper
once again and read the concluding words of the
speech.

" If you will bear with me a moment longer, I
should like to say one little inadequate word of
thanks to him from whose initiative this wonderful
demonstration has sprung, — my friend Sir Felix
Semon, with whose name link that of an institution
dear to me beyond all others,—the Laryngological
Society of London, and its chosen representative,
that social Atlas, the Garcia Committee."

This brought the first part of the programme to
a close, and the centenarian returned to his home,
which was inundated with telegrams and baskets
of flowers. Here he gave himself up to rest and
preparation for that still more trying ordeal which
was still to come.

That same evening Señor Garcia set out for
the Hotel Cecil, where a complimentary birthday
banquet had been arranged by the committee.

When the carriage had driven into the courtyard
of the hotel he alighted without assistance, entered
the outer hall, and walked nimbly down two or
three flights of stairs to the cloak-room.

There was a very large attendance, the Grand
Hall being filled with eminent musicians and
scientists anxious to do honour to the distinguished guest.

OPENING BARS OF AN ARIA WRITTEN OUT BY MANUEL GARCIA WHEN IN HIS HUNDREDTH YEAR, GIVING HIS ELABORATIONS OF THE ORIGINAL MELODY.

Mr Charters J. Symonds was in the chair.

In proposing the first toast, "The King," he said that his Majesty was always the foremost in every way in the recognition of merit, and that day he had anticipated their function, and had received Señor Garcia personally, conferring upon him a great honour—the Commandership of the Royal Victorian Order. His Majesty, in honour of Señor Garcia, had also sent Lord Suffield there as his representative.

The toast having been loyally honoured, the chairman said that two other European sovereigns had combined with our own King to confer honour on their guest. His Majesty the King of Spain had sent Señor Garcia the Grand Cross of the Order of Alfonso XII., and also a message which he would call on the Spanish Chargé d'Affaires to read.

The Marquis de Villalobar said it gave him great pleasure to convey to his illustrious compatriot the message which his Majesty, the King of Spain, had sent to him just now through his Minister of Foreign Affairs. It was as follows : " By command of his Majesty the King, congratulate personally Señor Garcia on the day of the celebration of his 100th birthday. Convey his royal best wishes to the grand old Spaniard who, by his invention and works, has glorified and exalted the name of Spain."

The chairman, resuming, said he had heard a whisper that the honour conferred by the King of Spain carried with it the title of His Excellency, so that in future they might regard their dear old friend as His Excellency, Señor Garcia. Again, his Majesty the German Emperor, mindful of the benefit which he himself not long since obtained from the knowledge of the instrument invented by Señor Garcia, had conferred upon him a great distinction. It had been brought to London by the most distinguished laryngologist in Germany, Professor Fränkel. It was the medal which was called the Great Gold Medal for Science. They would appreciate its importance when he said that previously it had only been conferred upon Professor Virchow, Professor Koch, Ehrlich, and Mommsen. These three Sovereigns had that day combined to recognise in Señor Garcia the ability which had influenced science and art in all countries. He gave them the toast of the King of Spain, and then of the German Emperor.

The toasts having been honoured, Sir Felix Semon proposed the health of the hero of the evening in a long and eloquent speech.

The toast was drunk with enthusiasm, and the company sang, "For he's a jolly good fellow."

Then, in an atmosphere of electrical excitement, Manuel Garcia stood up, and amid a thrilling silence made his response.

It was almost the only occasion in the world's history that a man of world-wide fame had ever attained his 100th anniversary. It was, more-ever, the first time that any centenarian, whether illustrious or "born to blush unseen," had been in such full possession of his faculties and bodily strength as to make his own reply to the hundreds assembled to do honour to his birthday. He was

almost overcome by emotion in making his response
in English.

"Sir Felix Semon, Ladies and Gentlemen,—
Words, it is said, are given us to conceal our
thoughts. They will admirably fulfil that purpose
if you take mine as a full and complete expression
of my feelings on this extraordinary occasion. But
words, whatever use we make of them, are not mere
masks. They are living things, intensely living
things to some—to those of us who hold the magic
ring that makes them slaves. They are as mighty
friends, friends such as you to me, who from the
ocean depths of your indulgence fling back to me
my own poor and trivial deeds, transfigured into
something 'rich and strange.'"

At this point Señor Garcia, who had become
almost inaudible, and who was evidently somewhat
exhausted by fatigue and excitement, handed the
MS. of his speech to the chairman, who read the
remainder. It ran as follows:—

"There are so many of you to be greeted,—
old friends out of the past, old pupils, comrades,
children! Ah, children! Sixteen societies of
laryngologists, and mostly come of age, calling me
'Father'! They will have it so, and I am pretty
proud of the title, I can tell you. Well, do you
think one solitary man could find fit word to answer
all these voices? But you can do it for me. There
is an old story some of you may remember, which,
when I read it, changed the aspect of things for me
by its very name, for that was a stroke of genius:

'Put yourself in his place.' What a different world
it would be if we all did that! Well, you try now.
Try hard. Think yourself each one hundred years
old to-day. Not the ladies. I will not ask them.
Though they may come to that they will never
look it, and they will never know it, and no one
will ever believe it. But you men can try. Fancy
you each lived one hundred years and woke to-day
to find yourself surrounded by kindly clamorous
voices, 'troops of friends'! What would you say?
I think you would say nought. Only the infinite
nought which circles all things could give an ade-
quate answer to you all. I shall say nought to this
great master of the brush, Mr Sargent, who with
his creative touches in a moment brought life from
void. It is a strange experience to see one's very
self spring out at one from nothing in a flash. I
shall say nought to this rash friend of mine, Sir
Felix Semon, who into the midst of a busy life
crammed all the work and worry of the labour of
love that has brought you here to-day. Nought,
nought to the friends so very near my heart, the
Laryngological Society of London, and the chosen
band whose terrible labours fill me with remorse
whenever I think of them, the Members of the
Garcia Committee. I shall say nought, nought,
nought to all of you, except just this, 'God bless
you every one!'"

The chairman next proposed "Our Foreign
Guests," for whom Herr Emanuel Stockhausen (son
of one of his most distinguished pupils), Dr Puttner,
Dr Harman Smith, Dr Goris, Dr Lermoyez, Dr
Poli, Dr Botella, Dr Burger, and Professor Chiari

responded. During the dinner a number of congratulatory telegrams were received. Among them was one from the Prime Minister.

Between the speeches of foreign delegates, which were delivered in various tongues, Mme. Blanche Marchesi, Mme. Ada Crossley, Mr Ben Davies, and Mr Arthur Oswald sang, and then that wonderful evening came to an end.

CHAPTER XXI.

LAST DAYS.

(1905–1906.)

ON the Sunday evening after the Centenary Banquet, Señor Garcia was present at a more private dinner, attended by the laryngologists, who had come together to do homage to the founder of their art. He was brighter than at the larger gathering, while he not only smoked a cigarette, as he had done at the banquet, but drank a glass of lager beer with relish. He told many interesting stories of his early days; and once, in trying to fix the time of some reminiscence, he said, "Oh, about twenty-three or thirty years ago: I do not like these little dates"! With the greatest good nature he signed his name on some forty menu cards. The following is the text of his speech in French :—

"Vous ne vous attendez pas, sans doute, à ce que je fasse un discours. Si j'ose prendre la parole, c'est pour vous exposer, en quelques mots, une pensée qui m'obsède et que le grand éclat donne à la presentation qui a eu lieu a fait naître dans mon esprit.

" Le rôle des personnages qui ont figuré dans cette célébration aurait du être interverti ; les félicitations, les compliments vous appartiennent, et c'est à vous et à vos sociétés qu'ils auraient du être adressés.

" Il est de tout évidence que le petit instrument doit les succès qu'il a obtenus absolument et uniquement à vous, Messieurs, et aux associations sur lesquelles vous présidez. Privé du puissant appui de votre science, il serait tombé dans un oubli complet (et ego quoque).

" Par suite je me considère comme un usurpateur insigne qui accepte ce qui, en réalité, vous appartient, et c'est par acquit de conscience que je le confesse.

" Ne pouvant pas changer ce qui est, je termine ces mots en exprimant ma très vive reconnaissance aux sociétés laryngologiques que vous représentez, et à vous, Messieurs, qui, sans souci des inconvénients des voyages, êtes venus de tous pays, même les plus lointains, pour féliciter le centenaire et, plus encore, pour l'honorer de leur approbation scientifique. Ainsi comblé, saura-t'il jamais manifester l'intensité de son appréciation, de sa reconnaissance ?

" Je ne pourrais conclure ces remarques sans exprimer mon admiration pour Sir Felix Semon, dont l'infatigable persévérance, unie à une rare puissance d'organization, a réussi, à travers de nombreux obstacles, à organizer cette grande démonstration, inspirée uniquement par le désir d'honorer un vieil ami. Merci ! Encore, Merci ! "

A few days later Señor Manuel Garcia went to dine with Hermann Klein, who had come over from New York for a few weeks, and here the centenarian renewed his acquaintance with his pupil's younger brother, Charles. The meeting took him back over thirty years, to those days in Bentinck Street when Charles Klein, then a sturdy, dark little fellow of eight, used to go out regularly to fetch the maestro's lunch of sponge - cake from a baker's round the corner in Welbeck Street. Much water had passed under the bridge since these days, and he had now come over from a sojourn of many years in America, a man of forty, and one of New York's most successful playwrights.

In the following July I went up to spend a Sunday afternoon with the centenarian. It was quite impossible to believe that he was indeed in his 101st year. He actually displayed more vivacity than at the time when I was commencing lessons with him, while even in those days my mother had asserted that he seemed more hale and active than he had been when she in her turn was studying under him twenty-five years before. Truly as he grew older he appeared to become younger.

Charles Klein came to call on the maestro on this same afternoon, and was put through many searching questions with regard to the latest phases of American thought and character. When tea arrived our host displayed the most extraordinary energy, jumping up and insisting upon getting a small table upon which the playwright might rest his cup and plate. The latter he watched with anxiety. When it was empty, he promptly fetched a plate of scones, and with the most wonderful humour and good spirits pressed the guest to take some more. As for his own wants, it was perfectly futile for one to offer to take charge of his cup. Nothing would satisfy him but that he should himself take it over to be refilled. When I rose to go, the maestro insisted on coming to the front door, as in the old days, and in shaking hands said, " I shall hope to see you here soon again."

For the next nine months Manuel Garcia led a life almost incredible in one of such age. He continued to rise early, go to bed late, and enjoy walks, drives, theatres, concerts, and dinners as thoroughly as a man forty years his junior.

His hale old age he would ascribe to his mental and physical activity, his moderate living (he did not touch wine or spirits until he was ninety), and his good digestion.

His piano continued to be a favourite friend, and frequently he would play for an hour in the forenoon and again in the evening. The selections would be mostly snatches from the old Italian operas—especially Rossini, Meyerbeer, and Mozart,—played from memory. His hearing was excellent, and his sight still comparatively good ; indeed, he spent a great deal of time in reading, for he took an interest in everything that went on in the world. His evenings would be passed in conversation, or a bout at chess—a game in which he had many a time in the old days tried conclusions with Sir Charles Hallé. Sometimes he would go out for a game of cards with his neighbours.

He went to visit many old friends, and one day actually walked up to the fourth floor in a block of flats, disdaining the lift. He went to register his

vote at the general election. During his walks he
used to offer adverse criticisms of the motor-omni-
buses which were beginning to make their appearance. 'Bus conductors used to get their own back
without knowing it, for they would point to "Mon
Abri" as they passed, and remark to the passengers,
"That's where the Centurion lives."

In the following autumn I was at work on the
little book of reminiscences of my mother and her
circle of friends, and at the close of November
wrote to Señor Garcia telling him that I wished
to devote a portion to his own career, as her chief
instructor in singing. This letter at once brought
a reply that he would like to see the MS. of that
part of the memoir.

Hence there came about what must have been
unique in the experience of book publishers, for
when the manuscript was finally returned to them
after revision, marked for press, it contained some
corrections in the handwriting of one who was
within three months of entering his 102nd year.

The coming of the new year appeared to bring
with it little visible diminution in the maestro's
mental and bodily activity. Indeed, during the
winter of 1905-06 he attended quite a number of
public dinners, including one at the Savage Club,
another given by the "Vagabonds" to Mr and Mrs
H. B. Irving, and a third at the Mansion House in
honour of the King of Spain, by whose special request the Centenarian was invited to be present.

On March 17, 1906, he celebrated the entrance
into his 102nd year by taking up a guitar and
singing a Spanish song, while a few days after

J'ai lu avec beaucoup de plaisir, l'intéressant volume que avez dédié à la mémoire de votre chère mère; c'est aussi avec grande satisfaction que j'ai appris qu'il a été apprécié par la presse; c'est une garantie qu'il aura le succès qu'il mérite.

Agréez mes compliments et mes félicitations,

Votre sincère

M. Garcia

FACSIMILE OF A LETTER WRITTEN BY MANUEL GARCIA
IN HIS HUNDRED-AND-SECOND YEAR.

this he attended the Philharmonic Concert at the Queen's Hall and keenly enjoyed the music. So active was he still, that he refused with indignation an offer to be helped up or down stairs; but the candle was burning with an unnatural brightness, which could not last.

In the middle of April a letter arrived from the maestro, the perusal of which brought fresh wonder at his amazing vigour. It had been written on the 16th April, and ran as follows:—

CHER MR MACKINLAY.—J'ai lu avec beaucoup de plaisir l'interessant volume qu'avez (*sic*) dédié à la mémoire de votre chère mère. C'est aussi avec grande satisfaction que j'ai appris qu'il a été apprecié par la presse; c'est une garantie qu'il aura le succès qu'il mérite.

Agréez mes compliments et mes félicitations. — Votre sincère   M. GARCIA.

About the same time Hermann Klein received a letter from the old teacher, and the handwriting, he tells me, was not quite so firm as usual. Indeed it is evident that Señor Garcia was not feeling at all himself at this time, for in the note he says—

" As to my health, it is less brilliant than I should like, but it is passable ; " while a postscript is added showing that he himself realised that his hand was rather shaky: "Can you read this scribble (ce barbouillage) ? "

After this there appears to have been considerable improvement, for on May 24 he wrote to congratulate Charles Klein on the success of his new piece at the Duke of York's Theatre, and on this occasion the handwriting was much clearer and steadier than it had been five weeks earlier.

(*Translation.*)

"MON ABRI," CRICKLEWOOD,
LONDON, 24*th May* 1906.

DEAR MR KLEIN,—My paper informs me that you have just obtained a great theatrical success. I congratulate you with all my heart.

Would you have the kindness to send me your actual London address? I have a little parcel for your brother, which I beg you will convey to him. It is a portrait that he has asked of me, which he desires to present to Mme. Sembrich.

One of these days, when I feel in the mood (*en train*), I shall go to see "The Lion and The Mouse."

My respects to Mrs Klein, and to yourself a hearty and cordial handshake. M. GARCIA.

In June Charles Klein sent a box for the Duke of York's Theatre, and Señor Garcia went to see the piece, which he thoroughly enjoyed. This was the last dramatic performance which he attended, and indeed the drama of his own life was drawing to a close.

* * * * * *

On Sunday, July 1, the end came : the beloved maestro passed away in his sleep, calmly and peacefully, at the age of 101.

INDEX.

THE END

PRINTED BY WILLIAM BLACKWOOD AND SONS.